THE REST OF FOREVER

CARRIE PULKINEN

CHAPTER 1

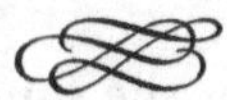

*A*pril Carter awoke covered in sweat, clutching the sheets. Her heart pounded at the vivid details of her way-too-realistic recurring dream. She looked at Jared, snoring softly in bed next to her, and her stomach churned with guilt. She'd had the most incredible sex of her life in that dream, and it wasn't with him. It never was.

Peeling the damp sheets away from her skin, she slid out of bed and tiptoed to the bathroom. Her boyfriend's alarm wouldn't be sounding for another fifteen minutes, and he'd be grumpy if she woke him early. She turned the knob and closed the door gently, slowly releasing the handle to minimize the noise.

The hot steam of the shower should've washed away the tension in her muscles, but she couldn't relax. Memories of her dream lover's hands caressing her body had her insides twisting in confusion.

Damian Perkins. Ever since he was hired on at her school, she'd been having dreams about the sexy history teacher. Dreams she shouldn't have been having. She didn't *want* to have them. She already spent her days working with him. He didn't need to be invading her nights too.

Trying to brush the once-velvet feel of his touch away, she vigorously rubbed her arms. She couldn't control her dreams, but she wasn't a cheater. Jared was the only man for her.

She shook her head as she shut off the water and dried herself. She wouldn't let it ruin her day. Not today. But why on Earth was she dreaming about Damian? Could she subconsciously—

No. Get a grip, girl.

She shook off the ridiculous thought and got ready for work.

Jared usually left the small apartment while she was in the shower, but since she woke up early today, she caught her boyfriend at the door. "It's a big day." She straightened his tie and kissed him on the cheek before he picked up his briefcase.

He wiped the lipstick off and loosened his tie. "The best of the year. Six o'clock is when it all goes down."

Her heart fluttered as she looked into his eyes. "Six? You're going to be home by then?"

"I'm taking off early for this, baby. See you tonight." He winked and slipped out the door.

April sighed and gazed at the ring finger of her left hand. There'd be a diamond on it tonight. Today marked the one-year anniversary of their first date. And if Jared followed the rules and spent three month's salary on her ring, it was going to be a whopper. A smile tugged at her lips as she picked up her bag and shoved her grade book inside.

With her hand on the doorknob, she glanced at the clock. Late again. *Those teenagers aren't going to teach themselves.* She darted downstairs to the parking lot.

The wind picked up as soon as her feet hit the pavement. Her scarf flapped in her face, blocking her vision for a moment, before it twisted and flew off her head. She gasped and jumped for the sentimental piece of silk, but it was no use. It floated across the parking lot, dancing in the wind. She trotted after it, determined to catch the gift her sister had given her before it landed in a muddy pothole.

Tires squealed as a car skidded inches from where she stood. The smell of burning rubber assaulted her senses, and a hard body slammed into her, shoving her to the ground as the vehicle slid to a stop. Her back collided with the concrete, and sharp pain shot through her spine as the air whooshed out of her lungs. She lay there for a moment, her heart frantically beating as she tried to slow her rapid breathing. The throbbing pain in her shoulder made it difficult, and she was definitely going to bruise. *Lovely.*

"You all right?" the driver called from the jet black Tahoe. She glanced at the man in the truck and slowly nodded her head.

"Yeah. She's fine," her savior said.

Gravel crunched as the car rolled by and exited the parking lot. April blinked and pushed up on her hands as her wavering vision refocused on the man who pushed her.

Damian.

Her coworker had appeared out of nowhere, and he was already on his feet, dusting off his pants.

He didn't even offer to help her up.

"Did you have to knock me down? You ruined my new clothes." She toyed with the torn hem of her designer skirt. Did he have any idea how long she'd had to save to buy this outfit? Luckily the tear was on the seam. She could fix it.

He snorted. "Thanks for saving my life, Damian. Oh, you're welcome, April. Don't mention it." He ran his hand through his tousled toffee-colored hair and narrowed his hazel eyes. "You know, you could show a little gratitude."

"You think you saved my life?" April scoffed. "The car was going, what? Twenty miles an hour? It would have stopped." She rose to her feet and brushed the gravel off her legs. As she swept the back of her calf, she winced at the stinging pain. Bright red scrapes extended from her ankle to the back of her knee. *Peachy.*

She opened her mouth to berate him some more, but her words caught on the lump in her throat as visions of their imaginary night together flashed in her mind.

The dream.

Heat flushed her cheeks, and she averted her gaze from his. She had no reason to be embarrassed. He didn't know she'd been dreaming about making love to him for the past three months. He couldn't know.

But there was something about the way he looked at her...that knowing gaze, like he knew all her deepest, darkest secrets. She shuddered.

"April, you...you know what? Never mind. I'll see you at work." He turned on his heel and marched to his '69 Mustang. Slamming the door, he peeled out of the parking lot without looking back.

"Unfortunately," she muttered as she picked up her muddy silk scarf and headed toward her own car.

That man grated on her every last nerve. It was bad enough she had to work with him, but then he had to move into her building. Like she didn't already put up with him enough. And his know-it-all attitude drove her insane. It wouldn't be so bad if he wasn't so damn good at his job. The kids loved him, and he knew more about history than her best college professor. She wasn't sure which irked her more: his I'm-smarter-than-you attitude or the fact that he really was.

She climbed into her car and adjusted the rearview mirror to check her face. At least her makeup still looked good, and she was having an amazing hair day, scarf or no scarf. She wasn't going to let her little run-in with Damian get her down. She was getting engaged tonight, and nothing was going to ruin her day. Not even a torn Prada skirt.

Damian knew better than to expect gratitude from April. Still, a little thank you wouldn't have hurt. If she only knew how much he did for her. How many times he'd saved her life.

Of course, she didn't know the things she did *to* him either. The way she made him feel. The reason he had to put space between them. He couldn't let any kind of emotional attachment form between them. If she hated him, it would be easy to let go of his Charge.

Easy for her, anyway.

He chuckled as he pulled into a parking space. Only three more weeks and he could get away from the certain disaster his heart was heading for. He'd be done with April and with this place.

He'd never understood the draw of small town life. Felicity, Texas, didn't have much of anything. While all the neighboring towns blossomed during the housing boom, Felicity stayed the same old small town it had always been. Probably always would be.

It was like living in a vacuum. People rarely got away. Even the lucky ones who went off to college eventually moved back.

Then there were the ones like April. She grew up in this hellhole and starting teaching at her own high school. Didn't she get enough of the place the first four years she spent there? Well, there were worse jobs. And worse places to live for that matter. Felicity did mean happiness. Maybe some people found it there.

April May Carter. What was her mother thinking giving her a name like April May? It had to be a Southern thing. Damian grinned. She hated being called April May. Every time her grandmother said her name, she'd cringe. She'd chew on her bottom lip like she did when she was trying to keep her mouth shut. He'd have to make a point to use her full name today, just to grate on her nerves.

April. The most stubborn woman he'd ever known. When she set her mind to something, there was no backing down. Even if she was wrong. But her strong will served her well as a teacher. The kids respected her, and she'd do anything in the world for them. Of course, that also had a lot to do with genetics. Damian knew April's grandfather, and he had that same strong will.

He strolled into his classroom with two minutes to spare and sat on the edge of his desk. The last student shuffled in just as the tardy bell rang, and Damian began his lesson.

"All right, guys. Let's talk about the fall of the Roman Empire."

Most of the morning went by in a fog. April did her best to teach her students about the Romans, but her mind was in a diamond store picking out her engagement ring. She'd already forgotten about the torn skirt she'd mended with a safety pin. Only six hours to go, and she'd have a rock on her finger.

April taught in the same room where she'd once learned. They'd torn down a few of the old school buildings and done some renovations, but it was the same old school. Nothing seemed to change in Felicity. Not the scenery. Not the people. Nothing.

Maybe once she had a ring on her finger, she could convince Jared to get out of this Podunk town. She loved working with the kids, but sometimes she felt trapped. She wanted more than small town life could give her. She wanted to help kids with real problems. Inner-city kids. She knew she could make a bigger difference there. But every time she'd mentioned it to Jared, he'd shrug, tousle her hair as if she were a child, and say, "We'll see, babe."

Her best friend Janice was already in the teacher's

lounge having lunch when she arrived. April beamed a smile, waltzed into the room, and settled into a chair next to her.

"Tonight's the night, Janice. I can feel it." She pulled a tuna sandwich out of her lunch bag and opened a Diet Coke. "He's even taking off work early."

"You're sure he's going to propose?"

"Of course he is. It's our anniversary. It'll be perfect. I bought a new dress that's amazing. Here, let me show you a picture." She pulled her cell phone out of her pocket and flipped through the photos. "I took this one in the dressing room. Isn't it gorgeous?"

Janice looked at the picture and shook her head. "How can you afford these designer clothes? We make the same salary, and I get most of my clothes from Target."

April shrugged. "There's nothing wrong with wanting to look good. I save my money, and Jared pays the rent. Designer clothes are my guilty pleasure. I'm not ashamed." She flashed a smile, but then rolled her eyes when she saw Damian walk through the door.

"Here we go. Asshole alert. Better put your boots on, Janice. It's gonna get deep real quick."

Janice smiled and waved at Damian. "Why do you hate him so much? He's not that bad."

"He's an arrogant prick."

"Well, I think he's cute."

"Yeah, until he opens his mouth." April shook her head. Damian wasn't cute. He was downright sexy, and it ate her up that she was attracted to him. There should've been a law against assholes like Damian being so hot. It wasn't fair.

"Oh, come on. You're just jealous they hired him as department head when John left, instead of promoting you."

April huffed and crossed her arms over her chest. "I'm not jealous. And I don't want to be department head. I've got too much invested in the kids to have to deal with all that bureaucratic crap. But since you brought it up, don't you think it's kinda unfair to bring in a new department head midyear? I mean, he's only been here three months."

"Yeah. I guess it is a little strange, but what can you do? Anyway...where's Jared taking you tonight?"

"I don't know. I think he wants it to be a surprise, because he hasn't mentioned it. I'm so excited! I'm finally gonna have a diamond on my finger. You're going to be my maid of honor, right? We can go dress shopping together. It'll be so much fun!"

Janice pressed her lips together and looked at April in silence. Then she took a deep breath and sighed. "Of course. I will be your maid of honor whenever you get married. I just wonder..."

April put down her sandwich and folded her hands on the table. "Uh-oh. Here it comes."

"What?"

She leaned back in her chair and crossed her arms over her silk blouse. "Whenever you *just wonder* about something, it's usually something I don't want to hear."

Janice shrugged and turned to toss her trash in the can behind her. "All right, then. I won't say it."

"No. Go ahead, because you're usually right. Seriously, Janice. Just say it."

"Okay. I just wonder about you and Jared. You talk

about getting a ring and about your wedding, but I don't hear you talking about being married to *Jared*. Do you really want to marry him, or do you just want to have a wedding?"

"Well, I...of course I want to marry him." Why wouldn't she? Jared was attractive and stable, and April would be thirty in three weeks. She certainly didn't want to wind up being a crazy cat lady. And she didn't want to end up like her mom—lonely and miserable.

She and Jared had their ups and downs like any couple. He was a lawyer, and he worked way too much. She'd even suspected there might be another woman a time or two, but he always had an alibi. Lawyers worked crazy hours, and she would have to get used to it. Eventually.

"Jared is educated, and he has a steady job. What more can a girl ask for?"

Janice arched an eyebrow. "Just last week you said he's more interested in sports than sex."

She waved her hand dismissively. "Passion is fleeting. Stability is the important thing when it comes to marriage."

"What's this? You ladies planning a wedding?" Damian turned a chair around backward and straddled it, leaning his forearms on the table.

"I'm sorry." April sat up straighter. "I don't remember including you in this conversation. Don't you think you've done enough to ruin my day?"

Damian narrowed his eyes at her and then smiled. "Okay. I can take a hint. Here." He pulled a thick stack of papers out of his bag and dropped it on the table. "I rewrote the nine-weeks exam."

April picked it up and flipped through the pages. "I haven't even covered some of this stuff, Damian. You can't change the test a week before I have to give it."

"I just did, April May," he drawled, mocking the Southern accent that was so prevalent in their town. "And you better catch up. I'd hate for a hundred kids to fail World History because their teacher couldn't handle her new boss." He grinned and raised an eyebrow.

Her blood boiled. How the hell did he find out her middle name? And she did *not* talk like that; she always made a point to speak without an accent. She wasn't a hillbilly, even if she did live in the middle of Hickville. He was baiting her, and damn it, she was going to take it.

"Believe me, I can handle you. And, you're not my boss."

"Close enough." He shrugged and rose from the table. "Have a nice lunch, ladies."

April glared at his backside and ignored the warmth pooling below her navel as he strode confidently from the room. She'd show him. Her kids were going to ace that exam if she had to stay up all night preparing her lessons.

Too disgusted to eat, she threw the rest of her lunch into the trash and picked up the stack of tests. "You see what I have to put up with?"

"Is there a lot you haven't covered?" Janice took one of the exams and flipped through the pages.

"Not really. But it's the principle. I think he does this crap just to get on my nerves. He's out to get me, Janice."

She snatched the test out of her friend's hands and slammed it down on the stack of papers.

Janice laughed. "I think he likes you."

"Oh, please." She rolled her eyes and waved off the comment, though the thought did send a tingling sensation shooting through her chest.

"I'm serious. No man focuses that much attention on a woman unless he's interested. And I think deep down, you like him too. Not that you would ever admit it to yourself."

Janice didn't know how right she was. April had already come to terms with her attraction to Damian. As much as she hated herself for it, she liked him. His abrasive exterior had to be a mask. She wondered what he was like underneath that mask as much as she wondered what he looked like underneath his Dockers and Polo shirts. Then there was the dream...

Could he really be interested in me? April shook herself. She couldn't let her mind go there. Not when Jared was about to propose.

"I do not like him. And even if I wasn't engaged, I still wouldn't go for a guy like that."

"Right, because who would like a guy like Damian? He's cute, smart, available...and you're not engaged."

April grinned and rose from the table. "Not yet."

Damian knew April could handle it. He'd only added a few things she hadn't covered, and she could teach them to the kids in a day. She was an amazing teacher, and he admired her drive and devotion to the kids. But he also loved watching her temper flare. The fire in her emerald eyes sparked to match her flaming red hair. The way she glared at him and turned up her nose when they passed in the hall. She hated him.

At least, he hoped she did.

He needed to get away from the woman. He was feeling things he shouldn't be feeling. Things he hadn't allowed himself to feel in so many years. Whenever she narrowed her sparkling eyes at him, he felt something stirring in his soul. A slow burn that would eventually incinerate him if he wasn't careful. He couldn't wait for these last three weeks to be over.

Although, teaching wasn't the worst job he'd ever had to stand in for. He enjoyed the kids, and teaching them about world history—the *real* events that actually happened—was enthralling. He was going to miss this job.

He sighed as he picked up his bag and locked his classroom door. April was going to miss this job too.

He needed to ease off and let her have fun with her last three weeks of teaching. Her life was about to change dramatically, and he still hadn't figured out how to tell her. She was different from the others. Stubborn. But it was part of being a Guardian, and he'd figure out a way. He'd done it hundreds of times. And he'd do it hundreds more.

Only, he wasn't doing a very good job of earning her trust. He'd saved her life at least a dozen times, but she'd had no idea it was him. He'd done a damn good job with her, in his own opinion. She'd turned out to be a good person deep down, and that's what really mattered. Her obsession with designer clothes and that loser boyfriend wouldn't matter in a few weeks.

In a few weeks, he could wash his hands of April May Carter, and move on to his next Charge. Still, he wondered about the wedding talk he heard at lunch. Could she really be engaged to that bozo? He'd cheated on her so many times, Damian lost count. And he knew for a fact the jerk had a fling going on with a legal assistant at his office.

Well, there was one way to find out for sure. April had probably already left the school, so he jogged out to the parking lot and climbed into his Mustang. He drove back to the condos, just to keep up the charade, and parked next to April's car. Then he glanced around to be sure no one would see. Closing his eyes, he took a deep breath and slipped into The In-Between.

CHAPTER 2

April dropped her purse on the bed and dashed straight to the closet. It was only four o'clock, and Jared wouldn't be home for another two hours. But she was bubbling with excitement and too hyper to sit around doing nothing. She pulled out her new Versace dress and spun around on her toes before she laid it on the bed. The dress was basic black and hit her a few inches above the knee. It had spaghetti straps and a black floral pattern embroidered on the material. She'd driven to Dallas to get it, so she had to be the only girl in town that owned one. And that made her giddy.

"Tonight's going to be perfect." She held out her left hand and wiggled her ring finger. What type of ring would he get her? She hoped for a princess cut, but she wasn't going to be picky. She'd appreciate whatever he picked out —as long as it was big and sparkly.

Dancing into the bathroom, she looked in the mirror. Her hair had fallen flat, and her makeup looked dull. A quick shower and blow-dry would fix that. She styled her hair, put on some makeup and her favorite Heavenly perfume. Then she smiled at her reflection. She looked like a million bucks. There was no way Jared would be able to resist her tonight.

His key jingled in the door, and she squealed with delight that he was home at five instead of six. He must have been as excited about the night as she was. She pranced into the living room and stood with one hand on her hip as he opened the door. "You're home early," she said in her most sultry voice.

"Hey, babe. You look nice." Jared dropped his briefcase on the couch and pecked her on the cheek as he brushed past her to the bedroom. "You going somewhere?" he called over his shoulder as he opened the dresser drawer.

"Of course I am, silly." April giggled. He was still putting on the charade, and curiosity spun through her mind. What amazing evening could he have planned?

"Where are you going?"

"Don't you mean, 'where are *we* going'?" April slinked to the bedroom and put her hand on the doorframe, trying her best to strike a sexy pose. Her smile faded when she saw Jared in blue jeans and an LSU T-shirt.

Her heart sank as she realized his plans weren't up to her expectations. Well, she could do casual. She'd throw a sweater on over the dress and wear flats instead of heels. No big deal. "I guess I'm a little overdressed."

Jared shrugged. "Depends on where you're going." He brushed past her again on his way to the door. "I've gotta get out of here if I'm going to make it before tip-off."

April furrowed her brow. "Jared, I thought we were spending the evening together."

"Well, I guess you can come if you want. But I thought you hated basketball." He slipped on his jacket and put his keys in his pocket.

Her heart raced, and her hands trembled. Tears welled in her eyes, but she would not cry in front of him. She was stronger than that. "Basketball? The biggest day of the year is about basketball?"

"Well, yeah." Jared grinned. "It's the final game of the college playoffs. LSU's gonna kick ass tonight."

She was being dumped for a basketball game, and she could hardly control the emotions that swirled inside her: anger, disappointment, humiliation. She didn't trust her voice, so she spoke in a whisper. "Jared, it's our anniversary."

"Aw, man. Is that today?" He put his arm around her and squeezed. "I'm sorry, babe. We'll celebrate it tomorrow, okay? How about I take you to Bob's Bar-B-Que and you can get one of those loaded baked potatoes you love? How's that sound?"

April straightened her spine and forced a smile. "Fine. Just peachy. Enjoy the game."

"Thanks, babe. Happy anniversary." Jared loped out the door.

"Right back at ya."

He'd be back. This was all part of the charade, and in a few minutes he'd walk through the door and tell her what the real plan was. He'd done the same thing on her birthday last year—pretended like he forgot, when he'd really planned her a surprise party. Tonight would be the same. It had to. He wouldn't have forgotten their anniversary.

Or would he? He'd blown her off for basketball before, so she shouldn't have been surprised. But on their anniversary? *That's inexcusable.*

She waited by the door for five minutes, but he didn't come back. He was going to draw it out. That was okay. She'd wait. She perched on the edge of the couch, trying not to wrinkle her dress, and turned on the TV. After flipping through all two hundred channels, she settled on watching the Ghost Hunters marathon on Syfy. She wasn't sure what she believed about the afterlife, but the show was interesting enough to hold her attention.

She made it through one hour-long episode before it hit her. Jared wasn't coming back. He'd chosen basketball over her. He'd rather be out with the guys than on a date with his girlfriend. Her stomach churned.

She slouched back on the couch, no longer concerned about the dress. Had Jared even mentioned their anniversary recently? Could she have conceived this whole idea of a proposal in her head? *No. He must have mentioned it.* She played their conversations of the last few days through her mind, but she came up with nothing. *Did* she imagine it?

The first tear slid down her cheek. Jared forgot their anniversary. He wasn't going to propose tonight, or probably any other night. The floodgates opened. She was an idiot.

With her head in her hands, she curled up on the couch and sobbed. How could he do this to her? After everything she'd done for him. Everything she'd tried to *be* for him. She cooked, cleaned, did his laundry. She put up with way more crap than she should have. Her entire life centered around this man. But she couldn't lose him; she couldn't be alone.

Her sobs turned into cries of sorrow, and she wrapped her arms around herself as if she'd fall apart if she let go. A feeling of warmth seemed to envelop her as she lay there on the sofa, reminding her everything would be okay. She would get through this. She always did.

Damian's heart broke right along with April's. As much as he loved to watch her temper flare when he ragged on her, he *hated* to see her hurt. Why was she so dependent on this guy? She was stronger than that. She didn't need that cheating bastard in her life.

She didn't know Damian was there, watching her from The In-Between. She couldn't feel his arms around her as he comforted her. He took a deep breath and sighed. She smelled delicious. Like flowers with a hint of vanilla. It was a scent he could wrap himself up and get totally lost in.

Scent and hearing were the only senses that remained fully intact in The In-Between, a dimension just outside the Earthly Realm. She couldn't feel him holding her, and he couldn't feel her body wrapped in his embrace. He was nothing more than a ghost in her world. A fleeting breeze. A sense of comfort. He couldn't feel her, but the desire to experience her body pressed to his...to feel her warmth envelop him...had him aching with need. Heat surged through his body, and he groaned.

He had to push those thoughts out of his mind. He

was her Guardian, and she was his Charge. Nothing more. His mission was to protect her, to comfort her. And right now, she needed him to do his job.

Though doing his job was a lot easier before she met him. She really was nothing more than a Charge to him before he crossed over and started interacting with her three months ago. But the moment her emerald gaze had locked with his, and her pink lips curved into that sensuous smile, something inside him stirred. He'd seen her smile thousands of times, but that particular one had been for him, and he would never forget it.

"You don't need him." Though she couldn't hear his words, the message still registered in her subconscious. He'd guided her through many heartbreaks and difficult decisions in her life by whispering in her ear, just as he did now.

"You're smart, capable, and beautiful, April. Don't let him get you down."

She sat up and wiped the tears from her face. She took a shaky breath, and with a look of determination, she marched to the bedroom. Damian started to follow, until he heard her dress unzip and fall to the floor. He'd give her privacy. Besides, seeing her naked would only stir up more emotions he didn't want to feel.

She emerged wearing jeans, a T-shirt, and that same determined look. She'd heard his message.

She swung her purse over her shoulder, and with trembling hands, searched for her keys. "I'll show him. I'm just gonna march my happy butt right up to that bar and give him an ultimatum. Either he's going to marry me, or...or else!"

"Don't do that, April. Leave him alone tonight." Her plan was bound to backfire, and he couldn't stand seeing her in any more pain. She needed time to think. In nearly thirty years she still hadn't learned hasty decisions were always bad ones.

"You know what you need? Food. You need to drive to Whataburger, and get yourself a big, juicy burger. Those always make you feel better."

April sighed. "Who am I kidding? That'll never work." She pulled out her keys and opened the door. "Whataburger, here I come."

"That's my girl." Damian breathed a sigh of relief. He was lucky to have a Charge that actually listened. He didn't know how the Keepers did it with Charges that were normal humans. Some of them listened. Some of them didn't. They could merely make suggestions and hope the Charges followed. He chuckled. April was anything *but* normal.

Just to be sure she didn't change her mind and follow through with her catastrophic plan to find Jared, he trailed her to the restaurant. Once she was safely inside with the burger in her hands, he decided to do some reconnaissance from The In-Between. Following someone else's Charge was against the rules, but some rules were made to be broken.

He closed his eyes and pictured Jared in his mind so he could Jump. In an instant, Damian dematerialized and found himself standing in the middle of a sports bar. Peanut shells littered the floor, and the smell of stale beer and cigarettes assaulted him as he made his way past the giant flat screen to the table Jared and his buddies shared.

He shook his head. He never understood the draw of bars. People drank pints of alcohol to dull their senses and slow their reflexes. What was the point?

As he approached the table of men, he noticed Jared's Keeper standing behind him. Eric was a good friend, though Damian kept him at arm's length like he did everyone else. Eric's last Charge had lived in Southern California, and he'd picked up the surfer boy image.

"Dude, how goes it?" Eric ran his hand through his chin-length blond hair.

"Three more weeks, man. Just three more weeks."

"I'm stuck with this dude till he croaks." Eric nodded toward Jared and shook his head. "He never listens."

"Well, you've only got what? Fifty more years, max? Hang in there. It'll fly by." Damian slapped Eric on the shoulder. Since both men stood in The In-Between, Damian felt his hand land on Eric's back—a sensation he never felt when comforting April.

Eric was cool enough to let Damian nose around in his Charge's business. Other Keepers would have reported him by now, but not Eric. He was lucky to have such good friends in the Angelic Realm.

"Uh oh. Here she comes." Eric jerked his head toward a tall blonde slinking up to the table. She wore a shirt cut down to her navel, and she had legs up to her earlobes.

"I'm outta here, dude. I'll be back when the game's over to try and convince him to go home. Later." Eric closed his eyes, and in a mist of sparkling, gold light, he vanished.

"Aw, hell." Anger surged through Damian's core when the woman slid onto Jared's lap. She played with his hair and kissed his neck before she nibbled his earlobe. Jared obviously enjoyed the attention as he ran his hands up and down her body. Damian watched them cuddle and down beer after beer as they watched the game. Well, Jared watched the game, anyway. The blonde spent her time watching Jared and stroking his crotch under the table. Did this guy have no shame?

April was in tears, curled up on the couch when Damian had found her, and he was mad. No...he was pissed. His temper had gotten him into trouble on several occasions, and he was lucky he was in The In-Between or the punch he threw at Jared would have knocked him out cold. Instead, his fist flew right through Jared's head like a ghost passing through a wall.

Damian was fuming with nothing solid to take out his aggression on. His hands balled into fists. His teeth clenched together with an audible click. He needed to hit something...hard. And he couldn't do that in The In-Between.

He checked in on April, who was sound asleep in her bed. Alone. The tear stains on her cheeks told him she'd cried herself to sleep, and he berated himself for not being there to comfort her. If he hadn't been so concerned with spying on her ass of a boyfriend, he would have known she needed him. His own emotions overpowered hers, and that didn't do her any good. He needed to get his head together and do his job.

He'd never been so involved in a Charge's life. He was letting the little things get in the way of the big picture, and that wasn't helpful for anybody. What was it about this woman that absorbed him so? It didn't matter. He was going to shape up, complete his mission to help her cross over, and move on. Just like he always did.

But she looked so peaceful when she slept. Almost angelic. Her skin glowed softly in the moonlight, and the tiny whimpers that escaped her throat as she breathed gave him chills. What would it feel like to be curled up in that bed with her? To feel her soft curves pressed to his body and run his fingers through her silky hair? He allowed himself to lean in and take one last breath of her intoxicating scent. Deeply buried emotions stirred in his core, burning to unearth themselves and wreak havoc on his heart. He closed his eyes and Jumped.

He reappeared in his rented condo in the Earthly Realm, where he could slam all his frustration into the punching bag that hung in the middle of his bare living room. He hit his target with an unearthly force, sending it flying up to the ceiling. Catching it on the downswing, he nailed it again. He beat it, over and over, until the tension drained from his muscles and his mind cleared.

With a heavy sigh, he leaned into the bag and pressed his cheek against the rough vinyl. What the hell was wrong with him? He cared deeply for all his charges, but with April he felt something else. And it would be a cold day in Hell before he let that something else grow into something he couldn't take back.

CHAPTER 3

With a heavy heart, April dragged herself to work. Jared never came home, which meant he probably got too drunk to drive and had to sleep at Greg's house. Maybe she was better off without him. Maybe she should pack up all her stuff and get the hell out of there before he got home.

Who am I kidding? She never had much luck in the love department, so she had to hold on to what she could get. So he forgot their anniversary. It wasn't like it was their *wedding* anniversary. And guys were notoriously forgetful anyway. Maybe she should cut him some slack. Still, it would've been nice if he'd shown a little more interest in the woman he loved.

When she pulled into the parking lot, Damian was already there, getting out of his car. *Great.* She sure wasn't in the mood for his mockery today. Oh! And he was waiting for her on the sidewalk. *Just wonderful.*

She strode across the parking lot with her head down, trying to avoid the confrontation, but he blocked her way.

She sighed and looked into his eyes, where she was met with sympathy and concern. So not like Damian.

"Good morning, April. How are you?"

"Fine. Just peachy." She forced a smile and stepped around him. He had that damn knowing look again. But how could he know?

He caught her hand, and she felt a jolt of energy flash through her body before she yanked out of his grasp.

"You don't look fine. Do you want to talk about it?" Again with the sympathetic look. What had gotten into him? Was she really that obvious?

"Why would I want to talk about anything with you? Now if you'll excuse me. I need to get to class."

She turned on her heel, flipped her hair in his face, and marched inside the building. She usually stopped by Janice's classroom to say hi in the morning, but today she hurried past the door. She didn't know what she was going to say, or if she could even talk about it without breaking down. That's just what she needed—to have Damian walk in while she was blubbering on Janice's shoulder. She couldn't give him any more ammunition in their war of wits. No, she'd never let him see her cry.

She dropped her backpack on the desk and sank into her chair. Her feet were already throbbing from the three-inch heels she'd worn to make herself feel better. They were the cutest shoes she owned, but at three hundred dollars, they should've at least been comfortable. Her pink silk blouse tucked into her black pencil skirt accentuated her curves in all the right places. She'd hoped the outfit would lift her spirits, but it wasn't helping.

Still, she put on her best smile and greeted her

students as they walked through the door. Her personal troubles had no place in the classroom. The kids deserved her full attention, and they would get just that.

The morning went by without incident. She was able to forget about Jared for a few hours and focus on the work she loved. If she could make it through the day, she'd be okay. She'd talk to Jared tonight, and they'd work it out. They always did.

She was holding up. And after the night she'd had, Damian was surprised April even came to work. He probably wouldn't have. Their encounter in the parking lot didn't go as planned, not that he expected her to open up to him. She said she was fine, but he knew she wasn't. She had on the pick-me-up clothes she always wore when she felt especially depressed. His mouth curled up in a slight smile because he knew that about her. He knew *everything* about her.

April was a confident, take charge woman. But when it came to men, she always settled. He never understood that. She was beautiful, smart, witty, sexy. The way she flipped her hair in his face that morning sent her fragrance rocketing through his senses, and he couldn't get her out of his head. If she got him this worked up, he could only imagine the effect she had on mortal men.

He shook his head. He needed to stop thinking about her like that. He wouldn't allow himself to entertain the idea of being intimate with April. Of being intimate with anyone. Not after what he went through with—*no. I'm not even going to think about that.*

He opened a bag of Gardetto's and graded the pop quizzes he'd given his morning classes. His favorite thing about being in the flesh, in the Earthly Realm, was food. And the more time that went by, the better the food got. Gone were the days of seasonless meats and bland potatoes, and he relished the exciting combination of flavors in his mouth.

He closed his eyes and concentrated on the tangy, salty goodness—an explosion of savory flavor on his tongue. In three weeks, he'd have no need to be in the flesh every day, so he intended to make the most of what little time he had left.

"'S'up Mr. P.?" A lanky boy in baggy jeans and Converse tennis shoes interrupted Damian's delectable moment with his bag of snacks.

"Not much, Richie." He raised an eyebrow at his student. "Shouldn't you be in class?"

"Nah. I'm an office aide." Richie raised one shoulder in a dismissive shrug. "I just wanted to stop by and see how my favorite teacher is doing." He put on a charming smile and pulled a chair up to Damian's desk. "How's your day going?"

Damian grinned. "You didn't do your homework, did you?"

Richie's smile slipped away. "No...but I have an excuse. See, I had to work till midnight last night. Then, my baby brother was crying all night, and my mom was at work, so I had to take care of him. And she didn't get home till seven this morning, so I was late for first period…can you give me another day?"

Damian rubbed the scruff on his chin and pretended to think about it. "That sounds like a valid reason to me. Can you get it done tonight?"

"Thanks, Mr. P. Yeah, I don't have to work tonight, so I can definitely get it done." Richie's face lit up, and he straightened his spine as he walked to the door. "Thanks for understanding."

"Of course."

Richie was a good kid, and he listened to his Keeper. His dad had run out on his family when the baby was born, and Richie had to take over the role of father to his siblings. He was mature beyond his years, and Damian was glad to be able to help him. Even if all he did was cut the kid some slack. Richie needed a good role model, and Damian almost hated having to leave him.

Richie wasn't supposed to be his concern, but Damian was concerned about everyone. He'd take the world under his wing if he could.

The bell rang, and he knew April would be meeting Janice in the teacher's lounge. Since she wouldn't talk to him, maybe he could eavesdrop on their conversation and find out what April thought about everything that happened last night.

He waited a few minutes, to make sure they'd be deep in conversation, then he sauntered to the lounge. He hesitated by the door, trying to figure out his best maneuver. He found an empty chair directly behind April, so he could listen without her knowing he was there. Silently, he slipped into the seat.

"I don't know what I was thinking, Janice." April thought she'd be in tears talking to her best friend, but she must've cried herself out last night. "I mean, I guess I should have been more upfront about it. Maybe reminded him about our anniversary a few days ahead of time."

Janice rubbed April's shoulder and looked at her with sympathetic eyes. "Do you really think it would have made a difference? It was the championship game. C'mon, you should know Jared by now."

April sat up straighter, ready to defend her man. Instead, she blew out a hard breath and slouched in her chair. "I guess not. Basketball is important to him. I guess I should have talked to him about it, and we could have planned something for the day before or after. Then I wouldn't have been so let down."

Janice shook her head. "No, April. *You* should be more important to him than basketball. He could have recorded the game and watched it later. Quit blaming everything on yourself and see the man for who he really is—a jerk."

She took a deep breath and let it out slowly. Anger burned inside her, and she knew she needed to cool off before she spoke. She didn't want to go off on her friend, but Janice crossed the line. How dare she call Jared a jerk? April lowered her voice to an almost inaudible level; it was the only way she knew to keep from yelling.

"Janice, I'd appreciate it if you'd keep your opinions of the man I love to yourself. You don't know him like I do. He's not a jerk."

Janice leaned forward on her elbows. "Do you really

think you love him, April? Really? Because I think you're in love with being in love. You want a wedding and a diamond and a husband, and you're so blinded by all your wants you'll put up with guys who treat you badly. You can do so much better."

She looked at her hands folded on the table and whispered, "No, I can't."

"Yes, you can." Damian's voice came from directly behind her, and she jumped.

She turned and glared at him, trying to suppress her aggravation. She didn't want him to see her moping like this. She didn't want him to see any kind of weakness in her. Why his opinion mattered so much, she wasn't sure. But she had no intention of explaining herself to the man who'd been a thorn in her side for the past three months.

"How long have you been eavesdropping?"

"Not long." Damian smiled and shrugged. "But really, April. If the guy makes you that miserable, why don't you leave?"

"He doesn't make me miserable...not that it's any of your business." She crossed her arms and turned her back to him, praying he'd go away.

Damian rose from the table and put his hand on her shoulder, sending an electric jolt rocketing through her body. Had his touch always done that to her? Had he ever touched her before today?

"Suit yourself, April. But you're beautiful. If you just had a little more self-confidence, you could have any guy you wanted." He turned and strode out the door.

April's jaw dropped open. "Did he just say I was beautiful?"

Janice giggled. "I think he did."

"Wow." Had he given her a compliment before? Had he ever been *nice* to her? Just hearing him say it made her heart race and her stomach do back flips.

"I told you he liked you."

"Shut up. He does not. He was just being...nice." She tried to fight the grin that threatened to blow her cover.

"Uh-huh."

Her cheeks flushed as heat rose in her body, and she knew it wasn't from lack of AC. It was freezing in the teacher's lounge. "I've...got to get back to my room. I'll see you later."

She clicked down the hallway as fast as her three-inch heels would take her, and not until she was in the safety of her own classroom did she remember to breathe. She shouldn't have reacted that way to a simple compliment. Coming from any other man, she doubted she would have. But this was *Damian*. How could a man she hated so much make her want him so badly...with two simple words?

You're beautiful.

April laughed at herself. It didn't matter if Damian thought she was beautiful. She was with Jared, and she was going to make things right tonight. That's all there was to it. She'd push those thoughts of Damian out of her mind and focus on fixing her relationship with the man she loved. What else could she do?

~

Damian berated himself all the way back to his classroom. Did he really just tell April she was beautiful? Well, she needed to hear it, and it was his job to comfort her. He was her Guardian, and he had to soothe her pains and keep her safe until she turned thirty. That's all he was doing.

Yeah, right.

That was the last mistake he'd make with her, for sure. He'd have to be more careful with what he said, or she might start to think—to know—he liked her. And he couldn't let that happen.

He finished grading the last of the quizzes to get his mind off his Charge and congratulated himself for doing such a fine job with his students. Every one of them made an A, and he knew they were going to ace the nine-weeks test. How could they not, with a teacher who'd lived through everything they were studying?

CHAPTER 4

April got to work extra early the next day to avoid having to talk to anyone. Jared didn't come home again last night, though that was no surprise. His nights out were becoming more and more frequent, and she doubted he slept on Greg's couch every night.

Could he be cheating on her?

If he was, she certainly didn't deserve it. She did everything she could to make that man happy. But maybe her best wasn't good enough. Maybe *she'd* never be good enough.

Or maybe he wasn't good enough for her. He'd been so distant lately—like he already had one foot out the door. She could give him a push. Send him packing. She'd seriously considered packing up her things and getting the hell out last night. But where would she go? Momma would surely take her in, and wouldn't that be peachy? Mother and daughter, two sad, lonely women in one house. They could start their cat collection together.

She'd invested a year of her life in this man, and what

did she have to show for it? Lonely nights and hurt feelings. She could have those things on her own, no man
necessary.

Though she'd managed to avoid both Janice and
Damian all morning, she knew she'd have to face them at
lunch. She meandered down the hallway to the teachers'
lounge and shuffled through the door. Janice was already
seated at their table, but to her relief, Damian wasn't
around.

"Hey, girl! Where'd Jared take you last night?"

April forced a smile and slid into her seat. She
unpacked her lunch and spread it out on the table,
opening her Diet Coke and taking a long drink before she
spoke. "He, uh...had to work."

Janice raised an eyebrow and crossed her arms. "Are
you serious? After the stunt he pulled on your anniversary,
he went to work? What a jerk!"

"He can't help it. He's a lawyer." She shrugged and
took a bite of her sandwich. Why was she defending him?

"There's always Damian... He works the same hours,
he's smokin' hot, and he thinks you're beautiful." Janice
grinned and winked.

Warmth spread through her body, flushing her cheeks
and awakening urges she shouldn't have been feeling. Why
did thinking about those two little words Damian
muttered in passing get her so worked up? "He does not."

"He doesn't strike me as the type of guy to say things
he doesn't mean."

That was true. He wasn't the kind to play games. She
sighed and rolled her eyes. "It doesn't matter."

Janice shrugged. "I'm just saying." She leaned forward

on the table with excitement in her eyes. "Know what you need? You need a girls' night out. Let's go to Big Willie's after work."

"A pool hall? I don't see how that will—"

"They have a live band now. And they're really good. We can do some dancing, have a few drinks. It'll be happy hour." Janice pretended to dance in her seat.

April cringed. She hadn't been to that place in too many years to count. "Oh, I don't know. I'm not really in the mood to go out. I want to talk to Jared and figure out if this relationship is worth saving."

"You'll be home before he even misses you. C'mon, April. If not for yourself, will you at least do it for me?" She looked at her with pleading eyes and batted her lashes.

Janice wasn't going to give up, so April gave her the same line she delivered to her students when she didn't want to say no right away. "I'll think about it."

Janice clapped her hands and squealed. "Yay! That means yes."

"No, it means I'll think about it."

"Hey, maybe Damian'll be there, and he can tell you all about how beautiful you are."

Lord, I hope not. Seeing him in a bar when she had some alcohol in her system could be dangerous.

She made it through the rest of her classes and hoped to slip out the door before Janice caught her. Racing around the room, she picked up paper balls and discarded candy wrappers and tossed them in the trash.

The sound of keys jingling outside her room stopped her in her tracks.

Crap. She wasn't fast enough.

"Are you ready to go?" Janice stood in the entrance to April's classroom, clinking her keys in her hand. She leaned against the doorframe and crossed her legs at her ankles. "I'm not letting you through this door unless you're coming with me."

April shoved a stack of homework papers into her bag and zipped it before turning her pleading gaze to her friend. "I think I'm just gonna head home and wait for Jared."

Janice widened her stance and crossed her arms over her chest. "You're not going to wait for anybody. Get your purse, and I'll follow you home since it's on the way. We'll ride to Big Willie's in my car."

"Janice."

"April." Her steely tone said there was no use arguing.

She sighed in defeat. "All right. Fine. But I'm not staying out late. I want to be home when Jared gets there."

They drove to April's condo, and she climbed into Janice's passenger seat. She slammed the door, buckled her seatbelt, and assumed the pouting posture. Her brow furrowed as she slouched in the seat and stared out the windshield. She probably looked like a bitch, but she didn't care.

"Oh, don't be such a grump. Randy's picking up the kids, and this is the first time I've been out in two months. You could at least *act* like you're having fun."

A twinge of guilt twisted her stomach. She sat up straight and forced a smile. "You're right. I'm sorry. I deserve to have a good time, don't I? Jared obviously did last night, since he didn't come home."

And if he could have fun, why couldn't she? If she went home, she'd just be moping on the couch, eating ice cream. And she sure didn't need the calories. Jared liked her to be rail thin, so she'd been dieting since the day she met him. With her natural curves and full bottom, being perfect for him was no easy task.

But she did everything she could to please him. How else was she supposed to get a husband? Janice had been married five years and already had two kids. Most of April's friends had settled down, and she was tired of being the single one. She'd been a bridesmaid in countless weddings. It was her turn to be the bride.

She already had her gown picked out. It was white, of course, with a full skirt and elaborate beading covering the bodice and train. She'd wear a cathedral-length veil, and the entire church would be filled with freesia and tulips. Her bridesmaids would wear lavender, floor-length dresses and carry bouquets of matching flowers.

It was going to be perfect. Her dream wedding. All she had to do now was get the man.

An image of Damian flashed in her mind, and she squeezed her eyes shut. She'd always done so well at suppressing the sexual attraction. His personality had been like a cold shower to any desire she might have had for his body. But, now... She shouldn't be so attracted to another man when she had a boyfriend. Damn him for saying she was beautiful; that made her want him even more.

"Hello? Earth to April." Janice waved a hand in front

of April's face, snapping her back to reality. "We're almost there."

"Oh, sorry. I was off in my own little world."

"And what was Damian like in dream land?"

April's jaw dropped. "I was *not* thinking about Damian."

"Oh, come on. You can't tell me you're not wishing—just a little bit—that he'll be here tonight. I saw your face when he said you were beautiful."

"I can honestly say I absolutely do not want him to be here." Because after a few beers, she might do something she'd regret.

"Riiight."

The Chevy Silverado bounced through muddy potholes in the unpaved parking lot and came to a stop on the side of the red wooden building. The peeling paint looked like the original coat from fifteen years ago, and the hand-drawn sign hanging over the entrance was just like April remembered it.

She put on her best smile and opened the door. "Let's go have some fun."

Big Willie's hadn't changed much since she was in high school. The same old arcade games lined the walls of the entrance, and April smiled as they passed the Street Fighter machine.

"I beat that game senior year."

"Yeah, I know. You wouldn't stop talking about it for like three weeks."

She put her hands on her hips and lifted her chin. "I was proud of myself."

"Uh-huh."

A dimly lit bar sat off to the left, and rows of billiard tables occupied most of the room. Lights hanging over the tables advertised various beers along with the neon signs covering the walls. A small stage stood just past the bar, and the wooden dance floor had been installed within the past five years.

They stopped at the bar, and Janice ordered two bottles of Miller Lite.

"Wow. Last time we hung out here, we weren't old enough to drink." April took her beer and ambled to an empty table.

"I know, right? We had to get drunk before we got here. Ugh. I cannot believe we used to drink Mad Dog 20/20."

"Oh, and Strawberry Hill. That was my favorite."

Janice made a disgusted face. "Yuck. I'll stick with beer, thank you very much."

"Because that's so classy." April giggled and took a swig. The effervescent liquid cooled her throat, and she closed her eyes to savor the experience. A night out was exactly what she needed.

"Do you know that guy?" Janice nodded her head toward a man in the corner.

April turned around, and her heart sank. Guilt tipped with a spike of dread made her slouch into her chair.

"You know him, don't you?" Janice's eyes lit up. "He's checking you out, girl. You should go say hi."

She grimaced. "No way. That's Greg, one of the lawyers at Jared's firm. If he sees me here, he'll tell Jared. Jared would flip out if he knew."

"Really? He goes out without you all the time."

"I know, but he gets jealous if I even mention going out with anyone but my mom."

Janice laughed and downed the rest of her drink. "You know, I think we should have a girls' night out at least once a month. Just leave the guys at home and have some wild and crazy fun."

"That sounds like a good idea."

From the corner of her eye, she saw Greg rise from the table, high five his buddies, and stumble toward her. She sank even lower in her chair and brushed her hair forward to cover her face. Her pulse quickened when he neared them, but he shuffled right past toward the restroom.

He didn't see her. Relief flushed through her, relaxing the tension in her shoulders. Why should she feel guilty, though? She wasn't doing anything wrong. She had never been unfaithful to anyone, and she never would. Cheating wasn't in her blood.

She sat up straight and drank the last sip of her beer. "Want another round?"

"Hell, yeah!"

April looked around for anyone else she might know —that Jared might know—and when the coast was clear, she made her way to the bar. She had no reason to be afraid. *Better safe than sorry, though.* She ordered two more beers just as the music started up. Of course, it was a country band. They were in Felicity, after all. She rolled her eyes and shuffled back to the table to find Janice dancing in her seat.

"Okay. Next time we go out, we're going somewhere that *doesn't* play country music all the time."

"Oh, shut up, April. You used to love it."

"Well, not anymore. My tastes have...improved." She straightened her spine and raised her chin in a gesture of mock-superiority.

"You like to think so."

She pretended not to hear her friend's teasing words. "What was that?"

"Oh, nothing." Janice grinned and slapped her hand on the table. "Hey, you remember that four corners dance we made up at Billy Bob's way back when?"

How could she forget? She'd felt like a star with all those guys drooling over her and the girls trying to keep up. "Oh, yeah. That was cool. Everyone started following us and learning the dance."

"Yeah, we had the entire dance floor doing it before the song was over."

April sighed. The reminiscence eased her anxiety, though she longed for those simpler times. For the days when all she had to worry about was making it to school on time and having fun. "Those were the days."

Janice's face lit up, her eyes sparkling as she leaned forward on the table. "Do you remember how to do the dance?"

"Yeah." Her voice was wary; she knew where this was going.

"Let's go do it!" Janice grabbed her hand and tried to pull her to her feet.

"Oh, no. No way. No one's even on the dance floor." She jerked her hand back and gripped the sides of her chair.

"So, we'll be the first. C'mon, April. Do it for me?"

"What if Greg sees me?"

Janice took her hand and pulled her up. "Are you kidding? That guy's so drunk he'll be in the bathroom all night. Besides, have you ever even spoken to him? Would he recognize you?"

April pursed her lips and considered her options. Greg probably wouldn't recognize her, especially since he was drunk. And if he did, he wouldn't remember tomorrow.

"Just one song? Please?"

She glanced around the room. Luckily, she didn't recognize any of the other patrons. If she made a fool of herself, at least it wouldn't be in front of anyone she knew. "All right. But just once. And if Greg sees me, you're gonna be in *big* trouble."

Janice led her to the dance floor, shaking her hips to the beat along the way. They stood side by side and moved their bodies in unison with the music. Joyful memories flooded April's mind as she performed the dance she hadn't done in at least twelve years. As much as she wanted to get out of that town, Felicity would always be home. Her roots were here, but the rest of her wanted to see the world.

By the end of the song, tears streamed down her cheeks from laughter. "Oh, thank you for making me do that. It was so fun!"

"You're welcome. I'm gonna go get us another beer."

"Okay. I need to use the little girls' room. I'll meet you back at the table."

April paraded to the short hallway that led to the restrooms. She was actually enjoying herself, which she hadn't done in ages. With a skip in her step, she made a sharp right and ran right into a solid, muscular chest.

She looked up to find Greg smiling down at her. He smelled like cigarettes and whiskey, and his hooded, bloodshot eyes gazed up and down her body. She backed away, but he pinned her to the wall with a thick hand on either side of her head.

Her heart leaped into her throat, and she chided herself. Greg was obviously drunk, but he was one of Jared's best friends. He wouldn't hurt her.

"Hey, Greg. What are you doing here?"

"I jus' won a case, so I'm celebratin'." His slurred words oozed to her ears, and his toxic breath clung to her skin like plastic wrap.

She tried to duck under his arm, but he caught her by the hand and spun her around. He grabbed her shoulders and pushed her against the wall. Her head hit the sheetrock with a thump. "I was watchin' you dance. You looked good."

Panic-stricken, she glanced down the hallway, praying someone would walk by and save her. But no one was around. Surely he'd let her go. He wasn't going to hurt her; Jared would kill him if he did. "Um, thanks, Greg. Look, I've got to get home. Jared's expecting me." She tried again to wiggle from his grasp, but he pressed her harder into the wall.

"Aw, you can stay a little longer, sugar." He yanked open the men's restroom door and shoved her inside. Her ankle twisted, and she crashed to the sticky, nasty floor. The fluorescent lights cast a sickly green glow across the metal stall doors and the icy tiled floor.

"Greg! What are you doing?" The smell of urine and

vomit assaulted her senses. Her stomach lurched, and the rapid pounding in her chest made her head spin.

He locked the door and slowly turned around as she scrambled to her feet. Anger burned in his eyes, and a wicked sneer stretched across his face. He walked toward her, his cocky gait closing the distance between them in two strides.

She backed into a wall. The only way to escape was to make it past Greg, get the door unlocked, and get out before he could catch her. Her chances were slim, but anything was better than the alternative staring her in the face. And he was drunk, so he'd be slow. Even if he was twenty times stronger.

With adrenaline pumping and every muscle in her body tensed, she spun around him and darted to the door. But he caught her around the waist, knocking her breath clean out of her. He turned her around, and she screamed with as much volume as her breathless voice would allow. But with the music blaring in the bar, she was sure no one would hear her cries.

Greg backhanded her and slammed her into the wall, sending sharp pain slashing through her head. Her vision wavered, and stars danced before her eyes. But she wasn't giving in without a fight. She clawed at his face, digging her nails into his cheek and dragging them down to his chin. It didn't faze him. Blood trickled into the stubble on his chin, and he grinned. Her heart hammered so hard, she thought it might explode. *Oh, my God! This isn't real. It can't be.*

"I love a woman who fights back." Taking both wrists

in one hand, he pinned her arms above her head and unbuttoned his slacks.

"Oh, God. No! Greg, don't do this!" Icy tendrils of terror climbed her spine and shot down her limbs. This couldn't be happening. Her pulse pounded in her ears and sweat dripped down her forehead. "Please!" she screamed.

He reared back and punched her in the gut. Her stomach heaved as the pain traveled up her body. She tasted beer in the back of her throat as it burned its way up her esophagus. Her knees buckled. She gasped for air. Had she not been pinned to the wall, she would have doubled over in agony.

"Please." She barely forced a whisper from her chest.

Greg reached into his pocket and pulled out a knife. He flipped it open and pressed the blade to her throat. "Stop talking. You're ruining the moment, slut."

She held her breath as he dragged the dull side of the blade down her chest to the opening of her shirt. She tried to think of something—anything—to make him stop. She sucked in a breath to scream again, but the sharp edge against her throat silenced her. She stifled a gasp.

"No more screaming or I'll cut you open. Are we clear?"

She nodded, trying not to swallow against the blade.

He pressed the knife against her shirt, and in one swift movement, sliced it down the middle. He laughed when she squealed, and he moved the cloth aside, exposing her bra. Holding the knife between his yellow teeth, he cupped a breast in his hand.

He twisted it, flesh and muscle stretching almost to the point of tearing. Tears stung her eyes, and she gasped and struggled against his grip. He plunged his rancid tongue into her mouth and pressed the blade to her throat once more—this time with the sharp edge. The sour taste of stale whiskey and ash trays nearly made her vomit. Instead, she went utterly still. She tried to catch her breath —to calm down enough to think clearly. If she was going to make it out of this alive, she'd have to cooperate.

"Oh, you're gonna play nice now?"

She didn't answer, didn't move. He dangled the knife in front of her face, then slid it between her breasts. Hooking the blade under her bra, he yanked it, snapping the material in half. She squeezed her eyes shut and swallowed hard.

Then he released her hands to take both breasts in his. Her arms fell limp to her sides.

"Oh, yeah. This is gonna be fun."

Eric settled on the floor in the corner of Jared's office and rested his elbows on his knees. "Dude. It's not that I mind you hanging out, but don't you have anything better to do?"

Damian shrugged and sat next to his friend. "Not really."

"Where's your Charge?"

"She's out with her friend. They're having a couple of drinks. Nothing exciting. She doesn't need me right now."

Though he wished she did. He didn't want her to be in any trouble, but lately he'd find any excuse to talk to her. But he knew Janice would take care of her, so he focused on his burning hatred for Jared instead. The distraction helped distance him from April.

"That's cool, bro. I'm just hangin' out cause the blonde paralegal's gonna come traipsing through the door any time now. It's useless, but you know I'll try to talk him out of it."

Damian slapped him on the shoulder. "I know. You're doing your best."

"How's she doing?"

"Who?"

"April. How'd she handle the whole anniversary thing?"

"Ah, not so well. But her friend is there for her, so that helps." He stared out the window of the fourth floor office. *He* should be there for her too. In the flesh. Not just from The In-Between. And he would be if his heart didn't race and his cock didn't swell every time he got near her. He wanted her in ways a Guardian should never want his Charge. He despised the other Guardians who Fell for theirs—especially the first one. The one who started it all. His entire existence, he'd sworn it would never happen to him. After all the agony he'd endured, he would never let his emotions interfere with his job.

And then came April.

"Have you told her yet? I mean, it might make it easier on her if she knew."

He raked his hand through his hair and shook his head. "No. I haven't found the right time. I will, though. I've got nearly three weeks left."

Eric nodded and looked out the window. "So, you still

see Ella, huh? I mean, when April visits her family, you must..."

Damian raised an eyebrow. "Yeah. I see her."

"She still single?"

"Yeah."

"Do you think she'd be interested? I mean, if I..."

"How should I know? I don't pay attention to that kind of stuff." He didn't mean to snap at his friend, but Damian avoided love and relationships at all costs. Even talking about them. He'd been in love once, and it would never happen again.

"No. I guess you wouldn't." Eric gazed at the floor.

Damian sighed and leaned his head into his hands. Then he felt it. April's adrenaline spiked high. Her frantic pulse pounded in his head, and without explanation, he left Eric at the office and Jumped to her. From The In-Between, he saw her pinned against the wall as a big man in a cheap suit fondled her. Where the hell was this guy's Keeper?

Rage exploded inside him. He didn't think twice about Jumping in, right in front of her. He tackled the man, who was twice his size, and pounded his fist in his face. The protectiveness he felt for April drove his aggression harder and harder. He picked the guy up and slammed him into the wall before dropping the unconscious drunk on the floor. Blood trickled from the corner of the guy's busted lip.

Damian turned to April, who cowered in the corner, clutching her torn shirt to her chest. She looked at him with wide, unblinking eyes, and she recoiled when he knelt in front of her.

"It's okay, April. I'm not going to hurt you." He put his hands on her shoulders and looked into her fearful gaze. His stomach churned. Guilt weighed heavy on his heart. He should have been there for her. Where the hell were his priorities? He'd let his own raging emotions hinder his connection to hers, and she'd been hurt because of it. "You're safe now. He can't hurt you anymore."

Confusion clouded her expression, and she whimpered. Her chest rose and fell erratically as she gasped for her breath. "Damian?"

"Yeah. It's me." He brushed her disheveled hair away from her face and trailed his fingers down her cheek.

She looked down and back into his eyes. Then she threw herself into his arms and cried. He held her as she clung to him, wave after wave of sobs flowing from her trembling body. She climbed into his lap and pulled her knees to her chest, as a small child would do in her mother's arms.

He stroked her hair and rocked her, doing everything he could to ease her pain. It killed him to see her like this. Pain and burning anger ignited inside him. How could he have let this happen to her? He should've been there sooner. Should've *felt* her sooner.

When her sobs slowed, she inhaled a deep, shaky breath and blinked up at him. She wiped the tears from her eyes and forced a tiny smile.

"Thank you." The fragile whisper was barely audible.

"Are you okay? Did he hurt you?" He pulled her away from his chest to examine her face. A large, purple bruise had formed on her right cheek, and she winced when he touched it.

"I'm okay. He punched me a few times; that's all." She shrugged and struggled to her feet, still clutching her blouse together at her chest.

How could she brush it off like it was nothing? "That's *not* all. He tried to rape you. We've got to call the police before he wakes up."

She looked at the body lying on the floor, and fresh tears welled in her eyes. He pulled her into a firm embrace and turned her away from the attacker. Her body trembled as she clutched his arms and buried her face in his aching chest. The sweet scent of her hair tickled his senses as he kissed the top of her head. She fit perfectly in his embrace, as if she were made to be in his arms. How many nights had he dreamed of holding her? But not like this. Not because he'd let her get hurt. A fresh wave of anger broke in his heart.

She pulled from his embrace, and her shirt fell open as she wiped her eyes, revealing the delicate dip of skin between her breasts. He forced his gaze to her face.

"Here, take my shirt." He unbuttoned it and slipped it off his shoulders.

"Oh, I can't do that."

"Sure you can. I've got an undershirt." He smiled and held it out to her.

She slipped it on, but her hands trembled so much she couldn't manage the buttons.

"May I help you?"

She nodded.

He carefully closed each button, pulling the shirt as far away from her chest as the material would allow. One bump of a man's hand against her breast would probably send her into another fit, and he couldn't watch her go through that again.

"There. Do you think you're okay to go out and talk to the police? I can stay with you a little longer if you're not."

"No, I'm ready. I just want to get this day over with." She straightened her spine and pulled on the knob, but the door didn't budge.

He reached up and undid the latch that locked the door. Without making eye contact, he swung it open and gestured for her to exit. Hopefully she wouldn't notice it had been locked.

"How did you get in here, if the door was locked?"

Damn it.

"Uh, it wasn't locked when I came in. The latch must've closed itself when the door slammed shut." It was a lame excuse, but it was the best he could come up with. With any luck, she'd buy it.

She narrowed her eyes and gave him a questioning look before shrugging and shuffling out the door.

He stayed with her as the police arrived, though Janice took over comforting her. The bar manager calmed down the crowd and kept an eye on Greg until the police took him into custody.

He hated watching her relive the horrific experience as she explained what happened to the officers. Her sobs and trembling voice broke his heart. He wanted to take her in his arms and tell her everything would be all right. That he'd stay with her always and keep her safe.

But she wouldn't want that. She'd politely smile and turn away, and he'd make a fool of himself. She couldn't stand to be in his presence. He'd made certain she would feel that way.

He gave the police his statement, and tried to convince April to go to the hospital. She refused the ambulance, muttering that she was fine, so he helped Janice walk her to the car. With April safely inside and buckled, Janice closed the door and turned to him.

"Thank you so much. You got there at just the right time."

"Would've been better if I was a few minutes earlier, but I'm glad I could help."

Janice grinned. "First you kept her from getting run over in the parking lot. Now you saved her from being raped. What are you? Her guardian angel or something?"

He let out a nervous laugh. "Something like that."

"Well, she's got someone up there looking out for her."

You have no idea.

"Anyway, I better get her home. Thanks again." She dashed around the truck and got inside.

April rolled down the window and stuck her head out. "Damian, your shirt."

"Keep it. I've got plenty." He waved as Janice backed out of the parking lot and watched until the taillights disappeared in the distance.

April sat silently on the ride home. She'd been violently attacked by one of Jared's closest friends, and he might have killed her if not for Damian. She was damn lucky he came in when he did. Such a whirlwind of emotions spiraled inside her—relief, fear, embarrassment, anxiety—she didn't know what to feel.

When they got to April's condo, Janice parked the truck and took her inside. The house was just the way she'd left it. Yesterday's mail was still on the counter, and her discarded jacket lay across the tan leather sofa. The flat panel hung on the wall, and the remote peeked out from between the couch cushions, where she'd left it the night before. Everything was the same, except for her.

She'd never had her purse snatched, much less been beaten and almost raped. And by someone who was supposed to be a friend. Cold shivers ran down her spine. She felt different somehow. Older. Violated. Would anything ever really be the same?

"Here's an ice pack. Put it against your cheek, and I'll find you something to eat."

She took the ice and lowered her aching body to the couch. It stung at first, but the cold soon dulled the throbbing pain that shot through her head like bullets in a firing range.

"Thanks, but I'm really not hungry." Her stomach churned too much for food.

"You've got to eat something. You don't want your body to go into shock, do you?" Janice handed her a small container of chocolate pudding and a spoon. "Just eat this, and I'll leave you alone."

April smelled the pudding and scrunched up her nose.

"C'mon. Give it a try."

Janice wasn't going to let up until every bit of that pudding was in her stomach, so she dunked in the spoon and licked at the velvety treat. It was delicious, and she must have been hungrier than she thought. Before she realized it, the container was empty, and Janice looked at her with a smug smile.

"When are you going to learn I'm always right?"

She exhaled and put the bowl and spoon on the coffee table. "Maybe some day. But don't hold your breath."

Janice folded one leg underneath her and looked at her with a somber gaze. "Do you want to talk about it?"

"Not really...I mean...I can't believe it was Greg. That somehow makes it worse. Is that weird?"

She wrapped her arm around April's shoulders. "Absolutely not. You thought you could trust him, and he betrayed you."

"Yeah. Jared's gonna be pissed when he finds out."

"He should be. His friend tried to rape his girlfriend. He should kick Greg's ass. And if he doesn't, I'll kick *his* ass. Did you get ahold of him?"

"I called twice, but he didn't answer. I left a message, so he should be calling back soon." April rested her head on Janice's shoulder. "I just don't know who I can trust anymore."

"Well, you know you can trust me. And you know who else? Damian. He tore Greg up."

She smoothed his shirt over her stomach and tingles ran up her spine. Could she trust him? His personality had done a 180 from the day before. He'd laid into Greg like he was defending his own girlfriend. Then he was so kind and gentle with her. His gaze never left her as she talked to the police. The way he looked at her...she saw more than sympathy in his eyes.

Of course, Jared would've done the same thing. Wouldn't he?

"You know what's weird? Greg locked the door before...and when Damian and I went to leave, it was still locked. Damian said it was open when he came in, and the latch must've closed when the door slammed shut."

"Sounds logical."

"I don't know. I had this weird feeling he was lying—that he was hiding something. Listen to me. I must've hit my head harder than I thought. Like Damian could've gotten through a locked door. It's not like he can walk through walls."

"It'd be pretty cool if he could."

She looked at the clock and checked it against her watch, letting out a sigh of disappointment. "Jared's late."

"Doesn't that happen a lot?"

"Yeah, I was hoping he'd come home so we could talk. I don't know, I think I'm going to lie down while I wait for him."

"Do you want me to stay till he gets here?"

"Nah. I could use some alone time, if you don't mind."

Janice patted her friend on the back. "Of course I don't mind. But, I'm just a text away if you need me."

"Thanks, Janice."

When the door clicked shut, she curled up on the couch and closed her eyes. She was beaten and bruised. Her body ached, and her head throbbed. She tried to clear her mind, but thoughts of Damian kept intruding. How he saved her. The way she fit into his arms like he'd been holding her all her life. How safe he made her feel. He sure didn't act like he hated her today. He acted almost like...he cared.

Don't be ridiculous.

She chuckled at herself. He'd probably be back to his same old annoying self at work tomorrow. And she was looking forward to that. After the day she'd had, she could use a little normal.

She dozed off on the sofa and woke with a start when Jared slammed the front door. She sat up and rubbed her eyes.

With his fists clenched and his jaw rigid, he stared at her. He was livid.

"Tell me why I just had to bail Greg out of jail." His voice seethed with anger, and his narrowed eyes glared at her. Surely he wasn't mad at *her.*

He stomped toward her, and she recoiled into the cushions. "He tried to rape me."

"You're full of shit, April. He was trying to teach you a lesson. You shouldn't have been dancing out there like a stripper. You deserved it!"

She gasped and raised her hand to cover her mouth. No one *deserved* to be raped. "I wasn't dancing like a stripper. I was just having a little fun with Janice. How...how could you say that, Jared?"

"He wasn't going to hurt you." He grabbed her by the arms and shook her. "What the hell's your problem? Huh?"

"He held a knife to my throat." She tried to hold back the tears, but it was no use. They streamed down her cheeks, and she sucked in a breath.

"A little pocket knife. You made a huge mess out of

nothing. Now he's gotta go to court. Do you know how that looks, when a *lawyer* gets in trouble with the law?"

"He beat me." She had to force the words out through clenched teeth. Why was he doing this to her?

"You brought it on yourself. Where'd you get this?" He grabbed the top of Damian's shirt and twisted it in his hand, pulling her off the couch. "This is that guy's, isn't it? The one you work with?" He shoved her back down and clenched his hands into fists. "You've got something going on with him, don't you? You're cheating on me."

"No! Jared, I would never." Her heart sank, and heat coursed through her veins. How could he accuse her of such a thing?

"Save it. I'm getting outta here." He stormed into the bedroom and rustled around. When he emerged, he carried a duffle bag in one hand and his keys in the other.

"Where are you going?"

"Out. I can't stand to look at you anymore." He swung open the door and slammed it behind him with such force a picture fell off the wall.

She sat there—unmoving—staring at the door.

Did that really just happen? Did Jared actually blame *her* for Greg's actions? He and Greg were friends, sure, but the bruise on her face was proof enough he'd hurt her. How would Jared have reacted if he'd seen it happen, like Damian did? Would he have defended her? Would he have plowed into Greg without thinking twice? Would he have held her and wiped away her tears?

If the way he just acted was any indication, she knew what the answer was. Now what was she going to do about it?

How could that low-life idiot have treated her like that? What the hell was his problem? No doubt he was heading back to that blonde bimbo.

Damian couldn't stand seeing her curled up in a ball, crying on the sofa. She deserved so much better.

He lowered himself next to her and wrapped his arms around her fragile frame. *"It's not your fault. You didn't do anything to deserve it. You're a beautiful person, and you deserve so much more. Don't listen to him, April. Leave him."*

With his encouraging words and comfort, it wasn't long before she sat up straight and wiped the tears from her eyes. She looked at the clock and shook her head.

"No use staying up and worrying over it. I might as well go to bed." She dragged herself to the bedroom and fell face-first onto the mattress. Groaning, she worked her way under the covers and curled onto her side.

"It's not my fault, Jared. You'll see."

Damian lay on the bed behind her with his arm across her body. *God, I wish I could feel her.* The memory of the way she fit in his arms tightened his chest, and he yearned to feel her warmth again. To feel her soft curves pressed against his body. She could've used some *real* affection. But as much as he wanted to give it to her, it wasn't his place. He'd have to settle for comforting her from The In-Between.

She took a few deep breaths and slowly drifted to sleep. The tension in her body relaxed, and her pulse slowed to a steady, rhythmic beat. Rest was exactly what she needed to chase away the fear and guilt that must've been coiling inside her. To be betrayed by someone who was supposed to love her. He couldn't imagine what she must've been feeling.

Well, yes he could...

He breathed in her intoxicating scent and closed his eyes. He was getting in too deep, and he needed to get away.

But as the last of the tension left her body, she exhaled and whispered, "Damian."

Hearing his name dance from her lips made his heart lodge in his throat. Was she dreaming about *him*?

"I'm here, April. You're safe."

A soft moan vibrated from her chest, and she nestled her head into the pillow.

She couldn't possibly be dreaming about him, could she? He'd tried so hard to make her hate him. What dream could possibly be twirling through her mind? She was sound asleep, and he knew it was safe to leave her alone.

But he stayed.

As much as he hated to admit it, he liked holding her, whether he could feel her body pressed to his or not. There was nowhere in the universe he'd rather be. And he desperately wanted to hear her whisper his name again.

Get it together, man. It's not gonna happen.

The sun set, and soft moonlight filtered through the window, giving her skin an angelic glow. Even with her tear stained cheeks and disheveled hair, she was magnificent. The soft rise and fall of her chest, her gentle breath, her fragile posture. He could've held her forever.

But he needed to leave. To get away from her before

his thoughts went any farther down the path he'd been avoiding all this time.

He pulled his arm from around her and prepared to Jump. She moaned and reached to the place where his arm had rested moments before.

"Please don't leave me, Damian."

He froze, his body paralyzed in anticipation, and swallowed down the lump in his throat. Did she sense him? Did she know he was there with her? No, it wasn't possible. Charges felt comfort from their Guardians, but they never knew why.

"Damian, please."

Liquid warmth flowed from his core, out to his limbs. His heart raced at the sleepy sound of her voice. He imagined it was how she'd sound in the morning, after a long night of lovemaking.

But he could *not* think about her that way. There was no way in hell he'd ever fall for a Charge. Not if he could help it.

But if she needed him to be there with her, he had to stay. It was his job, after all. And though he needed more rest than The In-Between could provide, he'd stay with her all night if she needed him to.

He draped his arm across her soft skin—wishing he could feel it—and inhaled her sweet scent. If he wasn't careful, this woman would be the death of him.

CHAPTER 5

When the alarm beeped, April's eyes fluttered open. She didn't remember setting it last night, but she must've done it during her oblivious trek from the sofa to the bed. As she sat up and stretched, she couldn't remember the last time she'd slept so well.

She swung her legs over the edge of the bed and smiled when she realized she still wore Damian's shirt. She lifted it to her nose and inhaled the warm cinnamon scent that always made her body tingle.

She'd had some vivid dreams that night—all of them about him. From innocent cuddling to steamy sex, she'd been with him all night in her mind. It should've disturbed her, but it didn't. Surely it was just her subconscious working through his sudden change in personality. He'd saved her life. It was natural for her to have *some* feelings for him now. And they'd probably fade as soon as she saw the real Damian. He couldn't compare to the one from her dreams.

She unbuttoned his shirt and basked in the deliciousness one last time before laying it on the bed. She'd wash it and bring it back to him tomorrow. Her own shirt was ruined, which ticked her off. She lifted the tattered rags from her chest and groaned. She took good care of her expensive clothing, and seeing her favorite shirt ripped to shreds was infuriating.

She shucked it off and tossed it in the trash along with her bra. She was going to have to replace those soon. Maybe a little retail therapy after work would make her feel better. Lord knew she needed it.

She stepped into the shower and washed her hair as best she could. Every muscle in her body ached from being thrown around and beaten the night before. Just raising her arms over her head was a chore. After she dressed for work in the most comfortable outfit she could find, she looked in the mirror at the giant, purple bruise across her cheek. It'd take several layers of foundation to cover that up. Her nerves were shot, but she *had* to go to work. At least it would get her mind off everything that happened.

Wearing enough makeup to make a drag queen jealous, she headed out the door. Hopefully no one would notice the discolored splotch on her face. She could always say the swelling was from a bad sinus infection. She stopped by a drive through for an Egg McMuffin and coffee before driving to work. That little cup of pudding didn't do much for her last night, and she felt lightheaded from the lack of protein. She cringed with every turn of the steering wheel. She never realized how much she used her stomach muscles until they were beaten and bruised.

She ate her breakfast on the way to school and parked next to Damian's car when she got there. Opening her door, she sighed. She was actually looking forward to running into him this morning. Oh, well. Maybe she could stop by his classroom on her off period. She wanted to tell him thank you again.

Honestly, she just wanted to see him. Maybe his cocky attitude could chase away her yearning to be in his arms. She shivered as the memories of her dream flashed through her mind. Would being in his arms be such a bad thing?

Janice met her at the door as she entered the building. "Hey, girl. How are you feeling?"

"Better. Thanks." April continued to walk down the hall, and her friend kept pace with her.

"What did Jared say when you told him?"

She blew out a hard breath and opened her classroom door. "Come inside for a minute." She closed the door and paced to her desk, where she dropped her purse and back-pack before turning around and staring at the floor.

"He blamed me." Her gaze flicked to Janice, and she cringed.

"What?" Janice's eyes widened, and her jaw dropped. "You can't be serious."

"Well, I am. He bailed the asshole out of jail, and Greg convinced him it was all my fault. He came home screaming at me, saying I deserved it for dancing like a stripper."

"You've got to be kidding me. April, that's not right. There's something wrong with Jared if he's taking Greg's side."

She shrugged and dropped into her chair. "I know. I don't know what to do."

Janice sat on the desk in front of her. "Well, Cleopatra. You've got to get out of denial first. I know you're dying for a happily ever after, but Jared is obviously not the one to give it to you."

"I'm not in denial. I know there's a problem. I've known there was for a while now; I was trying to be optimistic before."

Janice crossed her arms and frowned. "All the optimism in the world isn't gonna change his personality."

"Maybe not, but what if he's the best I can do?"

"He's not, babe. Not even close. So what are you going to do about it?"

Before she could form an answer, the bell rang to start first period.

"I'll talk to you later, Janice."

"Okay. I'm right down the hall if you need anything."

What was she going to do? Jared was supposed to be the one. They were supposed to get married, move to Houston, have a few kids, and live happily ever after. That's the way it was supposed to be. She'd have a diamond, a house, a nice car. And she'd dress her beautiful children in the cutest designer outfits money could buy. It was the American Dream. It was *her* dream.

If she couldn't make it happen with Jared, what if she couldn't make it happen with anyone at all? She couldn't spend the rest of her life alone, but it looked like she couldn't spend it with Jared either.

She propped open her door to greet her students, and pushed the thoughts from her mind. She had a job to do, and she wouldn't let anything get in her way.

Her first two classes flew by without incident. Third period wasn't so easy.

When Alex, an outgoing star student, sulked through the door, her nurturer senses kicked into overdrive. A worried frown replaced his usual shining smile, and his brow was drawn over watery eyes.

"Alex? Is something wrong? Do you want to talk about it?"

He nodded his head without looking her in the eye and drew in a shaky breath. "Yeah. Can we talk in private, though?"

Her stomach dropped at his request. Alex was one of the most open people she knew, and he never minded letting the entire class hear about the latest drama in his life.

"Of course. Why don't you go in my office, and I'll meet you there as soon as I get the class started on the assignment."

He nodded again, keeping his eyes trained on the floor to avoid the questioning glances of his classmates, and he shuffled to the office.

"All right, y'all. Get out your books and do the pretest for chapter thirteen."

When the class groaned, April crossed her arms over her chest. "Hey, I don't like it anymore than you do. But I was just informed this chapter is going to be on your nine-weeks exam, so if you want to pass you'd better get busy."

The students grumbled, but they pulled out their books and began the assignment. April joined Alex in her office.

"What's up?"

Alex shifted from one foot to the other, still not looking at her. He wiped his eyes and ran his hand through his short, dark hair before taking a deep breath and blowing it out. He finally raised his gaze to hers and spoke.

"It's just...You're the first person I thought of to talk to about this. I just don't know what to do."

"What happened, Alex?" She instinctively put a hand on his shoulder to console him.

He swallowed and wrapped his arms around his stomach like he was trying to hold himself together. "I...I think I might have HIV."

"Oh, Alex." She pulled him into a motherly embrace and held him for a long moment. "Here, sit down and tell me all about it." Teenagers were always exaggerating things. Hopefully that was the case this time.

He sniffled and wiped the fresh tears from his cheeks, then sat in the chair she offered him. April pulled up a chair right next to him and put her arm around him.

"Well...my girlfriend went to the doctor yesterday, and they told her she's HIV positive. She came over and started yelling at me, saying I cheated on her. She's telling everyone she got it from me."

"Did she?"

"No...that's the thing. I've never been with anyone but her."

His entire body trembled, and her heart ached at the terror in his eyes. "Oh, Alex. I'm so sorry. Have you gotten checked out yet?"

He was silent for a moment. "I haven't. I'm too scared.

It would ruin my life. I just...I don't know what to do, Ms. Carter. What should I do?"

"Does your dad know?"

"No. I was thinking about going to Planned Parenthood or something to get tested. What do you think?"

"Honestly? I think you need to tell your dad. He loves you, and he would want to know. No matter what the outcome, he'll take care of you."

He sighed and slumped in his chair. "I know. It's just hard to talk to my dad about stuff like that. I always talked to my mom before she died."

"It will be hard. But I bet it would be hard to say it to your mom too, don't you think?"

He shrugged. "Yeah. I guess it would."

"Please talk to your dad before you go. Her parents might end up calling him, and it's better if he hears it from you first. Okay?"

He inhaled deeply and sighed. "Yeah. Okay. You're right. Do you mind if I call him from your office? I want to get it over with."

April smiled and patted him on the back. "Take all the time you need. I'm gonna go check on the minions in the classroom."

Damian had avoided her all morning. He usually got right into their battle of wits before the first bell rang, but he couldn't do it today. And not just because he was exhausted from spending the night in The In-Between.

His usual sharp senses were dulled to that of a human, and he felt sluggish, tired.

The real reason he wouldn't rag on her today was that she'd endured enough pain to last a lifetime yesterday. Making her hate him didn't seem so important anymore. She needed a friend, and that's what he would be.

He'd have to be careful not to be too friendly, though. If she sensed his true feelings, she'd turn tail and run in the opposite direction. Which would be the wise thing for her to do.

When the bell rang to end third period, he traipsed down the hall to April's classroom. They shared a conference period, so it was the perfect time to talk to her. He walked through the door just as she was about to leave.

"Oh! Hey, Damian. I was just fixin' to come and see you."

He smiled and closed the door behind him. "Well, here I am." He knew his gaze was heavy, but he couldn't tear it away from her emerald eyes. His fingers trembled with the urge to touch her. To take her in his arms and hold her close. He shoved his hands in his pockets and fought the need to close the distance between them. This was a close as he needed to get to her. Physically and emotionally.

She let out a nervous giggle and backed up to her desk, gripping the edge and resting her weight against it.

"I just wanted to check on you. Make sure you're okay."

"Oh, yeah. I'll be fine. I'm tough." She grinned and folded her hands in her lap. "I was, uh...I was actually coming to say thank you. For last night. For being there for me when I needed you."

His breath caught, and his eyes grew wide. Did she know he'd spent the night with her? And was she thanking him for it? The idea of her *wanting* him to stay with her made his heart race and his palms slicken with sweat. But that couldn't be what she meant.

"I mean, if you hadn't gotten there when you did, he might've killed me."

Of course it wasn't.

She inhaled a shaky breath. "So, thank you...for being my hero."

He chuckled. He was the farthest thing from a hero he could imagine. Heroes used their brains, not their hearts. And if he'd used his when...He couldn't even finish the thought. But, if it made April feel better thinking he was a hero, then he'd let her.

"You're welcome."

She glanced at the floor, and then into his eyes. "Can I ask you a question?"

"Uh, sure." *But I might not answer it.*

"Why are you suddenly being so nice to me? It's... I don't know. I kinda like it." A tentative smile curved at her lips as she brushed her hair off her shoulder.

Uh-oh. He couldn't have her liking any part of him. But did he really want her to hate him? Deep down, he knew he didn't. He wanted her to love him. And that was selfish. How could he even entertain the idea of letting her in? Letting her know him, when he didn't even know himself.

"I'm not being nice. Just concerned about my

coworker. I wanted to make sure you're going to finish out the year, you know? Have you started teaching your kids the new chapter?"

Way to go, idiot. So much for earning her trust.

She straightened her spine as the smile slipped from her face. "Of course I have. In fact, I bet my kids will do better on the test than yours."

"Uh-huh. Wanna put money on it?"

She grinned. "Ten bucks says my class average will be higher than yours."

"You're on. But don't feel too bad when you lose. Your inferior teaching skills don't reflect on you as a person."

They looked at each other in awkward silence, and then her gaze tightened into a glare. What he wouldn't have given to be able to read her mind at that moment. The stubborn way she set her jaw and crossed her arms was so damn sexy.

"Well, I better go get ready for my next class." He flashed a smile and strolled to the door. Part of him wanted her to call him back. To tell him she saw through his charade and pull him into her arms and kiss him. The feel of her soft lips pressed to his would be enough to buckle his knees. But that was crazy. Even if it could happen, he wouldn't allow it. He'd never let her know how he felt.

She sucked in a breath before she spoke. "You're gonna have to do a lot of work if you want a chance at beating me."

"Dream on. You couldn't beat me if your life depended on it."

Well, so much for him being nice to her. She shouldn't have been surprised; she knew it wouldn't last. Damian was back to his old self, and the man from her dreams was just that—a dream.

But to be honest, it did hurt her feelings. A little. After what happened last night, and then her vivid dreams, she'd given in to the false hope he might actually care for her. Which was ridiculous. It didn't matter if he did, because Jared…Well, what about Jared? He'd probably come home tonight and apologize. He usually did whenever he blew up at her. But she couldn't forgive him this time. Not after he treated her like she was to blame.

The bell rang, and she stepped outside to greet her next class. Alex was the first student to step through the door. Tear stains streaked down from his puffy, red eyes as he moped into the classroom.

"How are you holding up?" April put her arm around him and led him further into the room.

"Fine. I'm fine." He wiped his eyes and took a deep breath. "Do you think I can stay in here this period? There's someone in my next class I don't want to see right now. It's…her."

"Of course. I'll e-mail your teacher to let her know."

"I'm just so scared, you know? I have all these plans to travel and be a writer…and if I'm HIV positive…" He pretended to examine his fingernails as more students poured into the room.

"You're going to be okay." April pulled him to her and

gave him a hug. "I'm sure the test will come back negative."

A harsh voice, spiked with rage, drew her attention from her student. "There you are. You're the reason this happened."

She turned around and found herself staring down the barrel of a gun.

Damian berated himself on the way to his classroom. When he went inside, he slammed the door so hard pictures rattled on the walls. What happened to his plan to cut her some slack? To lay off the jabs and just be her friend?

It all went out the window when she said she liked him. No, she didn't say she liked *him*. She said she liked the way he was acting. There was a difference, and he needed to remember that.

But how could he be her friend when simply looking at her set his soul on fire? The sooner her time here was up, the better. He needed to get away from her before he went down in flames.

He opened his door to let in his next class when adrenaline spiked in his core. Only it wasn't his adrenaline; it was April's again. Racing down the hallway to her room, he pushed against the raging flow of screaming students. A man held April and Alex at gunpoint. Six other students huddled under desks and in corners of the classroom, their gazes frozen on the gunman.

"It's not my fault, I swear." Alex's voice trembled as he

tried to reason with the attacker. "I'm not the one who gave it to her. It's someone else."

The man with the gun shook his head. "No. You're the only person my sister's ever been with, Alex. I know it was you. You gave my little sister a *disease*."

Damian calculated his options as they spoke. The man didn't know he was there, so he had the element of surprise on his side. He could jump for the gun. But the attacker had his finger on the trigger, and he was distraught enough to pull it. He could try to talk the gun out of his hand, but just hearing Damian's voice might be enough to startle him into shooting. Before he could make up his mind, April spoke.

"All right. Let's just think about this. Killing Alex isn't going to solve the problem. Shooting him won't cure your sister."

"Just keep outta this, Miss Carter." His hands trembled as if he didn't want to shoot, and it looked like April could convince him to turn over the gun. She took a step toward him, the gun pointing directly at her chest.

"Why don't you give me the gun, and we can talk about it? You don't really want to kill Alex, do you?"

"No." His voice was a whisper; tears rolled down his cheeks.

April took another step toward the man and put her hands on the gun. Damian held his breath as the man loosened his grip. April was doing it. She was going to get the gun.

"Good. Now give me the gun." Her soft voice should have soothed the man, but instead he panicked.

"No!" He tightened his grip, and his finger twitched.

He pulled the trigger, sending a bullet ripping through April's chest. Damian screamed and burst into the room as his Charge collapsed to the floor.

He tackled the man, sending the weapon skidding across the floor. Chaos consumed the room; students ran screaming and neighboring teachers rushed in. His temper raged out of control as he pounded his fist into the man's face. *Nobody* hurt April. She belonged to *him*.

The attacker was bruised and bloody by the time the teachers yanked Damian off him. He ripped from their grasp and darted to April where she lay in a pool of blood.

"Oh, no. April! No!" He pressed his hand to the hole in her chest to stop the bleeding, though he knew it was useless. The wound was fatal, and he could feel her life slipping away. The life he'd spent thirty years protecting, nurturing. Her death wasn't supposed to be painful. It wasn't supposed to happen this way. He was her Guardian, damn it!

He held her in his lap, and her eyes fluttered open.

She sucked in a pained breath and forced a whisper from her chest. "Damian? Am I dying?"

He sighed and pursed his lips. "Yes, April. You are."

"I thought so." She smiled weakly and grasped his hand.

He brushed the hair out of her face and caressed her cheek. The commotion in the room slipped away as he held his Charge in her last moments of life. She coughed, and blood spilled down her chin.

"I'm so sorry I failed you, April. But, don't worry. Your next life will start soon."

She sucked in a sharp breath, closed her eyes, and slipped away.

The police and EMS arrived not a minute after April died. They handcuffed the man and hauled him off, and Damian stormed to the door. The heat of anger pulsed through his veins, and with his jaw clenched tight, he focused on the exit. He had to get out of there so he could Jump to the Angelic Realm. He had some explaining to do.

An officer grabbed him by the arm as he went through the door. "Sir, you need to answer a few questions."

Damian's lip pulled up in a snarl, and he jerked his arm free. "I answer to no one."

He turned the corner and Jumped. It didn't matter that no one would be able to explain his disappearance. He'd never go back there. He had no reason to now.

CHAPTER 6

"How could I have let this happen, Mira? Damn it!" Damian slammed his fist into a white wall, leaving a gaping hole. "I've never lost a Charge." As soon as he removed his hand from the wall, the material liquefied into a thick ooze that filled the puncture, repairing the damage instantly.

"Don't be so hard on yourself. Look around; you're not the only one." Mira, the Guardian of the Slumbers, motioned for Damian to notice his surroundings. Beds covered with crisp, linen sheets filled the stark, white room. Five Charges of varying ages lay dormant on the beds, awaiting maturity so they could awaken again. "Many Guardians lose their Charges. It's nothing to lose your temper over, dear."

Damian chuckled at the woman with long, dark hair and lavender eyes. Though they were the same age, he respected Mira as he thought he would an older sister, if he had ever had one. She was the most caring Guardian of them all, motherly, which was why she Guarded the Slumbers, and everyone else for that matter. She was connected to every being in the Angelic Realm, could locate and help them anywhere.

"You're right, Mira. You're always right...but, *I* don't lose Charges. I shouldn't have lost April." He looked down at his only responsibility for the last thirty years. Her fiery red hair spilled out around her head, a vivid contrast to her pale skin and the bright white sheets she nestled in. Mira had changed April's clothes with a touch, a talent only she possessed, and a soft, white gown replaced her bloodied shirt and skirt. Even in Slumber she was breathtaking, and Damian marveled at her beauty. Her soft, pink lips curved into a perfect bow. Her delicate nose had a soft sprinkling of freckles, and her porcelain skin was flawless.

Mira put a hand on his shoulder. "This one's special to you, isn't she?"

He stiffened at the accusation. "No. No more than any other Charge." He shoved his hands in his pockets and turned away from April, afraid the distraction of her soft lips and perfect skin would give away his true feelings.

Mira smiled. "You can fool yourself, Damian. But you can't fool me. Remember that."

"You're crazy, woman. You know me better than that." Damian laughed and ran a shaky hand through his hair.

"Better than you know yourself...oh, we've got one waking up. What a joyous day!"

"Joyous. Right." He let out a cynical chuckle. "Go take care of him. I'll take care of April."

"I know you will." Mira gave him a knowing smile, turned and hurried across the room to greet the awakening Slumber.

Damian looked at April, peacefully sleeping, oblivious to the world she just entered. She died today, but the flush of her cheeks and her rose-colored lips made her look more alive than ever. Without thinking, he reached out his hand and gently caressed her cheek. The softness of her skin sent shivers down his spine, and he jerked his hand away. He had no right to touch her like that.

He wouldn't do it again.

He closed his eyes and imagined a stool next to the bed. When he opened them, his creation was there, so he sat down and sighed. Knowing April, she was going to freak out when she woke up. And of course she'd blame him, just like she blamed him for everything else.

It was his own fault she hated him. He did everything he could to push her away, when he should have been drawing her in. Making her trust him. Even after the last few days, when she was beginning to trust him, he had to mess it up by insulting her teaching skills.

He screwed up royally with April. He'd made more mistakes with her than he had made in his entire existence. Well, almost.

He had almost three weeks to think about what he was going to say to her. Three weeks to figure out how to earn her trust. Maybe he could convince Mira to do it. Then he'd be done with her now. He could move on.

No. April was his responsibility, and he'd stay by her side and see this mission through to the end—to her thirtieth birthday. And thank goodness that was coming soon.

"Hey, Damian." A young Guardian with spiky brown hair and light blue eyes approached him. "Paul wants to talk to you."

Paul. The leader of the Angelic Realm. He was the closest thing Damian had to a brother, but they rarely saw eye to eye.

"Tell him he'll have to come to me. I'm not leaving April alone."

"Whatever you say, boss." The Guardian scampered away, and in a few minutes, Paul returned in his place.

He looked at the Angel that lay by Damian's side, and a smile quirked at his lips before he frowned. "You attacked another human. That's two in as many days."

Damian straightened his spine, ready to defend his actions. "He shot her. What was I supposed to do?"

"Take care of your Charge. It's not your place to punish."

He raised his chin in a defiant gesture. "He deserved it."

"You don't get to judge." He let out a heavy sigh. "Look, brother. Your anger has gotten out of control. We've been looking the other way, letting you fight your demons. But it's gone too far. You don't belong out there."

Damian clenched his jaw and scowled at Paul. "Yes, I do. I'm the best Guardian you've got." He *had* to be out there. He would *not* let Paul take this away from him.

Paul put his hand on his shoulder. "I know. And that's why we've let it go on this long. It's time you took your rightful place as leader. We need you."

"No, you don't. You're doing just fine without me." He crossed his arms over his chest and widened his stance. He was standing his ground on the issue. No matter what.

Paul took a deep breath and leaned against April's bed. "But it would be so much easier if we had your help."

"You keep saying we. Is Mira in on this too?"

"We have discussed it, yes."

"That's funny. Because she hasn't mentioned a thing to me."

"Damian..."

"No. I don't belong up here. I need to be out there, helping people. It's what I was made for."

"You were made to lead, just as Mira and I were. You are hurting more than you are helping by not accepting responsibility for your position in the Angelic Realm."

"You know what? You're entitled to your opinion. But mine's the one that counts. As soon as April wakes up, Mira will give me a new Charge, and I'll be back on Earth doing what I'm supposed to do. I can't lead, Paul. I don't have it in me anymore."

"April is—"

"We're done, Paul."

"When are you going to let go, brother? You can't change the past. Your worries, your fears, your anger. Let them go."

"We're done." He glared at the man with white hair and ice blue eyes. Paul made a fine leader, and he certainly didn't need Damian hanging around, screwing things up.

"Okay. I will leave you be for now. But, this discussion is far from over."

"I've got nothing left to say."

Paul looked at him with a sympathetic gaze and shook his head. "Until tomorrow." Then, in a flash of shimmering light, he disappeared.

It was the same conversation every time. He'd do something to tick Paul off, Paul would try to convince him to stay in the Angelic Realm sitting on his butt and telling everyone else what to do.

It wasn't in him. He couldn't sit idly by when there were people out there who needed him. People he could focus all of his attention on and forget about the demons inside him. Because, honestly, he needed his Charges as much as they needed him. But no one else had to know that.

And if he was honest with himself, he'd admit he was scared. He was terrified of taking on any more responsibility because he'd failed so miserably before. If people depended on him, he'd ruin their lives. And he couldn't live with that.

Sitting here for three weeks with an unconscious April would be torture enough. He couldn't imagine spending his life with no distraction from the anger that burned inside him.

But sitting here with April was also torturous for another reason. The fire that burned in his soul when he looked at her perfect face. The emotions he felt coming to life in parts of him that had been dormant for so long. He couldn't let it happen.

He couldn't wait to get away, but he didn't want to leave her side. Life without April would be...unbearable.

CHAPTER 7

Searing pain slashed through April's chest as she tried to comprehend what happened. The last thing she remembered was the gun pointing at her. The trembling hand that held it. The sound echoing off the walls when the shot was fired.

She couldn't breathe. Couldn't move. The agony left her paralyzed while she choked on her own blood. Her body throbbed. Her chest burned like it was filled with flaming hot coals. Was the torment ever going to end?

She tried to scream, but couldn't find her voice. She was trapped. Panic rushed through her veins, and her blood ran cold. Why couldn't she move? Was she dead? Was she stuck in this torturous hell forever? *Oh, please Lord. Make it stop. I can't take it anymore.*

Then, as suddenly as the torment began, it slipped away. No pain, no fear. Only peaceful silence. Her body tingled with pleasure.

She was warm. Safe. Like she was wrapped in a cocoon of security—a sharp contrast to the agony she felt only moments ago. Nothing could hurt her now. In her mind, she drifted through the clouds. A midnight blue sky, sprinkled with glowing stars, stretched above her. Below, a body of water, translucent and serene, reflected the sparkling light from above. A gentle breeze caressed her skin, and the salty scent of the sea tickled her senses.

She was peaceful. Happy. And when a light began tugging her into consciousness, she fought it. She wasn't ready to wake up. Wasn't ready leave the calm of slumber. But the light insisted. And though she tried to resist, it pulled her closer and closer to awareness.

Her breath caught when she awoke, and she lay there for a moment, fighting the urge to open her eyes. She tried to keep her lids firmly shut, but they fluttered when she felt the small commotion around her. Someone was watching her.

With one last deep breath, she opened her eyes and tried to focus. The quiet room was devoid of color, yet somehow felt warm and inviting. She sat up and absorbed the surreal surroundings. Three other people in the room were sleeping, just like she had been, and several others watched over them protectively. She'd never been in a hospital like this, but it must've been a good one. Her body felt fresh, rejuvenated, despite being shot in the chest a few hours before. She felt her skin where the bullet entered. No pain. No stitches.

Hmm. Must have been a flesh wound. How long was I out?

Everyone in the hospital wore simple white outfits, including April. Her designer skirt and silk blouse were nowhere to be seen, but the gown she wore felt like velvet against her skin. She wondered what material it was as she smoothed the light, silky cloth down her legs.

"Happy birthday, April."

She'd recognize that voice anywhere, and she shook her head as Damian came into view.

"Great. I've died and gone to Hell, and the devil sent you to torment me for the rest of my existence." She rolled her eyes and swung her legs over the side of the bed. "And what happened to my clothes? That was a Versace skirt."

"It's good to see you've held on to your charming personality." Damian leaned against the bed next to her. "You got the death part right, but you're not in Hell. And I'm not here to torment you for all existence. I've been Guarding you all your life."

"Right, and I'm a superhero with magical powers...oh, God! Alex. Where's Alex?"

"He's fine. The bad guy's in jail. You're the only one who got hurt."

"Oh, thank God." Relief washed over her as that weight lifted from her shoulders. She'd have died if anything happened to Alex.

"Where am I really, Damian? What hospital is this?"

The corner of his mouth quirked into a crooked grin. "You're in the Angelic Realm. It's a place between Heaven and Earth."

"Yeah, right. What...is this like purgatory or something? What am I being punished for?"

"You're not being punished."

"Really? Then why are you here?" She'd had about enough of this game. She slid off the bed to search for her clothes, but there were no hooks or drawers where they could have been stored. She looked at Damian, who grinned at her with amusement sparkling in his eyes.

"Is this some kind of joke? Where are my clothes? I want to go home."

Damian sighed and pushed off the table. All humor faded from his expression as he approached her and put his hands on her shoulders. His touch sent warm tingles through her body, and she sucked in a sharp breath as she stepped away. That one chaste touch left her wanting more, and she had to fight the urge to slip into his strong embrace.

Not that he wanted to hold her.

He wore faded jeans that hung low on his hips, and his tousled toffee hair almost seemed to glow. His white T-shirt stretched across his sculpted muscles as he moved. He'd never looked so scrumptious.

She chided herself for feeling that way. Jared was still her boyfriend—for now—and she'd never be unfaithful. She just needed to find her clothes, check herself out, and get home before her thoughts drifted any further.

"April." He reached out a hand to touch her, but let it drop to his side before making contact. "This isn't a joke. You really are in the Angelic Realm, and I'm your Guardian Angel."

She searched his eyes for a trace of humor, but all she found was compassion. His lips didn't quirk into his teasing grin, and there was no hint of sarcasm in his voice. Was he telling the truth? Could she really be dead? *Oh, please.*

"I...I don't believe you. This is ridiculous." Why was he doing this to her? Was it some kind of sick joke? She pushed past him and spotted a door across the room. Adrenaline stung her muscles and she raced to the exit.

"April, wait." Damian caught her hand before she could push open the door. "Don't go out there. Please, let me explain."

"I've heard about enough from you, mister. Now, leave me alone. I want to go home."

He let her hand slip from his grasp as he took a step back. "If you must."

She huffed and swung the door open. Sparing one more glance at Damian, she expected to see his devilish grin, but what she saw surprised her. Emotions she thought she'd never see from Damian. Sadness. Worry. Understanding. The look in his eyes was magnetic, drawing her closer to him. She instinctively took a step toward him, her heart racing in her breast.

He was so serious, she almost stayed. She could feel the concern rolling off him, but it was more than that. She felt a connection. Like a cord connecting her heart to his. Did he actually care for her?

No. He couldn't. And it didn't matter if he did.

"Goodbye, Damian." She turned around, stepped through the door, and gasped.

If she thought the hospital room was surreal, this place was downright weird. She was in a fog, though the air was dry. She looked all around, but saw nothing. Nothing but white mist. Where the hell was she? The claustrophobic cacophony of nothingness sent chills down her spine. It was as if the world was closing in on her, though there were no walls—or anything solid for that matter.

The adrenaline tipped to panic as she sprinted through

the haze. Cold sweat beaded on her forehead. There had to be a way out. If she just kept running, she'd end up some- where. Anywhere but here in this void. She ran. And ran. But no matter where she went, the emptiness followed. It was in front of her. Behind her. Everywhere.

She was in Hell.

She could have kept running forever; she wasn't the least bit winded. But what was the use? She was getting nowhere, and now she couldn't even find her way back to the hospital.

She was lost and alone.

Tears stung her eyes, and she didn't try to hold them back. She dropped to her knees, and with her head in her hands, she cried. It wasn't supposed to be this way. This wasn't how her life was supposed to end. She was supposed to grow old and have lots of grandchildren. She would sit with her husband on their porch and rock while the kids played in the yard. She deserved a good life, damn it!

She let out a cynical laugh. Damian claimed to be her Guardian Angel. What a crock! God really screwed up on that one if he was.

But if Damian was her Guardian Angel, he'd be able to find her. She'd just have to call his name, and he would be there. Laughing at herself, she wiped the tears from her face. She must have been insane to even entertain that thought. If Guardian Angels existed, they wouldn't be flesh and blood and sinew and muscles like Damian. He was definitely all man. Still, he did seem to come out of nowhere when he tackled her in the parking lot. And how'd he get into the bathroom through the locked door?

You're being ridiculous, April. Pull yourself together.

Just to prove to herself that he wasn't her Angel, she whispered his name. If he was an Angel, it shouldn't matter if she whispered or yelled. That's how it was in the movies anyway.

"Damian. Help me."

"I'm here, April." He stepped through the haze, and the blood drained from her face. It didn't make sense. She'd been running for at least half an hour. Had he been following her all this way? Or was he...no, there was no way...

"How did you find me?"

His mouth quirked into a crooked grin. "I told you. I'm your Guardian. I can find you anywhere with just a thought." He dropped to his knees and held her hands in his.

"Look, April. I know I haven't been the easiest person to get along with. But I would never lie to you. You died. You were shot in the chest, and you died."

She wanted to run. To get as far away from him as she possibly could. But his intense hazel eyes held her there. He wasn't joking.

"I don't believe you." She pushed the whisper over the lump in her throat. She didn't *want* to believe him.

Damian sighed. "I didn't want to do this. But I've got to prove it to you." He rose to his feet, pulling her up with him. Though his grip was gentle, and she could have pulled free, she didn't. The warmth of his hands, the feel of his touch, soothed her.

"Don't let go." Damian smiled and closed his eyes.

In a blink, the haze receded, and they stood in a cemetery. The dreamlike scene was whitewashed—the sky a dark shade of ash and the grass even darker gray. She felt like she was standing in the middle of a black-and-white movie, and Damian was the only thing in color. His tanned skin and golden brown hair contrasted with the grayscale landscape, making him look like a Greek god.

"Where are we?"

"We're in a cemetery." Damian tucked a piece of hair behind her ear and trailed his fingers down her cheek, leaving a tingling path of heat on her skin. His touch was so gentle and kind, she inhaled deeply and leaned into his caress. The smile on his face dropped into a scowl as he pivoted and marched away.

"Damian, wait!" April called, and he stopped without turning around. She lifted her long gown and scurried after him. She couldn't bear to be lost again.

"I know we're in a cemetery, but why is everything black and white? Except for you..." She looked at her hands and realized her color was normal too. "Why are we in color?" She reached out to touch his arm, but he jerked it away. His rejection cut like a knife to her heart. She dropped her hand and took a step back, searching his eyes for a reason for his behavior. He met her gaze with confusion and compassion, which she didn't understand. How could his eyes say one thing, while his body said another?

Damian took a deep breath and let it out slowly. "We're in The In-Between. Think of it as another dimension. We're on Earth, in Felicity actually, but we're on a different plane than the rest of the world. We can see people, but they can't see us. They can't hear us or touch us, but sometimes they can sense us. And we can't touch them, either. We're like ghosts when we're in this realm."

"But I can feel you. I felt your hands holding mine."

"That's because we're both in The In-Between. It's how we Angels watch over our Charges without being detected."

"And you've been watching over me all my life?" She took his hand in hers and stepped toward him. This time, he didn't pull away. Something about his touch—about *him*—calmed her confusion and fear. The connection she felt to him was magnetic, pulling her in.

"I have." He tensed as her body moved closer to his.

Heat radiated from his skin, and she inhaled his dark, cinnamon scent. She shouldn't have been doing this. Logic told her to step away, but her body wanted to be closer. She was confused and possibly in shock. *I'm not in my right mind. I'm not responsible for what I do.* Her heart pounded in her chest as she stood on her toes and placed a tender kiss on his cheek.

"Thank you," she whispered into his ear.

He swallowed hard and turned his face toward hers, their lips so close she could feel his sweet breath on her skin. Was she really going to do this? Was she going to kiss him? *I shouldn't.* But oh, God how she wanted to. Heat flushed her cheeks when he leaned closer, placing his free hand on her hip. She closed her eyes and braced herself, the anticipation building until she thought she might explode.

Nothing happened. The warmth of his body turned cool, and when she opened her eyes he was gone.

"Damian? Where'd you go?" She spun around and found him standing, with his back to her, by a fresh grave.

She breathed a sigh of relief. He hadn't left her, and he didn't kiss her.

She moved toward him, stepping around the tombstones as she glided across the grass.

When she reached him, she placed her hand on his shoulder. "I'm sorry."

"For what?" He shrugged off her touch and paced around the grave.

"For what happened over there."

"Nothing happened." The way his brow furrowed over his eyes told her the conversation was over. *Ouch.*

Well, if he was going to pretend nothing happened, so would she. Nothing did happen, after all. And she was glad he didn't kiss her. She hadn't broken up with Jared yet. Still, she knew she wasn't the only one who felt the attraction. He liked her, no matter how hard he tried to pretend he didn't. A smile tugged at her lips as she stepped around the mound of dirt to stand next to him.

"Whose grave is this?" And why did he want her to see it?

His hard expression relaxed into one of sympathy as he looked into her eyes. "It's yours."

CHAPTER 8

"It can't be mine; I'm standing right here." She looked at Damian incredulously, as if she was waiting for him to tell her he was kidding.

But he wasn't.

"It's yours, April. Look at the marker."

She knelt by the grave and ran her fingers across the letters etched in the stone. Maybe she'd finally believe him. It was a harsh way to find out the truth, but April was stubborn. She needed to see this, or she'd never get out of denial.

"No...no, this can't be." The Southern drawl that she tried so hard to hide flowed into her speech like it always did when she was upset.

Sitting cross-legged on the ground, she stared at the grave marker in silence, and he let her have her space. He should have prepared her for the crossing over. That was his job, and he failed miserably. He was supposed to be the best Guardian of them all. One of the original four, created by God to watch over the humans from the beginning of their existence. He didn't make mistakes like this.

So why was he making them now?

April was different. Different from any Charge he'd ever guarded. Hell, she was different from any Angel he'd ever met, and that scared him. His own emotions terrified him.

She stood, wiping the tears from her cheeks, and turned to him. "How can I be here, with you, if I'm dead? Am I a ghost?"

"Not exactly."

She looked at the grave and held her hand to her heart. "And Momma and Shelly? They buried me here?"

"Yes."

"And Jared?"

He stifled a cynical laugh and gritted his teeth. "He was at the funeral."

"Oh, this is awful. Just downright awful!" She threw herself into his arms and nuzzled her head against his chest as she sobbed.

He wrapped his arms around her and held her while she cried. She was so warm and soft, and his heart broke to see her upset this way. Upset because he didn't do his job. Because he was so concerned with not developing feelings for her, he lost sight of his purpose. He'd never forgive himself. And as soon as April was in Mira's care, he'd make damn sure he didn't make this mistake again.

His body warmed with their embrace, and his heart raced in his chest. He'd comforted her like this hundreds of times: when she skinned her knee, when a boy broke her heart. But, this was different. She was actually *in* his arms. He could feel her. And she could feel him.

He inhaled her sweet scent and held her tighter. He was doing his job. He was comforting his Charge. So holding her brought *him* comfort too. No big deal. He'd take her back to the Sanctuary soon, and he could forget all about his feelings for April.

Yeah, right.

He'd never forget the way she felt in his arms at that moment, but that moment was all he had. He was alone by choice now, and he planned to keep it that way.

April's tears subsided, and she sucked in a shaky breath. "What do I do now?"

"If you'll let me take you back to the Sanctuary, there's someone I want you to meet." He stroked her silky hair one last time and grasped her hands in his.

"Is that the hospital where I was before?"

"Yes. But it's not a hospital. Let's go. Mira will explain everything." He closed his eyes and Jumped to the Sanctuary door. "This is it."

He opened the door and motioned for her to go inside. Every Guardian in the room turned to look at him as he led her up the aisle. He narrowed his eyes and tried his best to ignore the inquisitive stares of the Angels. Their gazes burned into his back as he created a white wooden chair next to the bed and asked April to sit. He clenched his fists so hard his knuckles turned white, and he spun around.

"What are you looking at?" His gaze locked on the Guardian closest to him.

"Looks like the mighty Damian makes mistakes too, eh?"

He gritted his teeth, trying to control the anger that burned inside him. "Mind your own business, Able."

"Just making an observation, man." Able raised his hands in surrender.

"I'll show you where you can shove your observations." He took a step toward the Guardian, but April caught him by the hand. Her touch immediately calmed him, and he regained his composure. He took a deep breath and created a privacy curtain around them.

"How do you do that?" She looked at him with wide eyes.

"Do what?"

"Just make things appear out of thin air. It's amazing."

"Not really." He shrugged and created a chair for himself. "We all can do it. Though some of us are better at it than others." He shouted that last part, just to grate on Able's nerves. He shouldn't have called Damian out like that.

"Mira." His patience grew thin while he sat in the curtained off room alone with April. She sat in the chair with her hands folded in her lap and her legs crossed at the ankles. An uncomfortable silence expanded between them, and he was relieved when Mira finally swept aside the curtain to enter the private room.

"I see you found our runaway." She smiled at April and patted Damian on the shoulder. "It's so nice to meet you, April. My name is Mira. I trust your Slumber was peaceful?"

"My Slumber?" April looked to Damian for an explanation.

"You were asleep for three weeks after you died. Today's your thirtieth birthday." He shook his head. He should have explained all this to her already.

April opened her mouth to speak, but closed it. She looked from Damian to Mira. "I'm confused. Does everyone go through this when they die?"

Mira smiled. "Only Angels, dear. You didn't make it to your thirtieth birthday, so you Slumbered until you matured. Just as the other Angels in this room are doing now."

Her eyes widened, and Damian stood to whisper in Mira's ear.

"Uh, Mira? She doesn't exactly know she's an Angel." He cast his gaze to the floor and heat flushed his cheeks. If he'd have done his job, she would have.

"Oh, I see." Mira furrowed her brow as she thought about the news. "But, she was only three weeks out. Surely you explained some of it to her."

He shook his head, afraid to look either of the women in the eyes. "I was...busy."

Mira crossed her arms over her chest. "Busy doing what?"

"Excuse me." April stood to address them. "I don't know what y'all are talking about, but I can tell you what he was doing. He was busy being an asshole and trying to make my life miserable. He didn't *explain* a damn thing."

He flinched at the accusation. Was that what she thought of him? "April, that's not true. I was—"

"Enough." Mira put her hands on their shoulders and

pushed them back into their seats. "The past is in the past. What matters now is that we help April get accustomed to her new life as an Angel."

"An Angel?"

"Right. Well, my job's done here, then. April, it was nice knowing you." He rose and turned to leave. The sooner he could get out of this mess, the better.

"Not so fast, Damian." Mira's frigid gaze stopped him mid-stride. "You're not finished."

He crossed his arms over his chest and glanced at April. She looked like she was about to cry. "I brought her over. It's your job to find a Keeper to train her."

"She's not a Keeper. She's a Guardian."

"A Guardian?" April's voice trembled as she spoke. "Like a Guardian Angel? Like *him*?"

Mira put her arm around April's shoulders. "Yes, dear. A Guardian Angel."

"You can't be serious." She looked from Damian to Mira. "I was...I'm not...It's not possible."

"No. It's not. Mira, this has to be a mistake. She's a half-breed." Damian heard the anger rising in his voice, but he couldn't help it. April couldn't be a Guardian. No human could.

"It's no mistake. She bears the mark... May I, dear?" Mira slid April's gown off her shoulder. "Come. See for yourself."

Damian huffed and moved behind her. There on her delicate shoulder lay the mark common to all Guardians— a halo encircling a crescent moon. The pale blue glow was almost iridescent, and it shimmered as she peered over her shoulder to try to see it. He touched a spot over his heart, where his own mark lay. There was no denying it; she was a Guardian.

"But... She'd have to be a direct descendent of..." The mere mention of the name made his blood boil.

"Of Micah. You're right."

Damian paced the small enclosure, thoughts tumbling through his mind. This couldn't be. "But how? I Guarded Trusten, and he wasn't..."

"Her paternal grandmother was. April is a Guardian, brother. And she is still your Charge."

"Hell." His face pulled into a scowl as he stared at April. She was a descendent of Micah. Of the Guardian who started it all. The reason for all the hell he'd lived through.

"Hello? I'm still here." Panic spiked in April's voice. "Can someone please explain what's going on? I have no idea what you're talking about."

Mira cast him a disappointed glance. "Your grandfather died when he turned thirty, as all human Angels do. Your mother carried the gene—it skips a generation—and she passed it on to you. Had you not been shot three weeks ago, you would have passed peacefully in your sleep on your thirtieth birthday."

"And my paternal grandmother?" Her chin quivered as she spoke. "I never knew my dad."

"Your father also passed the gene to you, from your grandmother, who was Micah's descendent. Because you received the gene from both parents, you developed Micah's Guardian ability. Hence your mark." Mira brushed the mark on April's shoulder.

He clenched his hands into fists at his sides. "You knew all along, didn't you?"

Mira inclined her chin.

"Why me? If you knew…after everything I went through." He inhaled a deep breath to calm his rage.

"She is special. The first of her kind. She needed the best Guardian watching over her. She still needs you."

"No, I don't need him. I'm not an Angel. I didn't sign up for this."

"You are what you are, dear. Damian will teach you everything you need to know. He'll be by your side until you are ready to be on your own."

April stood and clasped her trembling hands together. "But I don't want to be an Angel. And he…well, he hates me, so I doubt he'll teach me anything. Please, Mira. I don't want this. There has to be another way."

Mira pressed her fingertips together. "There is a way."

"Mira, no." Damian's heart dropped. Surely she wouldn't suggest…

Her gaze flicked to Damian before she addressed April. "You can Fall."

"Fall?"

Damian's jaw clenched. "No, she can't."

"She needs to know her options. She must have a choice."

"Yes! A choice. How do I Fall, Mira? What do I do?" The desperation in April's eyes crushed him. Had he been that awful to her? He'd only wanted to keep distance between them, not drive her away completely.

"You don't know what you're asking for." He turned to Mira. "Please, don't do this."

But Mira ignored his pleas. "You go to The In-Between, state your intent, and then you Fall. You'll be back on Earth, in your old life."

"That's it? And I can go home? Back to my kids? Back to…Jared?" She cast her gaze to the floor.

"It's not that easy." He had to stop her. He couldn't go through this again. "Everyone knows you died, April. Your mom, your friends…Jared. What are you going to tell them? How are you going to explain you're back?"

April shrugged. "I'll figure something out. My students need me; I have to go back."

"Do you? Because last I heard, you were planning on leaving Felicity anyway."

"Well, I was, but…but, I left things a mess with Jared. I have to go talk to him."

Damian pressed his lips together in a hard line. He tried to think of something—anything—that would stop her from doing the unthinkable.

"You know what? Go ahead and Fall. Go back to *Jared*. But, you'll be on your own. I won't Guard you anymore. No one will." Maybe April Falling would be a good thing. At least he'd be rid of her then. He'd never have to see her again. Then he'd only have to deal with the gaping hole she'd tear in his heart when she left.

"He is correct," Mira confirmed. "When you Fall, you lose your Guardian. You will have to survive without the help of an Angel."

April looked at Damian. The uncertainty in her eyes gave him hope, but only for a moment.

"I'll take my chances. I don't belong here."

Mira looked at him. "Damian, you will take April to The In-Between. Help her with the Fall."

Like Hell he would.

"No, I won't. If she wants to Fall, I won't stop her. But, I'm *not* going to help her." He gave April one last pleading look, but when she held fast to her decision, he simply turned and walked away.

Damian's attitude had been a roller coaster since April woke, and she'd had enough of it. One minute, he was kind and gentle. The next minute, his icy gaze and indifferent attitude made her wonder why she was ever attracted to him.

"What's his problem?"

"He has anger issues. Especially when it comes to the Fall. It is a...sensitive subject." Mira folded her hands and looked at April with an expression she couldn't read. Was it pity? Sorrow?

"What happened to him?"

"That would be for Damian to tell you. But if you are set on Falling, you will never know. You do realize you will never see him again? Can you live with that?"

She sucked in a shaky breath. She'd only known him three months, but in her heart it felt like he'd been there her entire life. Could she live without him? "I have to."

She smoothed the luscious material of her gown and looked at Mira. "Can I have my clothes back?"

"Of course, dear." Mira touched April's arm, and her

gown transformed into the outfit she wore the day she died, minus the bullet hole and blood.

"How did you do that?"

Mira smiled. "You can do it too. Just imagine what you want to wear, decide to wear it, and it will be there."

"Seriously?"

"Try it."

April closed her eyes and pictured the suede skirt and silk blouse from Neiman's she'd been saving for. A soft buzz tickled her skin as the garments transformed. When she opened her eyes, the outfit was hers. "Amazing. I'm in Heaven."

Mira chuckled. "No, this isn't Heaven. This is the Angelic Realm."

"I thought Angels lived in Heaven."

"No. God created us to mirror humans, so we could relate to our Charges on a personal level. We have the same emotions, desires, flaws. We sin, just like people do. We are by no means perfect, as you have seen. So Angels live here, in our own Realm, while human souls go to Heaven upon their deaths."

"Interesting. Well, it's Heaven to me if I can have any outfit I want. I've been eyeing this one for weeks."

Mira smiled halfheartedly, her gaze filled with pity. "Are you ready now?"

She swallowed as a heaviness formed in her heart. "Yeah. I guess I am."

"He will miss you dearly."

Her chest tightened, and tears stung her eyes. She'd miss him too. A voice in her head screamed at her to stay. She needed Damian in her life. Despite his temper, she knew he was a tender person deep down. She could see it in his eyes. Feel it in her soul.

But she didn't belong here. She wasn't an Angel. "I'm ready."

"Very well. Through that door is The In-Between. Imagine in your mind the place you want to be. State your intent to Fall, and then Fall. You will be mortal again, and you will live out the rest of your life on Earth."

April hesitated. Was Falling really what she wanted? If she ever wanted a chance at her dream life, it had to be.

"Will you tell Damian good-bye for me?"

A grin spread across Mira's face. "I think you'll have to do that yourself."

Before she could ask another question, Damian appeared in front of her. He clenched and unclenched his fists as he glared at her. Anger spiced with a hint of determination radiated from his body. "If you want to Fall, fine. But you need to see what you're going back to."

He grabbed her hand, and in a blink, they stood outside her apartment door. Normally bright red, the door was now gunmetal gray, and she instantly recognized they were in The In-Between.

"How do you do that? You just appear places, out of nowhere."

Damian shrugged. "You just do it. You think of where you want to be, and you're there."

"This is my apartment."

"You need to see what's inside, and remember...you've only been dead for three weeks."

He tightened his grip on her hand and stepped through the closed door, pulling her in behind him.

Crossing through the solid object felt like a cold breeze rushing across her skin, and it took her a moment to orient herself to her surroundings. She really was a ghost.

Damian exhaled a hiss. "Are you sure *he's* worth Falling for?"

She followed his gaze to the living room sofa. From behind, the couch appeared empty, but as she crept closer, she saw Jared...lying on top of a woman—the leggy blonde legal assistant from his office.

Her jaw dropped open as she watched him kiss her. As he fondled her in unspeakable places. This...this man she had wanted to marry was with another woman only three weeks after April's death. Jared had said he loved her. Surely he wasn't over her already. Her heart shattered. Anger fumed from her core.

"Are you okay?" Damian's anger faded to compassion as he rested his hands on her shoulders. The warmth of his touch soothed her, but she didn't want to be comforted.

"No, I'm not okay. Do I look okay to you?" She jerked away from him and stormed around the sofa.

"Jared! Get off of her!" Hot tears streamed down her face, and she tried to pull her boyfriend off the other woman. But she wasn't in his world anymore, and her arms passed through his body.

"Dammit, Jared! Why?" She tried again to grab him, but there was nothing to hold on to. Pain slammed into her chest like a brick as her emotions fell apart. She clawed at him, punched and kicked him, but it was like he wasn't there. No, like *she* wasn't there. She was dead to him. Kneeling beside the couch, she put her head against his back.

"Whoa! Did you feel that?" Jared's head snapped up when she touched him.

"Feel what, honey?" The blonde groped at him to regain his attention.

"My back just got really cold."

"Hmmm," she purred. "Maybe it's the ghost of that pathetic girlfriend of yours."

"Maybe so." Jared chuckled and shoved his tongue into her mouth.

Pathetic? She *was* pathetic for ever thinking he loved her. For thinking she could actually build a life with that...that creep! How could she have been so stupid? So blind?

She sat on the floor, pulled her knees to her chest, and cried.

"April." Damian knelt beside her and placed his hand on her back. "I'm so sorry."

"Why did you bring me here? You could have just told me instead of putting me through this hell."

"Would you have believed me?"

She wiped the tears from her eyes and stared at the wall in front of her. "I...it doesn't matter. Just leave me alone."

She rose to her feet and trotted to the door, but when she reached for the knob, her hand passed through it.

"Dammit." She took a deep breath and forced herself through the wall. She had to get out of there. She couldn't stand watching Jared making out with that tramp. Sure, she'd suspected he might be cheating. But having a suspicion and actually seeing him in the act stirred completely different emotions. She took one last look at the closed door; she'd never come back here again. Then, she spun around to leave and smacked into Damian's chest.

"Jesus, will you quit following me?" She stepped around him and marched down the stairs.

"Where are you going, April?"

"Somewhere far away from you." She couldn't bear to look at the man who probably knew about Jared's betrayal all along. How pathetic she must've been to him, planning a wedding that was never going to happen. Her ears burned with embarrassment, and she couldn't get away fast enough.

She jogged through the parking lot, though she had no idea where she was going. She turned to look at him one last time. "Please, just leave me alone."

"I'll be here when you need me."

I know. All she'd have to do was call his name, and he'd drop whatever he was doing and be there for her. But it was his job. As soon as he was relieved of being her Guardian, she'd be alone. Damian didn't care about her; he was doing his duty. He took care of her because he had to.

Fresh tears streamed down her cheeks as she headed to the one place she thought she could find comfort—her mother's home.

The sun setting behind the old house painted a fond picture. She grew up in this house, and the memories of her childhood always brightened her mood. But when she passed through the door, the sadness in the air engulfed her like a wet blanket wrapped around her skin.

Her mother lay curled up on the couch, clutching a picture frame to her chest. April recognized the frame; it was her college graduation photo.

"Oh, Momma." She dropped to her knees and reached out to her mother. "I'm so sorry, Momma."

"Hello, April." The soft voice startled her, and when April looked up, she peered into the bright blue eyes of an Angel. Her golden hair flowed in thick waves over her shoulders, and her belted white gown emphasized her small waist and delicate features.

"Oh! Uh...hi. Did uh...did Damian send you?"

The Angel smiled. "No. My name is Ella. Your mother is my Charge."

"So, you're her Guardian?" She tried to control her tears as she gazed at her momma.

Ella giggled. "Only a select few become Guardians. I'm her Keeper."

"Keeper?"

"Has Damian not explained anything to you? I heard his Charge had crossed over, but he usually has them prepared."

April toyed with a button on her shirt. "I guess I never gave him the chance."

Ella plopped on the floor next to her. "Well, there are two types of Angels: Guardians and Keepers. Guardians, like Damian, look after the rare people who will become Angels when they turn thirty. Keepers, on the other hand, only watch over regular people, who live their lives, die, and go to Heaven."

"Oh. So, does everyone have an Angel to look after them?"

"Everyone."

April looked at her mother, asleep on the sofa, and her heart ached. "Is she...okay?"

"She's improving, but it will take time. How are you coping?"

She laughed cynically. "Not very well, I guess. I just found out my boyfriend is a cheater, and he never planned on marrying me. And I pissed Damian off, so he probably hates me even more, if that's possible."

"He doesn't hate anybody. He just likes people to think he does."

"Yeah, right. Hey, is it okay if I stay here for a while? I don't want to go back. I just need to think."

"Of course you can. Take all the time you need."

"Will you let Damian know where I am?"

"He already knows." Ella grinned and winked at April. Then, she disappeared.

What was she supposed to do now? Damian was right; she couldn't go back to her old life. But could she be a Guardian? Would Damian be willing to help her? Maybe Mira would let her go to Heaven where all the normal people went when they died. Would she be happy there?

"Oh, Momma. I wish you could hear me. I don't know what to do."

CHAPTER 9

She didn't know how long she sat there and watched her mother sleep. But the sun was already setting behind the old rice mills when Momma awoke and looked at the picture still clutched in her arms.

Momma sighed, and a sad smile curved her lips. "You're in a better place, baby girl. No more fear, worry, or sadness. You've got nothing but happiness ahead of you now. I love you." She ran her finger down the face in the picture and kissed it. Then she set the frame on the coffee table and shuffled to the kitchen.

April couldn't stop the tears from flooding her eyes. If Momma only knew how wrong she was. Fear, worry, and sadness consumed April every second of her existence. There'd be no happiness for her. She was ripped away from her life. Her family. Torn away with no warning, no chance to say goodbye. Her family was miserable. *She* was miserable.

And for what? She wasn't going to Heaven. She'd never be the peaceful, happy soul her momma wanted her to be.

She was an Angel now. And who knew Angels could be so unhappy?

She sat on the floor, contemplating what to do next. Needing—more than ever—the warmth of her momma's embrace. Momma always knew what to do. She always had reassuring words for her daughter that would make her believe everything would be okay. Even if only for a moment.

April felt completely drained, both physically and emotionally, and she curled into a ball on the rug. She fought to keep her heavy lids open. Sleep overtook her as her body surrendered to its desperate need for Slumber. Her eyelids closed, and she slipped into peaceful darkness.

~

"April? Are you awake?"

"Hmm?" She pried open her eyes to find Ella kneeling in front of her.

"You need to rest. Come on, you can stay with me tonight." She took her hand and tried to pull her to her feet. April slid her hand from her grasp.

"I'm just gonna sleep here. I can't go back there."

Ella's brow furrowed. "That's not a good idea. You can't get the kind of rest you need in The In-Between."

April pushed up onto her elbow. "What do you mean? Sleep is sleep, and I'm so exhausted I could do it anywhere."

Ella shook her head. "It's not the same. You need Slumber, and you can only get that in the Angelic Realm.

The energy is denser there, and you can recharge. Here, you'll just feel drained."

She laid her head on her arm. "If you don't mind, I'll take my chances."

Ella sighed. "Damian's worried about you. Mira won't let him come get you. He'd pick you up and drag you back if he could."

"So he sent you to check on me."

She smiled and shrugged.

"Well, tell him I'm fine. He doesn't need to worry his pretty little head about me. I'm a strong woman."

"Suit yourself. I'll be back to check on you tomorrow. And when you realize you need some good Slumber, you're welcome to stay with me." She smiled and patted her on the shoulder. "Good night, April."

She laid down her head and was out again as soon as she closed her eyes. Wonderful, dreamless sleep consumed her mind as her consciousness slipped away.

She woke to the muffled sounds of Momma getting ready for work, and when she stood, her head spun. Had she really been asleep all night? It felt like she'd just closed her eyes. This must've been what Ella was talking about. But she couldn't go back. Not even for some much-needed Slumber.

She stumbled into the kitchen where Momma was drinking coffee and talking on the phone. The coffee smelled decadent, and she almost got a buzz from the scent. Everything about her childhood home smelled good. Familiar. From the lavender growing in the field behind the house to the fresh scent of the clean laundry just brought in from the line, this place—this *planet*—was home.

"No, Phyllis. You don't have to do that. Shelly's coming over today, and she's gonna stay with me for a while... Yeah, we'll be fine. I'll call you if I need anything."

April breathed a sigh of relief. Her sister was coming to stay with Momma. At least she wouldn't be alone. She'd always worried about her momma since she and Shelly moved out. She lived by herself in the three-bedroom house, and that must've been scary. April couldn't imagine being alone all the time. How sad Momma must've been.

April never knew her father. Shelly didn't know hers, either. Both women were products of her momma's failed relationships. Poor Momma. She never did find a man to love her. And after a while, she seemed to give up on love all together.

When she was twelve years old, April vowed her life would not turn out that way. She would find a husband, and they'd live together forever. They'd love each other forever. There was no way she was spending her life alone and miserable.

So much for that dream. Now she was alone, and she wasn't even sure if she was alive or dead. She didn't know how to be an Angel. So how could she build relationships with others like her?

With Momma on her way to work, she decided to visit the high school and see how her classes were doing. Hopefully they found good subs for both her and Damian.

She eyed the door and felt queasy. She'd never get used to passing through solid objects. It wasn't natural. But since that was how she got in, it was her only way out. She held her breath, closed her eyes, and forced herself through the door. The tingling sensation of her body moving through the wood made the hairs on the back of her neck stand on end. But she did it. She was on the other side.

She looked triumphantly at the old, weathered door and smiled. No lock could stop her now. She turned to make her way to school, but Ella stood at the bottom of the steps.

"How're you feeling?" Her warm smile and open posture put April at ease immediately.

"Okay, I guess. A little tired."

Ella sat on a step and patted the space next to her for April to sit. "It's only going to get worse the longer you stay here. Won't you come back with me? You won't even have to talk to him."

She shook her head and twirled a piece of her hair. "I can't go back. I don't belong there."

"Well, you don't belong here either. You're an Angel now, and your home is in the Angelic Realm."

April sighed. Ella wasn't going to let up, so she'd just have to go along with it. "I'll think about it, okay? Just give me another day or two to adjust." She rose from the steps and wandered down the path to the street.

Ella scampered after her. "Where are you going?"

"I was gonna go to the school. See how my kids are doing."

Ella giggled. "Well, you don't have to walk there, silly. You can Jump."

"Walking sounds a lot less strenuous."

"No! Not jump as in both feet off the ground. I mean Jump. As in imagine where you want to be in your mind, make your intent to go clear, and then just be there."

She stared at her in disbelief. She had to be joking. "Seriously?"

"Yeah. How do you think you got here?"

"Damian brought me. I never really thought about it." Funny, she never questioned his actions. She'd trusted him to take her where she needed to go without asking how. But that was because he was her Guardian. She was supposed to trust him.

"Well, *he* Jumped. And since he was holding on to you, you went with him. Pretty cool, isn't it?"

April wrapped her arms around herself. This whole Angel thing kept getting stranger. "It's kinda weird."

Ella beamed a smile. "Oh, you'll get used to it. When I learned how to Jump, I did it all the time. I just couldn't get enough of it. Do you want to try?"

"Um, I don't know."

"Oh, come on. It'll be fun." She reached for April's hand. "Where do you want to be?"

Home. Somewhere I belong. With Damian.

She shook herself to get the thought out of her head. "I was gonna go to my classroom."

"Okay. Close your eyes and picture it in your mind. Can you see it?"

She nodded.

"Now, just decide you want to be there. It's all about intent. Are you ready? Take us there."

A tingling sensation rippled through her body, and when she opened her eyes she stood in the middle of her classroom.

"Amazing."

Though it'd only been three weeks since her death, she expected it to be different. She thought *something* would have changed in her absence, but her classroom looked exactly the same as she left it.

A substitute stood in her place, delivering the lecture she should've been giving. Alex sat in his desk, diligently taking notes. He seemed different, though. He had an air of sadness about him that was so out of character. Of course, three weeks ago, he was nearly killed.

"I guess life goes on, doesn't it?"

Ella smiled sympathetically and rubbed her back. "Yes, it does. And so will yours."

"Will it?"

The bell rang, signaling lunchtime, and she watched Alex drag himself out the door. Hopefully his Keeper could make him feel better soon, like Damian had done for her.

"I wonder what Janice is doing."

"Let's go see."

They strolled down the crowded hallway toward the teacher's lounge. Every time a student passed through her, she felt a tickle in her core. She tried to step out of their way, but they never flinched—like she wasn't there.

"Don't worry. You'll get used to that too."

"It's all so weird. I mean, one minute I was a teacher,

convinced my jerk of a boyfriend was going to propose. And now I'm a ghost."

"You're an *Angel*."

"What's the difference?"

Ella sighed. She was obviously getting tired of her mopey attitude, and April didn't want to lose the only friend she had.

"I'm sorry. It's just hard to accept, you know?"

"I understand. But you have to try...look, there's Janice."

Janice sat at their usual table, but Crystal, an English teacher from two halls over, joined her. They smiled and laughed like she and April used to do. Crystal even sat in April's chair. She'd been replaced. Her heart sank, and she blinked back the tears.

Life really does go on.

Her best friend had moved on. So why couldn't she? Why was she so hung up on what everyone else was doing in her absence? She needed to figure out her future, but all she could think about was the past. She was about to Jump out and have a pity party for herself when she overheard Janice.

"God, I miss her. I still can't believe she's gone."

"I know. It just doesn't seem real." Crystal put her hand over Janice's.

Gone, but not forgotten. She'd heard enough. Janice missed her, and that was what she needed to know. No sense hanging around making herself miserable.

"Hey, Ella? I think I'm gonna go back to Momma's house. Shelly's gonna be there today, and I want to see her again."

She hugged her and smiled. "Okay. Take care of yourself. And remember you can come to my house when you need to Slumber."

Damian sat on the edge of his bed, staring at a crumpled piece of paper. He traced his finger across the image and sighed. He hadn't thought about it in so long. He'd occupied himself with Charge after Charge, helping his fellow Guardians when they needed it. He'd managed to keep so busy all those years, it rarely crossed his mind. But the effects of the haunting event were burned into his soul.

Then came April. She was wonderful. The most beautiful creature he'd ever seen. She was smart, charming, and full of spirit. She'd stirred up emotions in him that'd been dormant for so long, he'd forgotten what they felt like. Whenever she was near, his body warmed and desire pulsed through his veins. His heart quickened, and his arms ached to hold her. But his feelings for her brought the painful memories back to the surface.

A betrayal so wicked he'd been left a broken man. He'd lost the ability to trust. To feel. He wouldn't allow anyone to love him, when he couldn't even love himself. That's why he could not—would not—allow his feelings for April to bloom. He couldn't let her know how much he longed to hold her. She deserved better. She deserved someone who could give her the love she needed. Someone whole.

He couldn't let her love him, but he couldn't stand by and watch her fall apart. He had to go get her. He placed the crumpled paper back in the drawer and slid it shut, preparing to Jump.

But a frantic knock on the door stopped him. *Who the hell?* He strode to the door and threw it open to find a Keeper looking up at him. Her tear-stained cheeks and bloodshot eyes pleaded with him for help.

He stepped away from the opening and gestured for her to enter.

"Hi. I'm Jeana. I, uh...I need your help." Her voice, thick with tears, trembled as she spoke. "My Charge is about to commit suicide, and I can't talk him out of it. He isn't listening."

Damian took a deep breath and let it out slowly. "Guardians aren't supposed to interfere with humans. What do you want me to do?"

She clasped her hands together and stared at the floor for a moment before looking into his eyes. "I want you to cross over and stop him. Take the gun away. Talk to him."

"You know I can't do that. As much as I want to help you, I just can't." Sadness filled his heart, weighing heavy on his soul when he looked at the quivering Keeper, her shaky breaths growing shallow as she tried to contain her panic.

But it was expressly forbidden. Humans were left to lead their own lives with the simple guidance of their Keepers. If her Charge chose to die, it wasn't Damian's place to stop him.

But then again.

Why couldn't he help her? He could at least get a neighbor to go inside, couldn't he?

"Please." She threw herself against him and sobbed

into his chest. "I thought you might help, you know, since you're like Paul and Mira. The rules don't apply to you."

He patted her back and shook his head. "I'm not like Paul and Mira, and the rules do apply. I just don't always follow them."

"But, you *know* him. His name is Alex, and he goes to the school where you worked."

"Alex? April's student?" His stomach dropped. He put his hands on her shoulders and pushed her back to look in her eyes. "Tell me what happened."

"A lot of things. He's so depressed. He blames himself for April's death. Will you help him?"

It was a classic catch-22. If he helped him, he'd be breaking a cardinal rule—doing something no Angel was allowed to do. But if he didn't, he'd be letting an innocent child die by his own hand. He couldn't live with himself if he allowed that to happen.

Then there was April. Rules or no rules, if Alex died, April would be crushed. And he would not let her go through any more anguish. So by helping Alex, he was actually helping *his* charge. Nothing wrong with that.

"Please, Damian. Will you help him?"

"Yeah. Take me to him."

They Jumped to The In-Between in Alex's bedroom. He sat, curled up in the corner, toying with a pistol. His torn jeans and faded T-shirt were typical teenage attire, but the look on his face told a different story. Alex was no ordinary teenager. The burdens of death and humiliation weighed on his soul, and no child should have to suffer like that.

He turned the gun over and over in his trembling

hands before raising it to his temple. Closing his eyes, he rested his finger against the trigger. Then he put it down again and started over.

Damian watched him for several minutes as Jeana tried to whisper to him. Tried to convince him to put the gun away.

"He's not listening, and he's going to do it. I can feel it." She glided toward him and clutched his arm. "Please, Damian. His dad's out of town. No one's going to be home for days. Help him."

"I will." He crossed over, into the hallway outside Alex's room.

He had to plan his actions carefully. Last time he tried to stop a shooter, April wound up dead. He didn't want that to happen to Alex. She'd never forgive him.

He cracked open the door, lifting the handle to minimize the creaking. Then he slipped in through the small space and crept toward the boy. His soft voice meant to be gentle and reassuring.

"Hey, Alex. Whatcha doing?"

Alex's head snapped up when Damian spoke, and he whisked the gun behind his back. "Nothing. I'm not doing anything, Mr. Perkins."

He inclined his chin and peered at the crumpled mess of a teenager. "Then what's the gun for?"

Alex's eyes grew wide, and he swallowed. "I was..." He shrugged. "I just...I can't take it anymore. It's my fault Miss Carter died. Everyone hates me for it. She'd still be alive if I wasn't such a screw-up."

"You're not a screw-up. We all make mistakes." He knelt in front of him and put his hand on his shoulder.

"Why don't you give me the gun? Just to be sure you don't make another one."

Alex inched the gun from behind him, then jerked it back. "No. I deserve to die."

"No one deserves to die. Give me the gun."

He drew his brows together and pressed his lips into a hard line. "No."

"Do you think Miss Carter would want you to blow your brains out? Because I don't. I think she'd want you to live a long, happy life. Don't you?"

His lip trembled. Tears rolled down his cheeks, and he hesitantly placed the pistol in Damian's hand. "I miss her so much."

"So do I." He tucked the gun into the back of his pants.

Alex pulled his knees to his chest and wrapped his arms around his legs. "It's not fair. You know? That bullet was meant for me. I should be the one dead. Not her. She was the best teacher I've ever had."

"She was an amazing woman." *She still is.* "But you know what? It'll get easier. You just have to give yourself time. Can you do that for her?"

"Yeah. I guess I can. For her." He unwrapped his arms and ran a hand through his matted hair. "Did you really get fired for beating the crap out of that guy?"

Damian smiled and sat cross-legged on the carpet. "Something like that."

"I wish you would have killed him."

Part of Damian did too. Of course, he'd never take a life. But seeing April suffer, lying in her own blood, had unleashed a fury within him. He'd felt possessive.

Like she belonged to him and he'd kill anyone who hurt her.

Not an Angelic quality.

"Well, I'm glad I didn't. Then I'd be in even more trouble, don't you think?"

"Yeah, I guess so." Alex dropped his head back against the wall and rubbed his forehead. "God, I wish I could bring her back. I feel so awful. I'll never forgive myself."

"You have to, though. You need to mourn. However you need to do it: hate yourself, hate the killer, be mad. But then get over it. Otherwise, you'll spend the rest of your life bitter, angry, and alone. Trust me." *I know.*

"I don't know if I can get over it. I mean, she's dead because of me."

"Not because of you. She died because of the choices she made. She chose to put herself in front of the gun. She chose to try and talk it out of the killer's hands. She could've just as easily chosen to run and leave you alone with the guy, couldn't she?"

"I guess."

"We always look back on our lives and think of ways we'd change them. But there are no do overs in life. You can't change the past, but you can work on building the kind of future for yourself that Miss Carter would've wanted you to have."

But that's easier said than done.

Alex drew in a shaky breath and wiped the tears from his swollen eyes. "Yeah. I guess you're right. I guess I'll try for her... Hey, Mr. Perkins? How'd you know where to find me? I mean, my dad's out of town, and I came here straight after school."

He smiled and helped Alex to his feet. "I just had a hunch." With the gun tucked into the waistband of his pants, he walked him to the front door. "I don't want to leave you alone. Do you have any relatives nearby you could stay with until your dad gets back?"

"Yeah. My aunt lives three doors down. We're pretty close. I could probably stay there."

"Come on, then. I'll walk with you."

Shelly lay asleep in her bed, and April sat cross-legged on the mattress next to her. Though they appeared gray, the pale pink walls hadn't been painted since she'd moved out. But the floral duvet and polka-dot sheets were new. Her sister had been staying with Momma for the past six days, and April had kept her distance, watching them from afar.

They seemed to be coping better than she was. But they had each other for comfort. Their love for each other kept them going. Who did April have that loved her?

No one.

"Oh, Shelly. I really wish you could hear me. I need to talk to you so bad. I'm dead. And now I'm supposed to be some Guardian Angel. I can't even take care of myself. How am I supposed to take care of other people?"

She watched the gentle rise and fall of her sister's chest as she breathed.

"Jared turned out to be a jerk, which wouldn't have surprised you, I guess. You never did like him much. But there's this other guy. You'd really like him if you met him, I think. He's tall and incredibly sexy, and there's so much compassion is his eyes. He tries to hide it, but he's the most caring person I've ever met. The problem is he hates me, and I don't know why. I wish there was some way to make him like me, because he sets me on fire every time he touches me. I just don't know what to do. Why am I so attracted to someone who can't stand me?"

She lay on the bed and draped her arm across her sister. "I miss you, Shelly."

"April?" Shelly shot up in the bed and looked around the room. "April, is that you?" Her voice grew frantic as she shouted, "April!"

Her heart sprinted. Could Shelly sense her? Did she hear what she said? Was it possible?

Momma ran upstairs, clutching her shabby bathrobe to her chest. "Shelly? What's wrong?"

"I...don't know. I thought April was here. I *felt* her. Momma, she was here."

Momma sank onto the bed between her daughters and put her arm around Shelly. "I miss her too, sweetheart. But she's gone. It was only a dream."

"But it felt so real. Like she was sitting here talking to me, just like she used to do."

Momma sighed. Her slumped posture and the heavy circles under her eyes showed how worn out she was. "I dream about her too. But she *can't* be here. She's in Heaven now."

Shelly nodded and lay back on her pillow. "You're right. She couldn't be here, could she? She's probably floating on a cloud somewhere, eating cheesecake, and not gaining a single pound."

If only.

"Go back to sleep. Tomorrow's a new day." Momma closed the door, and Shelly closed her eyes.

April didn't want to upset her sister anymore, but she needed the companionship. She could lie there quietly. Sleep with her like she used to do whenever she had a bad dream. Because that's what this all seemed like. An excruciatingly long, bad dream.

She grew weaker every day. She finally understood what Ella had meant about not getting the rest she needed here. But she still wasn't ready to go back. She wasn't ready to let go.

Nestling into the pillow, she closed her eyes and drifted into a peaceful sleep.

~

"April? April, wake up. You need to come home."

The voice sounded distant, like part of a dream. But she'd recognize it anywhere. Damian had come for her.

"C'mon. You need to come back with me. Now."

"Mmm..." She rolled over and tried to ignore him. She was too tired to deal with him. Maybe in the morning...the thought trailed off as she slipped back to unconsciousness.

"All right. We'll do this the hard way." He slipped his arms beneath her back and knees and lifted her to his chest.

The jolt startled her; now she was fully awake. "What are you doing? Put me down!"

He glared at her and frowned. "It's for your own good. You're weak; you need Slumber."

"No! I'm not going back! Put me down!" She pounded her fists into his chest, but he didn't flinch. His hold was firm, his body warm. But she wouldn't give in to the comfort of his embrace. She kicked and screamed and clawed until he finally dropped her.

His tensed muscles caused his veins to stand out under his skin. He clenched his fists and snapped his jaw shut. "You know what? Fine. If you want to stay, stay. But you *will* come home eventually. Whether it's on your own or if I have to drag your limp, practically lifeless body there, you will come back."

He disappeared, and she curled up next to Shelly. Why did he hate her so? He couldn't *force* her to do anything. She was done trying to please men. She'd worked her tail off with Jared, and look where it got her. If she went back, it'd be because *she* wanted to. Not because Damian ordered her to do it.

CHAPTER 10

$\mathcal{D}$amian raked his fingers through his hair and paced across his chamber. Mira sat on a stool in the corner of the expansive white room, her gaze following him with each hasty stride.

"Why hasn't she come back yet, Mira?"

"These things take time. She's mourning the loss of her old life and hopefully coming to terms with her new one. She will return."

He huffed. "It's been two weeks."

"Patience is a virtue."

"Well, it's not one of mine."

"It never was."

Damian stopped and looked at the woman who knew him better than anyone. He considered Mira a sister; she was one of the original four. And she was the only Angel he came remotely close to sharing his true feelings with. The only one who was still around, anyway.

He looked in the large, oval mirror hanging on the wall and slammed his fist through it, shattering the glass.

But as everything did in the Angelic Realm, it reformed like water filling in the hole a thrown pebble makes.

"Aahhg. Nothing here breaks! I just want to hit something and watch it break!"

"And you know if you truly intend for it to stay broken, it will."

"How could I be so stupid?"

"Do you mean for not preparing April for the Crossing Over? Or for allowing yourself to have feelings for her?"

His gaze locked with Mira's for a split second before he had to look away. "I don't have feelings for her. She's my Charge. Nothing more."

"You are only fooling yourself, Damian." She rose from the stool to rub her hand on his back. "Don't be so hard on yourself. She will come around. You two will be very close; I can tell."

"Thanks, Mira. You're full of it, but thanks."

She flashed him a warm smile and Jumped from his chamber, leaving him alone with his thoughts. And that was a place he didn't want to be.

How could she accuse him of having feelings for April? Just because he was worried about the wellbeing of his Charge? Ridiculous. He was attracted to her, sure. But what man wouldn't be? She was gorgeous. Smart and witty. And when she let her guard down, she was kind and sweet.

When he held her in his arms, she was warm, soft. And she smelled like a blooming meadow with a hint of vanilla. So his arms ached a little with the need to hold her. No big deal. It'd been so long since he'd held a woman, he probably would've reacted that way with anyone.

Right.

He sensed her lurking in the high school, watching her classes being taught by a substitute. It killed him for her to be in so much pain, but Mira was right. It would take time. He'd already tried to coax her back several times after he'd tried to drag her home by force. But she completely ignored him. Acted like he wasn't even there. She wouldn't speak. Wouldn't even look at him, and the rejection stung.

But it wasn't about him, was it? If she wanted to be alone, he'd leave her alone.

No matter how badly he wanted to scoop her up in his arms and carry her back, he wouldn't do it. She'd come back when she was ready, and then they'd do things his way.

Ella curled one leg underneath her and lounged on a park bench—well, sort of floated above it. She'd been April's savior the past two weeks, helping her deal with the loss of her former life and filling her in on how the Angelic Realm worked. April sat on the other end of the bench, toying with the hem of her shirt.

"Damian should really be the one helping you with all this. You're his Charge; your mother is mine."

"I know." April sighed and turned to mirror Ella's posture. "I'm just not ready to talk to him. He knows everything about me. He knows about Jared."

"And he's going to kill me when he finds out I've been

involved with his Charge. This is such a no-no." Ella grinned. She obviously didn't mind bending the rules when it came to Damian.

"Thank you. I promise I won't tell a soul."

"Oh, he already knows." Ella shrugged. "But who cares? I won't be the first Angel he's gotten mad at. He asks about you all the time, you know. He's worried about you."

April crossed her arms over her chest. "Hmph. He's worried about his job, not me."

"I don't know...I mean, I don't know him that well, but he seems to really care for you."

"Yeah, right." He didn't have feelings for her. How could he? That spark she thought she felt in the cemetery must've been pity, not passion. Not that it mattered.

"How's Momma doing?"

"She's going to be okay."

"Who are you to her? You know, like how Damian pretended to be a teacher at my school. Who do you pretend to be?"

Ella giggled. "I forget how little you know about being an Angel. Keepers can't cross over to the Earthly Realm. The In-Between is the closest we get to our Charges."

"Really? So, you've never been human?"

"I have. I was born human, just like you. I ascended on my thirtieth birthday, and I've been a Keeper ever since."

"And Damian?"

"Oh, he's always been a Guardian. But Guardians are lucky. You get to interact with the people on their level. It must be incredibly exciting. You'll have to tell me all about it once you get your first Charge." Ella's eyes sparkled as she spoke. Guardians must've been revered among the Angels.

"And I know you'll do great because Damian is the best of the best. He'll be a great teacher."

April rolled her eyes. He was the best at making her feel like crap.

"And you're special too."

She raised an eyebrow. "How so?"

"No mortal has ever become a Guardian before. Not that I know of anyway. I mean, I've heard it can happen, but I think you're the first."

"I still don't understand how all this works. Why do some Angels start out human, if some are born that way?"

"For a human to become an Angel, it starts with someone who Fell."

"Why would they Fall?"

"Usually because they fell in love with their Charge. It doesn't happen very often. But once an Angel Falls, if they have children, they pass on an Angelic gene. Every other generation, one of their descendants will ascend and become an Angel. In your case, you received the gene from both sides, and one of those sides was that of a powerful Guardian."

Her new friend shrugged and shot her a smile. "And with all that Angelic blood swimming through your veins, you turned into a Guardian too. The rest of us become Keepers."

April sighed and looked at her hands folded in her lap. "I need to go back, don't I?"

Ella rested a hand on her shoulder. "Yes. You do. And

be patient with Damian. This is new for him, too. He's not used to getting close to Angels."

"Why not?"

Ella folded her hands in her lap and looked out across the park. The flush on her cheeks implied she'd already said too much. "I wasn't around when it happened, so I don't know all the details. You better wait till he tells you."

April chuckled. The more she learned about Damian, the more mysterious he became. Intriguing was more like it. He was going to be a hard nut to crack, but she was up for the challenge. If she could get sixteen-year-olds to tell her their deepest, darkest secrets, surely she could get a grown man to open up.

She was ready. Maybe if she focused on figuring Damian out, she could forget about how stupid she seemed to him. So what if he thought she was a pathetic loser? Maybe she could convince him she wasn't. She held her head high and rose to her feet.

"I'm going back."

"Yay!" Ella squealed and bounced with excitement. "Do you remember how to do it? Just close your eyes and imagine Damian in your mind. You'll be whisked right to him."

April couldn't fight the smile that spread across her face. She'd made up her mind. She was going to be a Guardian.

She closed her eyes, took a deep breath, and focused on making the Jump. Picturing Damian in her mind, with conscious intent, she Jumped to him.

Before she could even open her eyes, he smacked into

her, and they both toppled to the floor. She landed flat on her back with Damian on top of her.

"For Heaven's sake, April! You don't Jump into someone's home."

"Sorry."

He rose up on his hands, but he didn't get up. He just looked at her. His steely gaze softened and traveled from her eyes, down to her mouth, and back up again. His hazel eyes held hers, and he looked at her like she was a lost treasure he'd finally found. She tried to convince herself the spark she felt, the heat radiating from his body, was pity. That he felt sorry for her. But she felt his arousal growing, pressing into her hip, and she couldn't deny the hunger in his eyes.

Heat rose in her body, and just as she thought she'd be consumed by the flames, he hopped off her, pulling her to her feet. He dropped her hand and cleared his throat.

"It's okay. I'm uh...glad you're back." He adjusted his pants and ran his hand through his hair. He looked at her again, his gaze traveling up and down the length of her body, and he blushed.

If she didn't know any better, she'd think he was embarrassed. Of course, she was too, and she had to tear her gaze away from him. She looked around the room—everywhere but at him.

His house was interesting. A single, large mirror hung on one of the three white walls, reflecting the lush, green field that lay just outside his window. If you could call it a window. The entire wall was made of glass, and sheer alabaster curtains hung on either side. A plush white sofa sat near the middle of the otherwise bare room. She ran her hand along the wall as she padded closer to him.

"This is where you live? Where's your kitchen?"

The corner of his mouth tugged into a crooked grin. "Have you been hungry the past two weeks?"

"Well, of course I...I guess I haven't. Angels don't eat?" She moved closer to him, needing to fill the gap between them. He took a step back.

"No. We're pure energy. No need for food." He shrugged and took another step away from her.

"Well, that's a bummer. I sure do like to eat."

"Me too. We can eat when we cross over to the Earthly Realm, though. It's my favorite thing to do." He grinned, revealing a single dimple on his left cheek. Why hadn't she noticed that before?

"Really? What kind of food do you like?" She plopped down on the sofa and sank into the luscious upholstery. *What kind of material do they use to make stuff up here?* She'd never felt anything so soft.

"Nowadays, my favorite's Italian. Food just keeps getting better and better." He exhaled a nervous chuckle and inched his way closer to the sofa.

"Oh, yeah? What else do you like? Any guilty pleasures? I absolutely love Twinkies."

"I know." He laughed and slid onto the sofa, as far away from April as he could get. Why was he acting so nervous?

"Right. I forget you know everything there is to know about me. It really isn't fair, you know." She turned to face him, folding one leg underneath her.

"I don't know everything. I know *what* you've done.

But unless you speak your reasoning out loud, I have no idea *why.* I could never read your mind."

A tiny flush of relief loosened the tension in her muscles. He'd seen every pathetic thing she'd ever done—like staying with Jared—but at least he'd never heard her idiotic thoughts.

"Hmm... Still doesn't seem fair. I don't know much about you at all. Hey, I know! Let's go cross over, or whatever it is that we do, and go have some Italian food. We can talk over dinner and you can tell me all about Damian. What do you say?"

She froze. As soon as the words left her mouth, she wished she hadn't said them. Did she just ask him out on a date? She sure didn't mean to, but the way his body tensed and his gaze shifted about the room, it looked like she'd done just that. *Crap.*

"That's not a good idea. We're not supposed to cross over unless we have a Charge. We haven't been assigned one yet, since you've been MIA."

She stared at her lap and picked at her fingernails. "I'm sorry. I didn't mean it like that." *Nothing like being rejected by a super sexy Guardian Angel to crush your self-esteem.*

"Doesn't matter. If there's anything you want to know, you can ask me now. Then we have to go see Mira so we can get our Charge."

"*Our* Charge?"

"Yeah. I have to help you with your first one till he crosses over."

"How long will that be?" A strange chill flushed through her veins, and she wasn't sure if it was excitement because she had to spend more time with him or dread for the same reason.

"I don't know. That's why we have to go see Mira. Hopefully she'll give us one who's almost thirty. Some Guardians have multiple Charges, since there are so few of us. Maybe we can lighten someone's load and pick up one who's about to cross over. If the Guardian is willing to let him go."

"Is Mira your girlfriend? Or wife? Or whatever Angels have?" Not that it mattered, but it would be good for her to know if he was available. Just in case.

Damian chuckled. "Mira? No. She's like a sister. She works with Paul assigning Charges and taking care of the Slumbers. Mira is Paul's wife."

"Do you have a wife?"

"No." His casual expression hardened. "Come on. We need to go talk to Mira." He stood, and without looking at her, he strode to the door.

She obviously hit a sore spot with him, and she intended to find out why that simple question put him off like that.

"I'm sorry if I upset you, Damian."

"I'm not upset. I just want to get this over with. And the sooner we get started on your training, the sooner we can finish it and be done with each other." He opened the door and motioned for her to exit.

April brushed past him and turned to glare at him as he closed the door. So he wanted to be done with her, did he? Well, that was just fine with her. She didn't need to waste her time on a guy who obviously hated her. The sooner she could be rid of him the better.

"Lead the way, then. I don't want to do this any more than you do."

Damian grunted and marched ahead with his fists clenched so hard his veins protruded on his arms.

~

"Welcome back. It's so good to see you again." Mira hugged April like she was an old friend and shot Damian an "I told you so" look.

He rolled his eyes. Mira was right. She always was. Sometimes he wondered if she had the gift of premonition along with her ability to be connected to all of the Angels. Most Angels could only connect to their Charges, Damian included. He could sense April's moods, know when she needed his help. He could find her anywhere by simply picturing her beautiful face and fiery red hair.

He'd miss that connection when it was gone. Being that close to April almost made him feel whole again. Almost. He'd get over it, though. He had to.

"What do you have for us, Mira? April's ready for her first Charge."

"No, she's not."

"What? Of course she is." Desperation raised his voice. He *needed* her to be ready.

Mira pressed her fingertips together and smiled at the pair. "She is not ready."

"I really am, Mira. I'm okay with all this now. I'm ready to be a Guardian." April straightened her spine and held her head high.

"I believe you are indeed ready to be a Guardian. But

you are not prepared for a Charge. You need training. Damian will teach you everything you need to know. Then, you may have your first Charge."

Damian groaned. He should have known it wouldn't be so simple. Mira was up to something.

"Does it have to be him? Can't anyone else train me? Surely there's—"

"No." Thankfully, Mira didn't let her finish. The rejection hurt, though he hated to admit it. He needed to get as far away from April as possible, but all he wanted to do was to make her his.

"It must be Damian," Mira said. "You are his Charge; you are his responsibility. Besides, April." She put her arm around her shoulders and turned her to face him. "He's the best. Consider yourself lucky to have his guidance. In thousands of years, he has never lost a Charge."

"He lost me."

The defiant look in her eyes sparked his temper. He gritted his teeth and clenched his fists. He had to get it under control. "You know what, April? You...oh, just forget it." Who was she to judge? He'd lost her because she was so stubborn. Because she thought she was bulletproof. She always had.

"What, Damian? Why don't you just say it? It's because I'm right. When I needed you the most, you failed me."

He took a deep breath and counted to ten. *I will not go off on her.* She was baiting him, just like she did when she was human. Nothing had changed. He could handle her then, and he could handle her now.

"April, you have no idea how many times I've saved

your life. You would have been dead a long time ago, if it wasn't for me."

She crossed her arms over her chest and shifted her weight to one leg, her silence an invitation for him to enlighten her.

"You remember when you were thirteen? Your sister ran out in the street chasing a ball. You pushed her out of the way before the car could crush her. But why didn't it hit you? Both of you landed on the other side of the road, didn't you?"

She brought her hand to her mouth. "That was you?"

"Yeah. It was. You told your mom a man pushed you out of the way. Do you remember that? They thought you bumped your head, but you insisted. They never did believe you."

"Oh, Damian, I..."

"And how about when you were sixteen? You let your friends talk you out of wearing your seatbelt. You didn't need one. Until Jamie plowed her car into an oak tree. How long did she spend in intensive care? And you walked away without a scratch. Do you remember why?"

"I...I felt arms...*your* arms wrap around me. You held me in the car. Oh, Damian! I'm so sorry. I shouldn't have said that." She rushed to him and flung herself into his arms, squeezing him tight. "I'm so sorry."

God, she smelled delicious. The sensation of her body pressed to his was almost unbearable. He stroked her back, her soft, silky hair. The anger drained from his veins as his heart pounded in his chest. Never in his life had simply being near someone affected him so.

"It's okay, April. You didn't know."

She pulled from his embrace and peered into his eyes with an expression he almost mistook for love. But it wasn't that. He'd decided long ago he'd never let anyone love him, and he'd never fall in love. He wouldn't get burned again.

And he wouldn't burn her. Letting her love him would be like strapping a pack of C4 with a long fuse to his chest and lighting it. He'd be okay for a while, but eventually everything would blow up in his face.

She cast her gaze downward as her cheeks flushed with rosy color. Pressing her pink lips together, she turned to Mira, who'd watched the entire exchange with a smug grin.

"Okay, Mira. Tell me what to do."

"Be open to learning. Absorb all you can. And be patient with him. Remember...Angels aren't perfect. We *all* make mistakes." She cut him a sideways glance.

"Right, well I guess we need to find her a place to rest."

"She's going to stay with you." Mira's level gaze told him there was no sense in arguing. She'd made up her mind, and she wouldn't budge. "You can make her a room off your living quarters, next to your bedroom."

He sighed in defeat. How in Heaven's name was he supposed to distance himself from her if she was going to be living with him? Could this situation get any worse?

"And you will tell her anything she needs to know about you, Damian."

Yeah. It just got worse.

"Mira..." He hoped his tone would be warning enough

that she was treading in forbidden territory. He didn't talk about himself. Not to anyone.

"You must establish trust. How can she trust you if she doesn't know you?"

He closed his eyes and took a deep breath. Hopefully she wouldn't have too many questions. "All right. Let's get out of here, April. Before she lays down any more mandates."

April grinned as she walked with him to the door.

Women. They were all out to get him.

CHAPTER 11

The thrill of excitement and a hint of fear clouded April's mind as she followed Damian out the door and into the heart of the Angelic Realm. The view took her breath away. With the rich hues and saturated colors of the natural surroundings, it was as if she was seeing for the very first time. Her gaze had never held anything so exquisite, and she had to stop to admire the vivid scenery.

"Wow. It's so beautiful." Her eyes widened with wonder at the rolling hills covered in a myriad of fragrant flowers. The sky was the deepest blue she'd ever seen. To her right, a sparkling lagoon with cascading waterfalls sat nestled in the center of a majestic rock formation. Several Angels splashed in the crystal water, while others roamed about the picturesque scene. April was in awe.

Damian turned to her with a look of annoyance, but when his gaze met hers, he grinned. "Yes, it is. Sometimes I forget to stop and look. We really are blessed." He reached for her hand, and a jolt of energy shot through her.

Why did that always happen when he touched her? She considered asking him, but he'd probably have thought she was nuts. Instead, she let him lead her back to his home. *Their* home for the time being. Living with Damian would be weird, even if they weren't sharing a bedroom. But part of her was relieved she wouldn't have to be by herself. She'd depended on Jared for so long, she didn't know how to be alone.

But she would not be dependent on Damian. She had no delusions of making a life with him. Not like she did with Jared. Hell, with the way Damian was hot one minute and cold the next, she couldn't tell if he liked her or hated her. She wondered if *he* even knew.

"There's so much color here. Why does everyone wear white? And why are all the buildings white? Seems like you'd take advantage of all the beauty, and make your stuff more colorful."

He shrugged. "You can't beat natural beauty, so why even try? White is simple and pure. The way our lives are supposed to be." He let out a cynical laugh.

"But you can wear anything you want. Any designer is yours with just a thought. It's a dream come true." She grinned as she closed her eyes and changed her outfit. The buzzing, tickling sensation against her skin made her shiver.

He chuckled. "I guess when you can have anything—create it with your mind—acquiring material things isn't that important."

"Hmm... Well, I love nice clothes. It's not against the rules for me to wear colors is it?"

"No. I don't know anyone else who does it, but you've never been one to follow the crowd."

"You wear blue jeans."

His smirk flattened as he looked down at his own clothes and raised one shoulder in a dismissive shrug. "I like to do things my way."

"I can tell."

They continued to walk hand-in-hand until they reached a familiar meadow. She recognized the field as the one she saw outside Damian's window. A moment later, his home came into view—a simple white structure as plain on the outside as it was on the inside. Even in its bareness, though, the home felt like just that—a home.

"Here we are." He opened the door for her and followed her in. "Let me make you a room, and then we can get started." He waved his hand in front of the wall, and a door appeared, identical to the one farther down.

He made it look so easy. With some practice, maybe she'd be able to make her own home someday with flower beds and a picket fence. She could still have her dream home here in the Angelic Realm. Maybe even her dream life.

"This is just temporary. Once you're trained you'll get your own place." His serious expression made her smile.

"Of course."

He took a deep breath and closed his eyes. Several moments passed in silence as he focused on building her room. When he finally opened his eyes, he motioned for her to go inside.

"There you go. But it's just temporary."

"You already said that."

He blew out a hard breath and swallowed. She padded past him into her new room. The walls were white, as she expected, but her breath caught at the splash of color he created. A queen-size bed sat in the center of the room and was covered in a luxurious lavender duvet. Matching sheer curtains draped across the bright window, and a bouquet of pink and purple tulips sat on the bedside table.

"What do you think?" His breath against her ear made her jump.

She spun around to face him and found herself inches from his body. An electric charge danced between them, drawing her even closer.

"It's perfect." And it was. The gesture was so sweet, her heart jumped into her throat. He knew lavender was her favorite color. The flowers, the color, everything about the room was so *her*. He knew her. Sure, he'd been watching her her entire life, but he hadn't simply observed. How could he possibly hate her if he'd taken the time to know her so well? The simple act of designing her room so perfectly revealed a tenderness in him she'd never seen before.

She gazed into his eyes and felt like she would drown in them. His intoxicating scent drew her in. The warmth of his body held her. She couldn't help herself. She inched forward, her mouth so close to his she could feel his rapid breaths against her lips. When he didn't pull away, she kissed him.

Their lips met, and the rest of the world slipped away. Fire shot through her limbs as his tongue slipped inside her mouth. His hands came up to cup her face, his touch ever so tender. She slipped her hands behind his neck and pulled him closer, deepening the kiss. The passion inside her flared to life, and she pressed her body to his.

He inhaled deeply and slid his hands into her hair. His tongue traced the contours of her lips, his warm breath tickling her skin. He tasted like cinnamon, and she leaned into him, drinking in all she could of the exquisite Angel.

The feel of his sculpted muscles against her chest made her knees weak, and she stumbled into the wall when he jerked out of their embrace. Anger fumed from his body as he clenched his fists and paced her bedroom.

"That shouldn't have happened. It was a mistake." He spoke through clenched teeth, his eyes trained on the floor. He wouldn't even look at her.

"I'm sorry. I...I don't know what came over me. I just..."

"It won't happen again." His steely gaze met hers for a split second before he disappeared.

Great. Smooth move, April.

She plopped onto the edge of her bed and put her head in her hands. What the hell was she thinking?

She'd kissed him.

He did one sweet thing for her, and she'd lost control and kissed him. And what a kiss. Embers still burned in her core from the passion that surged through her body. She'd never felt anything like it. The way he touched her...like she was fragile. Precious. She'd never seen that side of him, and it left her wanting more.

Get it under control, girl. He's not for you.

Hopefully they could forget the kiss ever happened

and get on with her training. She needed to get far, far away from him before she lost more than her human life. She would not lose her heart.

Past the meadow and over the rolling hills, Damian found solace in the stillness. The golden sun warmed his skin as he stretched out on the soft grass. He knew April could find him with a simple thought, but he prayed she wouldn't. He needed to be alone. As far away from her as possible, so he could sort out the emotional mess he'd made of his heart.

How could he have let that happen? He should've known better than to make her room like that. He knew she'd love it. He knew it would melt her heart just a little. And deep down, that's what he wanted, wasn't it? Deep down, he wanted her to like him.

Was he insane? April was a giver, and plenty of men were happy to take. She'd never been with a man who showered her with the tenderness and affection she deserved. And that was a shame.

But he shouldn't be the one giving it to her. She was his Charge. Nothing good ever came from an Angel falling for his Charge. Not in his opinion anyway.

He'd have to be more careful, before he got in over his head. He was already in it deep enough.

But Lord, she tasted good. Like honey and vanilla. The way her body reacted to his touch made his cock swell. The way she pressed against him. How she gasped when he returned the kiss. The passion was driving him to go back and drown himself in her essence.

But he wouldn't. He couldn't. He didn't spend that many years building a fortress around his heart to have it torn down by a pretty face.

Who was he kidding? She was so much more than that, and he knew it. The question was, would he be able to get out of this with his heart intact, or would April tear him to shreds like Juliet did so long ago?

He lay back on the grass and closed his eyes. He needed to clear his mind, focus on something else. But his thoughts kept drifting back to April. Her soft lips and warm skin. Her silky hair running through his fingers. Squeezing his eyes tighter, he tried to force the image from his mind, but it was no use.

"How's it hangin' dude?" Eric's voice brought a welcome distraction.

He opened his eyes and peered up at the tanned skin and messy blond hair hovering over him. "I've been better. How 'bout you?"

"Just taking a break. Mind if I join you?"

"Sure." Damian sat up and sighed.

"Trouble in paradise?" Eric lowered his large frame to the ground and rested his forearms on his knees.

He chuckled. "Yeah. You could say that. What about you? How are things going with your winner of a Charge?"

"Ah. It's goin', dude. But you know Jared. He wouldn't listen to me if his life depended on it."

"Some of them are like that." Damian gazed out over the rich, green landscape. As much as he'd hoped his friend would distract him from his thoughts, he couldn't focus on the conversation.

"But, dude. Sometimes I wish I was a Guardian, so I could cross over and knock him out. Or at least convince him to move to Malibu."

He smiled. "You're still hung up on California? Texas isn't so bad."

"Have you seen the surf in the Gulf, dude? It's flat and brown. I miss the waves on the west coast." Eric looked out over the field, lost in thought.

The two men sat in comfortable silence, and Damian almost forgot Eric was there. Thoughts of April swirled through his mind, tearing at his heart. He couldn't deny his feelings for her anymore, but he couldn't risk the heartbreak letting her in would surely cause. If he wasn't enough for Juliet, how could he expect to be enough for April? The sound of Eric's voice pulled him from his inner torment.

"So listen, dude. Do you think you can put in a good word for me with Mira and Paul? I really want to go back to Cali."

He nodded his head. "I'll see what I can do."

"Awesome. I'll catch ya later." Eric Jumped to Heaven knew where, leaving Damian alone with his thoughts.

What on Earth was he going to do about April?

It'd been nearly an hour, and Damian still hadn't returned. Well, if he was going leave her all alone, she might as well end her pity party, get off her butt, and go explore.

She closed her bedroom door and tiptoed through the living room. It was a silly action, but she felt like she was intruding in Damian's space. When she passed by his bedroom door, the temptation to take a peek inside almost won over her good sense. She still didn't know anything about him, and her curiosity drove her crazy.

Why did he act that way? She'd have understood if he didn't kiss her back, but he was just as into it as she was. So why the angry reaction? She shook her head as she walked out the door. He felt *something*. There was no way he could kiss her like that without feeling anything. But what was she going to do about it?

She strolled through the meadow toward what she wanted to call the town. They didn't eat, and they could create anything they needed out of thin air, so there weren't any stores or restaurants. But she saw a gathering of Angels near the lagoon, so she headed that way.

Anxiety twinged in her stomach. She didn't know these Angels. She had no idea what to say to them, or how much they knew about her situation. She came close to turning tail and running back to Damian's place, but she spotted Ella through the crowd.

Relief washed over her, and the tension in her shoulders eased. In the two weeks she spent in The In-Between, she and Ella had become good friends. A familiar face in a crowd of strangers was just what she needed. Someone she could confide in.

"Hi, Ella. Whatcha doing?" April fidgeted with her hair, twirling it around her finger like she always did when she was nervous.

"April! It's so good to see you." Ella pulled her into a

warm hug then wrapped her arm around her shoulder and led her away from the crowd. *Thank goodness.*

She took April up a path to a rocky platform above the waterfall. The view was amazing. The landscape was so pure, untouched save for the small white houses scattered throughout the lush fields of green. Fluffy clouds floated in the bright blue sky, and the cool breeze caressed her skin. She took a deep breath as the rhythmic sound of the water cascading into the lagoon soothed her frazzled nerves.

"So... How's your training going? How are things with Damian?"

"Eh...not so good."

"Really? I thought you'd catch on pretty quickly. Don't worry. It'll come to you when you're ready."

April smoothed the seam of her royal blue skirt. She felt out of place as she watched the other Angels in their simple, white garments.

"It's not that. He actually hasn't taught me anything yet. It's just that...well...I kissed him."

"What?" Excitement bubbled in Ella's voice. "You kissed *Damian?*"

"Shh... Will you keep it down? I don't want the whole world to know."

"Sorry." Ella giggled. "April, what happened? Did he kiss you back?"

"Umm...yeah, he did. It was...nice." Blood rushed to her cheeks. Should she have told Ella this? What would Damian think if he knew? "You won't tell anyone, will you?"

"No, of course not. But, April...you kissed Damian!

He's like someone you admire from afar. The ultimate goal that's always out of reach. I've never seen him show the slightest bit of interest in any woman. You're so lucky!"

April cleared her throat and looked at the ground. "I don't think so, considering that after we kissed he stormed away saying it was a huge mistake and it would never happen again. I haven't seen him since."

"Oh." Ella's shoulders slumped as her excitement deflated. "Well, that's a strange way to react. You're sure he kissed you back?"

"Positive." Shivers ran down her spine at the memory.

"Huh." She shrugged and rested her hand on her hip. "Well, I'm sure you two will work it out, once you're speaking again. He can't hide from you forever."

"Yeah, but I'm not sure if we should talk about it. He's so...I don't know. He's a hard nut to crack. I don't think I'm going to say anything. Pretend like it didn't happen, you know?"

Ella nodded. "I see. Ignore the problem, and it will go away."

"Something like that."

"You know it won't work. You two are going to have to talk about it sooner or later."

"I'm going with later." April looked out at the setting sun over the horizon and yawned. "Hey, Ella? Why is that Angels don't eat, but we still need to sleep?"

"We don't eat because we're pure energy. But we still need time to recharge. We're still connected to our Charges, and we'll wake up the instant they need us. But everybody needs to rest. Even Damian. I bet he'll be home soon." Ella winked and grinned.

April sighed. "Yeah, I should probably go back. I'll see you around?"

"Definitely." Ella hugged her and made her way down the path.

She couldn't keep avoiding the inevitable, but she wished she could avoid the inquisitive stares from the other Angels at the lagoon. She could just Jump there. It was her home too, after all. He couldn't get mad at her for Jumping into her own bedroom. She closed her eyes, took a deep breath, and pictured the lavender duvet on the bed Damian created for her. When she opened her eyes, she was there.

Damian watched the sun set over the hills and blew out a hard breath. He knew he needed to go back to her. Not just because she was his Charge, but because he owed her an explanation. And he had no idea what to tell her.

He took his time walking back to the house, rolling his thoughts over and over in his mind. What was he supposed to say? Should he tell her the truth? That he wanted nothing more than to hold her in his arms and make her his forever? That his body ached to be close to her, and his heart burned with desire? That he was scared to death because he'd had his heart ripped out once before, and he couldn't go through that again? He could lay it all out for her. Just like that.

Yeah, right.

He couldn't make himself that vulnerable. Was it *really*

what he wanted, anyway? Part of him did. *Most* of him did.

Maybe she'd bring it up. She'd admit it was a mistake, and they could move on. But what if she didn't? He'd have to figure something out soon, because he was about to walk through the door.

He turned the knob and tentatively pushed it open, bracing himself for whatever rage April planned to take out on him.

He was met with silence.

"April?" He entered the living room, but she wasn't there, so he padded across the thick, white carpet and tapped on her door.

"Come in."

He crossed the threshold and found April curled up on her bed reading a book. A plain, white lamp sitting on her bedside table provided the only light in the room. His eyes adjusted to the darkness, and he noticed she had changed clothes. Instead of her designer skirt and blouse, she now wore a simple, pale pink nightgown.

Her silky hair spilled around her shoulders, and her pink lips curved into a tentative smile as she rose from the bed and put the book on the table.

"Hey." Her voice was a whisper, but it danced in his ears like the sweetest music he had ever heard.

Good Lord, she was beautiful. He bit his tongue to keep from telling her just that. Swallowing down the lump in his throat, he forced himself to speak. "Hey. Listen, about what happened earlier..."

"Nothing happened." April shrugged and brushed past him on her way to the living room.

That sure wasn't the reaction he expected. And having his own words thrown back at him frustrated him to no end. He followed her into the living room and sat next to her on the sofa.

"I just wanted to apologize."

"There's nothing to apologize for, Damian. Nothing happened. Now, are you going to teach me anything tonight or can I get back to my book?"

So, that's how she's going to be. Her stubbornness shouldn't have surprised him. But he'd expected her to be as torn up about the kiss as he was. He'd wanted her to be.

Or did he?

Hell, he didn't know what he wanted anymore.

"It's getting kind of late, so I thought we'd save the lessons for tomorrow. But, if you have any questions, maybe I could answer them."

"Nope. No questions."

"I mean...is there anything you want to know about me?"

April blew out a breath. "Nothing comes to mind right now. So if we're done here, I'd like to call it a night." With that, she stood and strode to her bedroom, closing the door behind her.

Well, hell. That didn't go at all as he expected. Damn it, why did he have to kiss her? If he'd walked away before she got so close, he could have avoided this situation altogether. But he didn't. He couldn't. The warm desire emanating from her body had paralyzed him, and he'd wanted to kiss her. He gave in to his weakness, and look where it got him. Getting a cold shoulder from the one woman who drove him crazy.

He groaned as he rose from the sofa and marched to his bedroom. He threw open the door, and it slammed against the wall with a bang. Pausing in the doorway, he half-hoped April would come out to see what all the noise was about.

She didn't.

CHAPTER 12

The morning sun filtered through the sheer lavender curtains, washing April's room in a soft orange glow. Was it the same sun she basked in on Earth? Or was it some distant star in a far off galaxy she'd never heard of?

There were so many things she had to learn. So many questions raced through her head, she didn't know where to start. Of course, the one at the front of her mind was the kiss. She shivered.

Damian had tried to talk about it, but she'd blown him off like it was nothing. Wasn't that how he acted after their almost kiss in the cemetery? Why would he want to talk about the one that actually happened?

They didn't need to discuss it anyway. All he would say was it was a mistake. He'd made that clear before he disappeared to God knew where for three hours.

She'd just have to keep pretending it didn't happen. So what if he was more thoughtful than any man she'd ever met? He was only being nice to her because she was his Charge. How would he act toward her if she wasn't?

With a heavy sigh, she threw the covers back and slid out of bed. She looked in the mirror at her wrinkled nightgown and disheveled hair. She'd gotten used to not needing to shower or brush her teeth anymore, but she hadn't been concerned about her looks in the two weeks she spent in The In-Between. Now she was, and she was a mess.

She started to create a hair brush, but thought better of it. If she could change her clothes with just a thought, why couldn't she fix her hair too? Closing her eyes, she imagined herself wearing a pale yellow V-neck with denim capris. She didn't want to stand out too much, but she wasn't ready to give up wearing color just yet. Then, she pictured her hair flowing over her shoulders, soft and shiny and tangle-free.

A smile spread across her face when she opened her eyes. The mirror reflected the exact image she saw in her mind.

"Amazing."

She couldn't put it off any longer. She would have to face Damian sooner or later, and she might as well get it over with. Hopefully he wouldn't try to talk about the kiss again. She couldn't handle yet another rejection.

Her look of resolve reflected back at her, and she nodded her head and pushed back her shoulders. She could do this.

She crept to the door and slowly twisted the knob. Part of her wished Damian would still be asleep so she could delay the confrontation a little longer.

No such luck.

He perched on the edge of the sofa, wringing his hands as he stared out the window. He wore blue jeans and a white dress shirt, untucked with the sleeves rolled up to his elbows. His golden-brown hair glistened in the sunlight and the emerald flecks in his hazel eyes sparkled when he turned his head.

As soon as he saw her, he jumped to his feet.

"Good morning, April." He looked her up and down, and his crooked grin melted her heart.

Get it together, April. Don't get swept up in his charm.

"Good morning." She had to force her voice over the lump in her throat. "Umm...so, where do we start?"

"Well, did you think of any questions you wanted to ask me?"

Why did you kiss me and run away? Why do you hate me so much?

She instinctively took a step toward him, her body aching to close the space between them. "How old are you?"

His smile widened, and he sat on the sofa, patting the space next to him. She accepted the invitation and settled onto the couch.

"I'm the oldest Angel in existence. Well, Mira, Paul, and I are."

"So your parents weren't Angels?"

"I never had parents."

April laughed, but his serious expression said he wasn't kidding. "You're serious?"

He shrugged. "Yes. In the beginning, God created four Angels to watch over the people. I'm one of those four. He eventually created more, and they had children. That's how we have so many Angels today."

She furrowed her brow as she tried to comprehend what she was hearing. Damian was *created* by God? No wonder everything about him was so perfect. Well, everything except his attitude toward her. "Wow. That's...impressive."

"Not really. I'm just like everyone else."

"But Mira said you're the best."

"The best at my job. Not the best person." He cast his gaze down to his hands folded in his lap.

Damian was always so confident. Cocky. Not now. Her heart fluttered at his raw honesty. *I will not let myself fall for him.* She almost wished he'd be mean to her, so she could squelch this burning desire to wrap herself in his arms.

"You said there were four original Angels. Who's the other one?"

His jaw snapped shut, and he grinded his teeth. His hands clenched into fists as he took several slow, deep breaths.

"Micah." The name came out as a growl.

"Who's Micah?"

He closed his eyes and went utterly still. The only movement he made was the rise and fall of his chest as he blew out a hard breath.

"Micah was my brother. But he Fell. Everything changed after that."

"How so?"

Damian groaned and shot to his feet. With long strides he paced the length of the living room. "He was the first Angel to Fall. He started it all. If it wasn't for him, there'd be no need for Guardians. We'd all be Keepers like we were supposed to be. No one would Fall for their Charges, and Juliet…"

He clamped his mouth shut and stared out the window. With his forehead pressed to the glass, his heavy breaths created a white fog on the pane, expanding and contracting with each exhalation.

So that's why he was so upset when April wanted to Fall. He was in pain. Instinctively, she rose to her feet and padded across the room to comfort him. She slid her hand across his back and rested her head on his shoulder.

"I'm sorry. I didn't mean to upset you."

He didn't move. "Not your fault. I've got my own personal demons to deal with."

"Do you want to talk about it?"

"No. Let's get started on your lessons." Without warning, he spun out of her embrace and marched to the door.

Once again, April stumbled with his quick retreat.

"You've got to quit doing that." She smiled at him, hoping to defuse the awkward moment.

The corner of his mouth curved into an almost grin. "Sorry." He took her hand and led her out the door.

Good Lord, that conversation had gotten too personal. How close he almost came to telling her about Juliet. What was he thinking? He didn't talk about her with anyone. Not even Mira. The pain was too much to bear.

But when she touched him. When she laid her head

on his shoulder in comfort, he felt just that. Comfort. Like a warm blanket wrapped around his soul. It was something he hadn't felt in hundreds of years. Six hundred and fifty-three, to be exact.

When April touched him, he wanted nothing more than to curl up in her arms and let her take the hurt away. To let her love him till he felt no pain at all.

Like he could ever let that happen. A Guardian was supposed to take care of his Charge. Not the other way around.

He shook his head and led her to the middle of the grassy meadow behind his house. That would be the perfect spot to practice crossing over to the Earthly Realm. He turned to face her and took both her hands in his.

Her emerald eyes sparkled in the sunlight, and her plump, pink lips were so kissable, he had to look away. He cleared his throat before he spoke.

"When you're a Guardian, you have to be able to get to your Charge at a moment's notice. You'll know he needs you, because you can sense his emotions."

"Or hers."

Her teasing grin made his heart skip a beat. But their relationship had to stay professional. He needed to get through this so he could spend the rest of the day in solace —away from April and the sweet temptation of her soft skin and warm body.

He let out a dramatic sigh and shook his head. "Or hers. Now, stop interrupting me."

"Do you ever Guard men? Or do you always pick women?"

"I Guard whomever is assigned to me. I don't choose. Mira does."

"Does she ever assign you to men?"

"Yes. Now can we please get on with this?"

Hurt flashed through her eyes before she composed herself. "Okay. Just tell me what to do."

"Right. Well, you have to be able to get to your Charge from anywhere. When you're in The In-Between, it's easy because you're technically already there. You just have to cross over from where you are. But when you're here, in the Angelic Realm, it's harder. If you can do it from here, you can do it from anywhere."

"Why's it harder?"

"Because you have to imagine just the right place, without actually seeing it. And you have to be sure you cross over somewhere no one will see you do it. People freak out when you appear out of thin air."

"Okay. So, how do I do it?"

"Let me show you first. You know that dirt road past the rice field behind your mom's house?"

"Yeah." She gave him a wary look.

"That's where we're going to go. It's secluded enough that no one will see us. Are you ready?"

April shrugged. "Sure." She was trying to play it down, like she wasn't nervous. But the sweat beading on her forehead and the quickening of the pulse in her neck gave her away.

He grinned. "All right. Here we go." He closed his eyes and pictured the location, and they crossed over. They appeared in the dirt beside the road, and April squealed.

"Why'd you put us in the mud? My shoes are going to be ruined!"

He chuckled. "You can make new ones when we get back. Remember?"

She rubbed her arms and stared at the ground. "Oh, right."

"So, that's all you have to do. And getting back home is easier. Do you want to try it? Can you take us back to the meadow? Or are you too afraid of getting dirty?"

She narrowed her eyes and crossed her arms over her chest. "I'm not afraid of anything, mister. Maybe you're just afraid I'll be better at it than you."

Her challenging stare made him grin. She'd taken the bait and gotten ticked off. That was the April he loved.

Wait. Not love.

He pushed the thought aside as soon as it entered his mind.

"All right, then. Let's see what you've got. Take us home." He held out his hand, and she placed hers in his palm.

She closed her eyes and drew her brows together. In a blink, they were swept into Damian's living room.

"Well, it's not quite the meadow, but it'll do for now. With a little practice, you'll be able to get the location more exact."

A smug smile slid across her face. "Oh, I brought us exactly where I planned to. You said to take us home, and here we are."

He laughed. "Okay. I see how you're going to be. If you think you're that great, then you can do it on your own. I'm going back. When you're ready, Jump to me. Okay?"

"No problem."

He Jumped to the side of the road by the rice field and waited for April. Several minutes had passed when a semi rumbled down the road. He prayed April wouldn't Jump right when the truck rolled by. The driver might have a heart attack if he saw her appear out of nowhere. But she'd have no way of knowing he was there.

He was about to Jump back to see what was taking her so long when she appeared in the middle of the road.

Right in the path of the oncoming truck.

Her eyes went wide a second before the semi slammed into her. The truck skidded and came to a screeching halt, but before the driver could jump out of the cab, Damian whisked her crumpled body into The In-Between.

He exhaled a curse when he looked at her battered, bloodied form. She'd felt every bit of that pain, and she'd remember it. Though he'd never died himself, he could imagine what it felt like to be crushed by a massive vehicle going sixty miles an hour—excruciating.

The truck driver jogged up the road to the place he *thought* he crashed into a woman. But there was nothing there. Damian watched as the guy looked around, scratched his head, and stumbled to his truck in a confused daze.

That was a close call.

He scooped April's lifeless body into his arms and Jumped to the sanctuary. Mira could clean her up, but Heaven knew how long she'd have to sleep it off. She was going to blame him, but that was April for you. He actually looked forward to the confrontation.

Laying her on a bed, he brushed her matted hair away from her face. He should have made her practice more before letting her Jump alone. He deserved to be blamed for the accident.

Mira appeared behind him and looked over his shoulder. "What happened?"

"She Jumped in front of a truck." He spoke to Mira, but his gaze lingered on April's bloody face.

She winced. "Poor girl."

"Yeah. Can you clean her up?"

"Of course." Mira placed a hand on April's cheek, and in a flash of shimmering light, a long white gown replaced her tattered clothes. All traces of injury disappeared, and the rosy glow returned to her cheeks.

"Thanks. But, can you make the dress lavender? It's her favorite color."

She tilted her head to the side and grinned at him. "What?"

"Oh, nothing." She touched April's hand, and color saturated the dress.

He could see why she loved the color so much. She was beautiful in it. "How long do you think she'll be out?"

"An hour or two."

Damian nodded. "I'll wait with her."

"I know." She gave him a knowing smile, turned and glided away.

"Oh, April May. What am I going to do with you?" He sat on the edge of the bed and stroked her cheek. He knew he shouldn't. He had no right to run his fingers through her silky strands of crimson. But the warmth of her skin, the softness of her hair only made him want her more.

How he longed to touch her like this when she was awake. When she could touch him back. Not that she ever would. Not after the way he'd behaved.

He needed to start using his head. Falling in love was the last thing he needed, but it was exactly what he was doing.

CHAPTER 13

*A*gony throbbed through every limb, and her head pounded with so much force she thought it might explode. April tried to cry out for someone to help her, but she couldn't breathe. Was she dead again? Would she wake up, or was the pain her eternal punishment? Every bone was broken, every muscle bruised. Anguish paralyzed her. The intensity increased, throbbing harder and harder, and when it reached the point that she couldn't take it anymore, it ceased. Sweet relief flooded through her body.

She floated through the night sky, coming closer and closer to consciousness. The twinkling stars above reminded her of the light that was sure to be pulling her out of Slumber soon. She fought the urge to open her eyes, but a warm touch trailing down her skin fully awakened her.

She knew it was Damian. Who else would it be? His warm, masculine scent wafted around her, and she hoped he hadn't noticed her breath catch when she awoke. His touch was tender, caring. Warm shivers ran down her spine when he stroked her hair and pressed his lips to her forehead.

She could have lain there like that all day, basking in Damian's sensuous touch. She knew when she opened her eyes, the tender moment would cease, so she forced them shut a little longer, memorizing the feeling of his hands on her skin.

When she finally allowed her lids to flutter open and smiled at him, he shot off the bed like he'd been bitten by a snake.

"What in Heaven's name were you thinking Jumping into the middle of the road like that?" While his voice held a touch of his usual anger, his eyes held nothing but compassion.

She swung her legs over the edge and perched on the side of the bed. "I didn't mean to. I was shooting for the opposite side of the road, but I guess I underestimated the distance."

"You think? You have to be more careful."

Pounding pain shot through her temple, and she pressed the heels of her hands against her forehead to subdue it. "Why does my head hurt?"

He forced out an exasperated sigh. "You were run over by a truck. The pain's in your imagination. It'll go away in a while. I can't believe you did that. That poor trucker thinks he's crazy now."

"Would you lay off?" The pain in her head subsided, but Damian was intent on being a pain in her neck. He was trying to drive her away, to act like he didn't care for her. But the tenderness in his touch when he thought she was in Slumber told a different story. And then there was her dress.

Lavender. Mira would've dressed her in white.

Her heart fluttered, a smile tugging at her lips as she smoothed the silky material down her legs. "Nice dress. Thank you."

"You know what? You just…oh, never mind." He threw up his hands and marched through the door.

She stole a quick glance at his backside as he stormed away. Delectable. But his mood swings were making her seasick. Why wouldn't he just pick a way to treat her and stick with it? She'd have preferred he be mean to her all the time rather than getting her hopes up only to shoot her down.

Well, no she wouldn't.

She stroked the soft dress one more time and looked up to find Mira standing next to her.

"How are you feeling, dear?"

"Like I've been run over by a truck."

Mira smiled and wrapped her arm around April's shoulders. "The pain will cease soon. How about your heart?"

"Excuse me?"

"How are things with Damian?"

She let out a cynical laugh. "That's a good question. One minute he acts like he hates me, and the next minute I think he might actually care for me. I don't know what's going on with him."

Mira pressed her lips together and shook her head. "I don't think he knows either."

"What do you mean?"

She sighed. "Be patient with him. He may seem strong and confident on the outside, but on the inside he's quite fragile. If you're feeling better, you are free to go."

"But..."

Mira disappeared in a flash of warm light.

April pushed off the table and shuffled to the door. She wasn't going to let one little mistake stop her. Even if the mistake had flattened her like a pancake. Her pride wouldn't let her go back to Damian until she was sure she could cross over on her own.

When she exited the building, she cut around the corner to a secluded spot and tried again. She pictured the road by the rice field in her mind, and she Jumped to the exact spot she'd hoped for.

That wasn't so hard. She crossed back to the Angelic Realm, and had to try one more time, just to be sure it wasn't a fluke. She made it to the road and back again like it was nothing. Easy.

Damian was distracting her before. That was the problem.

Excitement bubbled up inside her. She could go back to Earth any time she wanted to. How cool was that? She could check on Momma and Shelly and make sure Alex and the rest of her students were doing okay. She hadn't lost them after all.

With her confidence restored, she Jumped to Damian, who was lying in the field behind his house. With his hands behind his head and his ankles crossed, he stared up at the bright blue sky, lost in thought. Sunlight glinted off his shiny hair, and his white shirt stretched tight across his chest, hinting at the chiseled muscles lying beneath. Her heartbeat quickened at the sight of the Angel in the grass. If only she could get inside his head and figure out how he really felt about her.

Damian stared up at the clear, blue sky, but all he saw was April's face. The rosy glow of her skin. The perfect pink bow of her lips. His hands trembled with the need to be back in the sanctuary caressing her soft, supple body.

He felt her presence before he saw her, and he rose up on his elbows as she made her way toward him. She was a vision in the lavender gown that hugged her curves, revealing a slender waist and full breasts. His fingers ached to touch the soft, warm flesh. His mouth watered to feel her nipples harden like pebbles under his tongue.

He smiled when she knelt on the grass beside him. She placed her hand on his chest, and he sucked in a sharp breath as the jolt rocked through his core. How could she affect him like that with a simple touch?

"I'm sorry I screwed up. I promise it won't happen again." She started to move her hand, but he covered it with his, holding it against his body. He needed her touch more than he liked to admit. More than she would ever know.

"I'm sorry I was so hard on you. It was your first time. Every other Guardian's had years of practice by the time they reach thirty. I forget how new all of this is to you. You're unique, April. You're special."

Her cheeks flushed with color, and she grinned. "I can do it now, though. I've been practicing."

Of course she had. She was the most determined person he knew. "Do you want to show me?"

"Okay. But I want to try something first." She rose to her feet, and her gown turned gleaming white. "Stay here."

Yeah, right. He knew that look in her eyes. She was up to something, and he sure as hell wasn't going to let her do it alone.

April Jumped, but he could follow her. As long as he stayed in The In-Between, she'd never know he was there. She hadn't learned to sense the Angelic plane from the Earthly Realm.

He recognized the room immediately. Bookcases lined the walls from ceiling to floor, and a long mahogany desk sat off to one side. A man sat in a high-back leather chair, facing the wall, and April stood across from the desk—in the flesh.

What did she think she was doing? This was sure to get them both in trouble.

Jared finished his phone call and turned around. He froze when he saw her standing there; the phone dropped to the floor.

"A...April?" Fear spiked in his voice, but he still didn't move.

She put her finger to her lips and whispered, "Shhh." Then she giggled and Jumped back home.

Jared blinked. He squeezed his eyes shut and opened them again. Then with trembling hands, he picked up the receiver and put it back in the cradle.

Damian groaned and Jumped back to find April sitting on the sofa in their living room with a smug smile on her face.

"Just what do you think you're doing? You...you can't do that. It's against the rules."

She shrugged. "I didn't know there were rules. No one told me. Besides, Jared needs to learn his lesson somehow."

He raked his hand through his hair and paced the room. This woman was going to be the death of him. "You can't show yourself to people who knew you when you were human."

"Why not?"

"Well, because."

"Because why?"

"It freaks them out. You're *dead*. Angels are supposed to protect people, not mess with their minds." The sharp tone of his voice startled him. He didn't mean to yell at her, but sometimes she was so stubborn.

"He deserves it." Her gaze fell to her hands folded in her lap.

He sank to the floor in front of her, resting his hands on her knees. "Look, April. I know you're hurting."

She inhaled deeply and looked into his eyes. Tears welled up, threatening to spill over, but she blinked them back. "Do you know how long he was cheating on me? Tell me."

He exhaled sharply and shook his head. "Do you really want to talk about this?"

"I need to know." Her voice was a whisper across her lips.

He closed his eyes for a long blink and looked up at her sad eyes. The pain he saw there ripped at his heart, and he wanted more than anything to make it go away. To show her she deserved so much better. To be the man she deserved. "Five months."

She sucked in a shaky breath and nodded. "And you knew all along?"

"Yes."

"Why didn't you tell me? You were pretending to be human for three months. In all that time, you couldn't find a way to tell me?"

"Would you have believed me?"

Her silence was answer enough.

"And I did try to tell you. Every time you had doubts. Every time you confronted him, and he gave you excuses. I planted those thoughts in your head. But you wanted to believe him so badly, you accepted any story he told you. I tried, April. I really did."

"It doesn't matter. What Jared did was wrong, and he needs to learn his lesson. If seeing the ghost of his dead girlfriend is what it takes, that's what he's going to get." She crossed her arms over her chest and stared out the window.

He slid onto the couch, so close to her their thighs touched. Without thinking, he put his arms around her and pulled her to his chest. It was how he always comforted her before—from The In-Between. Why should it be any different now?

He didn't expect her to come to him so easily. She wrapped her arms around his neck and snuggled against him, tears streaming down her cheeks. "Please hold me, Damian. I need you to hold me."

He was more than happy to oblige. He pulled her into his lap and held her tight as she cried. She felt so good in his arms. So right. He stroked her hair and kissed the top of her head as her warmth consumed him. He'd comforted plenty of Charges over the years, but never in all his life, had a Charge provided so much comfort in return. Guilt twinged in his gut; he was enjoying the moment, while she was in pain.

He didn't know how long he held her, but they both dozed off in the warmth of each other's arms. When he woke, the sun had already set behind the hills, and April still clung to him.

She needed Slumber if her energy was to regenerate properly. And though he hated to let her go, he knew she needed to be in bed. He slipped his arm under her legs and inched forward enough so he could pick her up. The movement roused her from her sleep, and she hugged him tighter.

"Don't leave me." She looked up at him, and her tear-stained cheeks broke his heart.

"You need to rest. You'll feel better in the morning."

"No. Please, Damian. I need you."

She cupped his face in her hands and pressed her lips to his. Heat flashed through his body like lightning, and when she parted her lips he had to taste her. She was sweet, like honey; he couldn't help but drink her in. And when she broke the kiss to look in his eyes, he pulled her back for more.

She pulled away with a small gasp that left him breathless, and straddled his lap. Trailing kisses down his neck, she slid her hands underneath his shirt. Her touch raised goose bumps on his skin, and he shivered with the need to be with her.

He wanted her. He wanted her so badly, he could hardly stand it. But not like this. Not when she was reacting to hurt caused by another man.

He put his hands on her shoulders and gently pushed her back. "We can't do this. Not now." The sting of rejection in her gaze almost made him change his mind.

"Why? I want you, Damian. Don't you want me?"

"More than you can imagine. But you're hurting. If we do this now, you'll regret it. And I don't want you to have *any* regrets when it comes to me. Okay?"

She nodded and blinked back the tears that threatened to flow from her emerald eyes.

"Come on." He lifted her from the sofa and carried her across the room. "Let's get you to bed."

Soft moonlight spilled through the open window, basking the room in silver. He slipped her under the covers and kissed her forehead. "Good night, April."

She grasped his hand and pleaded with her eyes. "Will you stay with me? I don't want to be alone."

He shouldn't. Not if he wanted to make it out of this with his heart in one piece. But the pain in her gaze held him there. He couldn't leave her. Not when she needed him so badly. Charge or no Charge, he couldn't stand seeing April hurt.

"Okay, sweetheart. I'll stay." He crawled into bed with her. And with her back pressed to his front, he wrapped his arms around her and held her through the night.

CHAPTER 14

She'd never felt more secure in her life. The warmth that embraced her felt like a dream, and she wasn't ready to leave the safety of her Slumber. But the morning sun cascading through the window called her to start the day.

She rolled onto her side, opened her eyes, and found herself face-to-face with her Guardian Angel. Her chest tightened at the sight of him lying next to her, her heart fluttering against her ribs.

"Hey." His voice was raspy with sleep, and his concerned gaze caught hers.

She smiled and reached for his hand. "So it wasn't a dream. You stayed with me all night."

"Yes."

"Thank you. Umm...I'm sorry for the way I acted. For...you know."

He laced his fingers through hers, and pulled her hand to his chest. "It's okay. You needed me, and I comforted you. Just like I've done your whole life."

"Of course." *Because it's your job.* She pulled her hand from his grasp and rolled out of bed.

"I'll always be here for you, April."

"I know." She smiled halfheartedly and changed her clothes. She knew he was trying to make her feel better, but it had the opposite effect. She needed him to be there for her because he *wanted* to, not because he had to. "Well, I guess we better get started if we want to get this training over with, right?"

"Yeah. I guess so." He slid out of bed and shuffled to the living room, where he dropped onto the sofa.

April followed and sat on the opposite end, curling one leg underneath her. "So, what's on the agenda for today?"

He took a deep breath and stared at his clasped hands. Silence stretched between them as she awaited his response.

"Damian?"

"Hmm? Oh, right." He shook himself as if coming out of a daze and turned to her. "You need to practice finding your Charge. You have to be able to Jump to him at any moment."

"But I don't have a Charge."

"No, but you're linked to me. So we're going to play a little game of hide and seek. I'll Jump to the Earthly Realm, and then you have to find me."

"Sounds easy enough."

He grinned and looked at her with challenge in his gaze. "We'll see."

Before she could ask any questions, he Jumped to the rice field in Felicity. He'd make it easy for her the first few times. Not that she was making anything easy for him. After spending the night with her—feeling the warmth of her supple body pressed to his all night—he knew his heart wasn't going to make it out of this in one piece.

Within seconds, she stood before him with a smug smile on her face. "I told you it'd be easy."

"Uh-huh." If that's how she was going to be, he'd have to make it harder. He grinned, winked, and Jumped to a mountain in the middle of Wyoming.

Slipping inside a small crevice carved out of the red rock, he stepped into a spacious cave. He'd spent days in this cavern after what happened with Juliet. The constant dripping of water and the stale scent of bat dung and rotting foliage had his head spinning with painful memories.

Why on Earth did he come here? Habit? Masochism? Whatever the subconscious reason, he had to get out of there. He slid out of the gap in the rock and found April waiting for him on the outside.

He chuckled at the nervous look on her face. "Took you long enough."

She crossed her arms over her chest and shifted her weight. "I don't do small spaces."

"That's right, you're claustrophobic. Sorry about that."

He Jumped to a spacious pasture in rural Ireland. Saturated with vivid green, the rolling hills went on for miles. Sheep, thick with wool, grazed on the sweet grass, and the sound of waves crashing into a distant shore reminded him of home.

April appeared behind him and wrapped her arms around his waist. "Gotcha." An electric jolt rocked through his body, shocking away the pain his last Jump had caused.

"Not for long." He pulled from her entrancing grasp and turned to face her.

Her lips curved into a kissable grin. "You can't hide from me."

I don't want to. Good Lord, she was beautiful with the look of sheer determination in her eyes. She was going to be an amazing Guardian. She was already an amazing woman.

"We'll see about that." He Jumped again and appeared on a secluded beach on a small island off the coast of Australia. The cloudless sky and fine, white sand made the scene picturesque. Pristine. He sensed April finding him, and before she appeared in front of him, he slipped into The In-Between.

When she arrived, she looked around in confusion. She hadn't learned to sense the difference between The In-Between and the Earthly Realm. She knew he was there, but she couldn't see him. She turned around in a circle, her hand covering her brow to block the glare, but he was nowhere to be found.

Sunlight glistened on her fiery red hair as the breeze blew it over her shoulder. When she looked out over the crystal blue water, her breath caught. She was a vision of beauty standing in the sand, admiring the wonders of nature.

The curve of her slender neck made his mouth water. Her scent mixed with the salty air caused his head to spin.

His heart skipped a beat, and blood rushed to his groin. He couldn't help himself.

He appeared before her, pulled her into his arms, and kissed her. She gasped from the initial shock, but she slid her hands over his shoulders and let him in.

He was setting himself up for heartache, but at that moment, he didn't care. April was all that mattered, and she was in his arms. The aching need to hold her transformed into an unquenchable desire to be inside her. To be part of her. He cradled her face in his hands and kissed her like the delicate treasure she was.

Then, in one swift jump, she linked her legs around his waist, throwing him off balance. He fell on his back on the sand, and April fell on top of him. She bit her bottom lip and looked into his eyes. The feel of her supple curves pressed against him drove him wild with need. Her tongue slipped out to moisten her lips, and he groaned.

It was too much to bear. He couldn't control himself. Using one hand for leverage, he placed the other one on her back and rolled her over. She spread her legs, allowing his pelvis to settle between them, and she moaned softly when he pressed his arousal into her.

He needed to stop. He knew he did, but he couldn't. She tasted too good. Smelled too sweet. Lying beneath him with a smile on her lips and wet sand in her hair, she looked too damn sexy. He wanted her.

He teased her, brushing her lips with his tongue. She grinned and caught his bottom lip between her teeth. A fire ignited inside him, a burning need he'd never felt before. He had to have her. As he leaned in to take her mouth with his, a chilling wave crashed over them, drenching them both in salty water.

Her eyes widened with shock as she sputtered the water from her mouth. She laughed, and the moment was gone. He stood and helped her to her feet, both of them gasping from their laughter. She squeezed the water out of her hair and furrowed her brow as she looked at him.

"Why can't I change my clothes?"

"Because we're on Earth. We have to be home to do that."

"Huh. I'll race you there. On your mark, get set, go!" She disappeared.

He shook his head and ran his hand through his dripping hair.

Well, Damian. What are you going to do now?

April changed her clothes and sat on the sofa. She didn't really want to race him; she wanted a moment alone to gather her thoughts. That kiss was intense, and this time he initiated it.

Could he be falling for her? Did she want him to? Surely what he did on the beach wasn't out of duty. Her lips quirked into a smile. Damian had feelings for her, whether he would admit it or not.

His bedroom door opened, and he stepped out wearing faded jeans and a white T-shirt. Though he wore the same outfit almost every day, she never tired of seeing him in it. He looked good no matter what he wore. *He'd look even better in nothing at all.*

A shy smile curved his lips as he hesitated in the doorway. He ran his fingers through his hair and shoved his hands in his pockets. "Hey."

"Hi there."

He shuffled to the couch and sat next to her. Chewing his bottom lip, he stared at his hands folded in his lap.

He was obviously trying to think of something to say, but all she wanted to do was kiss him again. His nervousness was endearing; she was finally seeing behind his mask, and she liked what she saw. She placed her hand on top of his, and he looked at her.

"Did I pass the test?"

He grinned and placed his other hand on top of hers. "With flying colors."

"So, what next?"

"I guess we need to lay down some ground rules. Answer any questions you have."

The warmth of his hands encasing hers made her head spin. She'd had a million questions to ask that morning, but now all she could think about was the beach. "Okay. What are the rules?"

"We talked about one of them last night. You can't appear to people who knew you as a human. When you Jump, you have to be sure no one sees you. But if they do, you can wipe yourself out of their memories. We can practice that when it happens. And the most important one to remember is that we serve our Charges. It's our duty to keep them safe and comfort them. Duty must always come first."

She shrugged and folded her leg beneath her. "Sounds simple enough. Is there anything else?"

"That about covers it. Do you have any questions?"

There was one. The question that had been burning in the back of her mind since he told her about Micah and the Fall. The question she knew he didn't want to answer, which made her need to know even more.

"Who's Juliet?"

All expression dropped from his face, and he stared right through her. He sucked in a breath and shot off the sofa. "Right, well I'm going to talk to Mira about getting us a Charge. I think you're ready. Don't you?" He reached the door in three long strides and turned the knob before she could speak.

"Wait. I have one more question." If he didn't want to talk about Juliet, she wasn't going to push it. Not yet.

He sighed and turned to face her, his jaw clenched tight, his hand still on the knob.

"When I first got here, and you were arguing with Mira about me being a Guardian. You said I couldn't be because you Guarded Trusten. Did you mean my grandfather?"

Damian's posture relaxed, and he took a step toward her. "Yes. Would you like to meet him?"

"Really? My grandpa is here?" Though he died before she was born, she'd heard so much about the man, she felt like she knew him already.

Damian smiled. "Yes. He's a Keeper. Do you want to go see if he's home?"

"I'd love to." She took his outstretched hand, and they Jumped.

Damian knocked on the white door, and April bounced with excitement. She was finally going to meet the man her Nana loved so dearly. The man April compared all others to, though she'd never met him. What would she say to him? When the door opened, her heart lurched into her throat, and she ducked behind Damian's large frame.

"Well, hello Damian. To what do I owe the honor of your visit?"

"I've got somebody who wants to meet you. April, meet your grandfather." He stepped beside her and put his hand on her shoulder.

She was speechless. With wavy, dark brown hair and deep, chocolate eyes, Trusten was a far cry from the wrinkled old man she'd expected to see. "Grandpa?"

His warm smile put her at ease, and she took a step toward him. "Nana told me so much about you. I just can't believe I'm actually standing right in front you. It's a pleasure to meet you."

"Ah, April. The pleasure is all mine. Won't you come inside? Both of you." He stepped out of the doorway for them to enter.

She glanced at Damian, who nodded, and she entered her grandpa's house. The interior was white, just like everything else there, and a leather sectional was situated in the center of the living room.

"Please, sit down. I knew this day would come. That one of my grandchildren would become an Angel. And since Damian is still with you, I presume you must be a Guardian. Can it be?"

April settled onto the sofa with Damian by her side. He put his hand on her knee and smiled like a proud teacher.

"Yes, she is. The first of her kind." He rubbed her leg, sending warm shivers up her body.

"I feel like I already know you, Grandpa. Nana talked about you all the time. She loved you so much. Did you know she never remarried? She said the memory of you was all she needed."

"She's a strong woman. How is she doing these days?"

"Eighty-three and feisty as ever."

Trusten took a deep breath, and a smile of reminiscence spread across his face. "She always was a lively one. So, tell me about you, April. How are you faring in the Angelic Realm?"

"Oh, I'm doing good, I guess. I haven't gotten a Charge yet, but Damian's been teaching me the ropes."

Trusten's gaze fell to Damian's hand on her knee, and his smile widened. "Damian was my Guardian. Did you know that? Oh, my Charge needs me. I'm afraid I'm going to have to cut our visit short. Come back and see me, will you?"

"I will."

They rose from the couch, and Trusten hugged her tightly. "He's a good man, April. Hold on to him." He stepped back, waved good-bye, and disappeared.

She would love to hold on to Damian, if she could ever make him hers. As she followed him out the door, he turned to her and ran his fingers through her hair. Her knees went weak, and she wanted nothing more than to throw herself into his arms. Did he have any idea what his touch did to her?

"I have to go talk to Mira and Paul. Will you be okay on your own for an hour?"

"I guess. Can't I go with you?"

He smiled and tucked a piece of hair behind her ear. "No. We're kinda in charge of assigning all the Charges and making sure things are running smoothly. You know, since we're the oldest and all. We have to talk shop."

"Oh. You're a very important Angel."

"I'm not that important. I'd rather not be on the council at all, but I don't have a choice."

Her fingers twitched. She hesitated to touch him, but she glided the back of her fingers down his cheek. "It's okay. I'll be fine."

He caught her hand in his. "I'll be home in one hour. I promise. And then we can see about getting ourselves a Charge."

"Sounds great."

She expected him to vanish, but he just stood there looking into her eyes. He trailed his fingers up her arms and cupped her face in his hands. His gaze traveled from her eyes to her mouth, and he leaned forward, placing a tender kiss on her lips.

Her heart pounded in her chest as she opened her mouth. His sweet cinnamon taste made her mouth water for more. And when his tongue brushed hers, she trembled.

A soft moan of protest escaped her throat when he pulled away, and he smiled. She started to speak, but he put a finger to her lips.

"One hour." Then he was gone.

She stumbled out of her grandpa's yard and onto the path that would lead her home. Why was he doing this to her? If he didn't stop, she might end up falling in love with him. She chuckled at herself and shook her head.

Might? Come on, April. You're already on your way.

She needed to talk to him. To figure out what he wanted and why he was being so darn fickle. He couldn't just kiss her whenever he wanted and then turn around and gripe her out. They needed to set up some boundaries. But first, she had some business to attend to.

Damian stood outside Mira's door, unable to make himself knock. What was he thinking, kissing her like that again? He wasn't thinking, and that was the problem. Being with her felt so right, he couldn't help himself. But he had to. He was a broken man, and April deserved to be with someone whole.

He took a deep breath and knocked on the door. Mira answered immediately.

"I was wondering if you were going to stand outside all day. Come in and tell me what's on your mind."

He hesitated before he crossed the threshold. It was silly. Mira knew more about him than anyone. And if there was anybody he could share his secrets with, it would be her.

Stepping inside, he glanced around. Potted plants sat on tables in every corner of the white room. Lush, green ivies hung from baskets near the massive window, their long, leafy tendrils cascading down the glass. Mira placed a bouquet of fresh-cut wildflowers in a vase and smiled at him.

He ran his fingers through his hair and shoved his hands in his pockets. "Where's Paul?"

"Oh, he's out making the rounds. Checking in on the Keepers." She laced her fingers together and studied him. What was she looking for?

"What brings you here?"

"I think April's ready for her first Charge. For *our* first Charge. Do you have someone for us?"

"Indeed, she is ready. And I have someone in mind. He's two years out. You'd be relieving another Guardian who's on double duty."

He sucked in a sharp breath. He'd have to spend two more years with April. Two more years of her living in his home. Two more years of spending every single day with her. He didn't know whether to jump for joy or run away screaming. He swallowed, and the corners of his mouth curved into a smile.

"But that's not the only reason you came. What else is on your mind, brother?"

"That was it. I'll let April know we can get started." He took a step back, but Mira's gaze held him.

"If getting a Charge was the only reason you came, you would have brought her with you." She sighed as she glided toward him and rested her hand on his shoulder. "You can talk to me. You know that."

She saw right through him. He did want to talk, but he had no idea where to start. He couldn't sort his own feelings out, much less explain them to her. Where did he begin?

She leaned against the table and folded her hands. "You've told her everything?"

"Yes. She can Jump. She can find a Charge. I told her all the rules. She's ready."

"And about Micah?"

His skin crawled. "Yeah. She knows about that."

"And Juliet?"

His jaw snapped shut, and his hands instinctively clenched into fists. "You know I don't talk about that. Not to anyone."

"How can you expect her to love you if you won't be completely honest with her? Relationships need a strong foundation of trust. You of all people should know that."

He crossed his arms and gazed at the floor. "I don't expect her to love me."

"Why not? You're in love with her."

He opened his mouth to deny it, but he couldn't form the words. Mira was right. He did love April. He was completely and unconditionally in love with her. But she deserved better. "So, warn me away. Tell me I shouldn't get involved with her, like you did with Juliet. Tell me she'll break my heart."

Mira smiled sadly and shook her head. "I can't tell you that this time, brother."

"Why not?"

"Because it isn't true." She had cautioned him to stay away from Juliet, but he hadn't listened. Mira was connected to every Angel in the Angelic Realm; she could see inside everyone's hearts, and she knew Juliet's wasn't pure. He'd thought he loved her enough for the both of them. He'd never been more wrong.

He paced her living room, wringing his hands, his insides tying in knots. "She deserves better than me. If I wasn't good enough for Juliet, how can I expect to be good enough for April?"

"April is not Juliet. You'll do well to remember that."

"What do I do, Mira?"

"It's not for me to tell you. If you can admit to yourself that you love her, you have to make a choice. If you want to be with her, you need to tell her everything. How you feel, your past. Everything. Let her decide if you are enough for her. Or, if you prefer to spend the rest of your existence alone and miserable, you must tell her you aren't interested. And stop leading her on."

He raked his fingers through his hair. Alone and miserable or the rest of eternity with the woman he loved. And all he had to do was tell her the truth, then she could decide for herself if he was worth her love. "That's not much of a choice. I'm going to tell her. I'm going to tell her *everything*. Thanks, Mira."

He straightened his spine and marched out the door with purpose. He was in love with April. His heart sprinted at the thought of making her his. Of spending every night with her wrapped in his arms. Of her warm, naked body pressed against him as they made love. He could finally shower her with all the love and attention she deserved—if she would have him.

He took the long way home, trying to figure out exactly what to say. He didn't have to tell her about his past yet. He didn't want her to be with him out of pity. No, he could just profess his love, hope that she felt the same, and save his heart-wrenching memories for another day.

When his house was in sight, he picked up the pace.

His limbs couldn't carry him to her quickly enough, so he Jumped to the front door. Adrenaline coursed through his veins, and his heart beat in overdrive. This was it. He was going to do it. He was going to tell April he loved her.

He swung open the door and rushed into the living room, but April wasn't there. She wasn't in her bedroom either. Closing his eyes, he focused on finding her, and when he did his heart dropped to his stomach. *Why did she go back there?* With a groan, he Jumped to The In-Between.

There was April, standing in her old living room—in the Earthly Realm—while Jared made out with the blonde from his office. Her expressionless face told him nothing of her reasoning. She opened a drawer and pulled out a picture frame.

"What are you doing, April?"

Her eyes widened; she sensed his presence. "Damian. I'm sorry."

When she spoke, Jared looked up, his eyes bulging with fear. He scrambled to his feet, his back against the wall, while the blonde sat there and stared.

"I can't believe I wasted a year of my life on you." She clutched the frame to her chest and Jumped home.

Damian met her in her bedroom and watched her lay the frame face down on a table. She looked at the floor and toyed with the hem of her white sleeve. "I'm sorry. I know I'm not supposed to do that, but—"

"What is this?" Acid laced his voice, but he couldn't hide it. He picked up the frame and stared into the happy faces of April and Jared embracing on the beach.

His heart shattered into a million pieces.

A sickening feeling settled in his stomach as he set the frame on the table and forced himself to look at her eyes. "You're not over him yet."

"No. Damian, it's not that. I just..." She reached for his hand, but he jerked it away.

"Don't touch me." How could he have been so stupid to think he would ever be good enough for someone to love him?

"Damian, please let me explain."

"You know what? Don't worry about it. Mira will have a Charge ready for us in the morning. I'm going to bed."

"But, it's not even dark out." Her arms dropped to her sides as she gazed at him with pleading eyes. A small part of him wanted to hear what she had to say, but he knew her words would only cut him deeper.

"I'm tired." He turned on his heel and marched to the door.

"Damian, wait. Can't we talk about this?"

"Nothing to say." He pulled her door shut and hurried to the refuge of his own bedroom.

Once inside, his anger exploded. His fist plowed through the pliable wall over and over again. How could he have been so stupid? To think for a moment that she could love him was ridiculous. Her old life still consumed her. She hadn't let go, and if she kept going back to Jared she never would. He was an idiot. His heart was in her hands now, and she was tearing it to shreds.

He collapsed onto his bed and draped his forearm across his eyes, blocking out the light that filtered in through the glass ceiling. The brightest star in the sky couldn't shine into his heart like April did. What in Heaven's name was he going to do now?

He'd do the same thing he'd been doing for the past thirty years: keep her safe and comfort her when she needed him. That's all he could do. So what if holding her meant more to him now than it ever had before? He'd learn to deal with it.

He linked his hands behind his head and stared up at the darkening sky as a tear slid down his cheek. He was unlovable. Juliet had seen to that. When she left, she took a piece of him so big, he would never be whole again.

To think April might be able to fill the gaping hole in his heart was the most ridiculous idea he'd ever had. She had her own demons to deal with. She didn't need to take on his, too.

April climbed into her bed and curled up under the covers. That wasn't the reaction she'd expected from Damian at all. She'd expected him to be angry. She broke a rule, after all. And he was completely ticked off the last time she did it. She'd expected him to yell at her. To tell her how stupid she was.

Instead, he acted hurt. She had betrayed his trust, but it wasn't that big of a deal. She didn't *do* anything. And Jared deserved to be freaked out after everything he'd put her through.

Still, the anguish that filled Damian's eyes when he looked at the picture made her wonder if his feelings for her ran deeper than the physical. She pushed the thought out of her mind as soon as it entered.

No need to get your hopes up, April. He doesn't love you.

But she loved him, didn't she? There was no use in denying it. She was in love with Damian, and nothing would change that. All she could do was enjoy the time she had left with him and try not to tick him off anymore.

But how could she enjoy it when every time he touched her skin, he touched her soul? Every time his lips brushed hers, he broke another piece of her heart. She'd never known a love like this before. She never would again.

CHAPTER 15

From The In-Between, April eyed the man. He appeared to have sandy-blond hair and dark brown eyes, though she couldn't be sure through the grayscale. He was attractive, but she could tell he was incredibly sad.

"That's Daniel." The Guardian pointed to the muscular man in baggy jeans and an Abercrombie T-shirt. He trudged through the park like every movement was spiked with pain. Then he slumped onto a bench and stared at the sandwich in his hands.

"*That's* the Charge we're relieving you of?" Damian rolled his eyes.

"He's the one. Good luck, April. He's twenty-eight, so you've got him for two years. The main thing you have to do is protect him from himself."

"What's wrong with him? Why's he so depressed?" April asked.

"His wife was murdered about a month ago. No one knows who did it. Her sister's been trying to console him ever since, but he's so distraught, you'll be lucky to keep him alive till he ascends."

"Wow. Giving me a challenge right off the bat." April's voice cracked with nervousness. She was sure she was ready for a Charge. But now that she was responsible for the safety of another human, her confidence slipped through her fingers.

The Guardian shrugged. "You'll do fine. Mira thinks you can handle him, and you've got Damian to help you out."

She glanced at Damian, but he wouldn't meet her eyes. He hadn't said two words to her since he caught her taking the photograph from Jared's apartment, and her chest ached at the distant look in his eyes as he stared at their new Charge.

"Well, he's all yours. I've got to attend to my other Charge now. Have fun." The Guardian winked and Jumped out of The In-Between.

She turned to Damian, who picked imaginary lint from his shirt. "What do we do now?"

He shrugged and stared straight ahead.

She put her hand on his shoulder, and he tensed at her touch. "Damian, please talk to me. Let me explain what I was doing yesterday. I went there to—"

"You don't need to explain anything. Come on. You can practice whispering to your Charge." He strode toward Daniel without looking back.

April sighed. She couldn't spend the next two years with Damian like this. She'd have to find a way to make it up to him. To prove that he could trust her.

"Are you coming?" He crossed his arms over his chest and fumed with resentment.

She shuffled toward him and looked at Daniel, who still stared at his sandwich. Peanut butter and jelly. The scent of the sandwich wafted into her nostrils, and she took a long, deep breath. Peanut butter was one of her favorite foods. The only thing that could make it better was to smother it in chocolate. How long had it been since she'd eaten? Not since she was alive.

"How come I can smell his sandwich? I thought we were supposed to be ghosts here."

"Smell isn't affected by the dimensional shift." He still stared straight ahead, his hands clasped behind his back.

"What do I say to him?"

"Anything you want."

Frustration irked her, but the cold shoulder he gave her tore at her heart. "Look, Damian. You can hate me all you want personally. But when it comes to *our job* I need your help. Please."

He blew out a hard breath and finally looked at her. His pain-filled eyes held her gaze, and she wanted to run to him. To make the hurt go away. But he wouldn't let her near him, and she didn't know why.

"See if you can get him to eat. He's been staring at that sandwich for fifteen minutes."

"Okay, I'll try." She leaned over and placed her hands on Daniel's shoulders.

"Daniel? I know you're hurting, but you need to eat. Go ahead and take a bite. You love peanut butter."

Daniel exhaled and bit into his sandwich. Without raising her head, April cut her gaze to Damian to gauge his reaction. He smiled and nodded his head, but when she straightened and faced him, the smile faded.

"Good job. I think that's all we can do for him right now."

"So, now what do we do?"

He stared out across the park and lifted one shoulder. "We go home. Wait till he needs us. We'll check in on him later."

"Okay. Can we talk when we get home?"

He shook his head. "I'll find you when it's time to visit Daniel again." Then he disappeared.

Damian settled into the grass on his favorite hill and gazed at the bright blue sky. The sun warmed his skin, but it did nothing for the chill in his shredded heart. April was right. He couldn't let his hurt feelings interfere with their work. His duty to their Charge had to come first.

He'd just have to get used to his arms aching to hold her. The yearning without the fulfillment of her touch.

He should've gotten onto her about Jumping to Jared again. She needed to know how inappropriate her actions were. And to bring that photo back with her? He couldn't even think about it, much less reprimand her for it. He knew what it was like to be betrayed by someone you loved.

He needed to clear his mind, and an exercise in meditation might do the trick. He closed his eyes and inhaled deeply. Focusing on nothing but his breaths, he slipped into a meditative state.

When he opened his eyes later, he felt a presence beside him. Startled he had company, he cleared his throat and sat up.

"Dude, I hope I didn't wake you." Eric flashed a smile.

Damian rubbed his face and ran his hands through his hair. "It's cool. What time is it?"

"Five thirty."

"I must've fallen asleep. April's probably wondering where I am."

"Nah. She's all right. I saw her walking through the meadow with Trusten a few minutes ago. So, he's her grandfather, eh?"

"Yeah. He is."

"But he's a Keeper. And she's..."

"Long story. How are things going?"

Eric's smile stretched even wider, and his eyes sparkled with excitement. "Ah, man. I don't know what happened to Jared, but he's starting to listen. He broke it off with that chick from work, and he even went to confession."

"Well, that's a good thing, right?"

"Dude, he's not even Catholic. I don't know what got into him."

Damian sighed and rubbed the back of his neck. "I do. April."

"April?"

"Yeah. She's been crossing over and messing with him. She even stole a picture of the two of them from his apartment."

"Why'd she do that?"

"I don't think she's over him. She hasn't let go yet."

Eric put a hand on his shoulder. "Aw, I'm sorry, man. I know you care about her."

Was it really that obvious? Was he so transparent with his feelings everyone else knew he was in love with her, when he'd only recently been able to admit it to himself? If so, why didn't she see it? He shook his head. He couldn't even form a response in his mind.

"Well, whatever she's doing, it's working. I'm okay with it if she keeps it up. Even if it is against the rules."

"All right. I won't try to stop her on your account." Though he was definitely not okay with it.

"Thanks, dude. And good luck with her. Just give her some time. I think she'll come around. Catch ya later."

Damian stood and dusted the grass off his jeans. It was time he went back to April and made amends. She deserved better than the way he was treating her. He focused on her smiling face and found her reading a book in the meadow by their house.

He appeared in front of her and sat cross-legged on the ground. "Where's Trusten?"

"He had to go." She shrugged, her gaze never leaving her book.

"Romeo and Juliet?"

"Who can resist a good tragedy?" She still wouldn't look at him.

He let out a cynical laugh. After what happened with *his* Juliet, he'd had more than his share of tragedy. He scooted over to sit next to her.

"I'm sorry, April."

"For what?" She licked her finger and turned the page.

He sighed and wrapped his arm around her shoulders. "C'mon. You know what for. I was a jerk, and I'm sorry."

She finally looked at him. "What's going on with us? One minute you hate me, and the next minute you're making out with me. I need to know where we stand, because I can't handle all this back and forth business. You either like me or you don't."

I love you. Should he tell her the truth? He didn't have anything to lose. His heart already belonged to her. He took a deep breath, and with his fingers on her chin, he lifted her face to his.

"April, I..." An alarm went off in his soul. Daniel was in trouble.

When April gasped, he knew she felt it too.

"Take us to him."

She reached for his hand, and they Jumped to The In-Between.

Beer and whiskey bottles littered the living room of Daniel's house, and a myriad of prescriptions lined the coffee table. Daniel sat on the edge of the couch with his elbows on his knees. A whiskey bottle dangled from one hand, and a container of pills sat in his other trembling palm.

"Go whisper to him. Convince him he's going to be okay."

But she knew better. She'd seen her cousin in this condition, and whispering wasn't going to cut it. What

Daniel needed was tough love, and she knew exactly how to give it.

"I have a better idea. I'm going in."

"In? No. You can't show yourself to him yet. He's two years out."

"He's trying to kill himself."

"So whisper to him, and tell him not to. That's how Angels work."

She crossed her arms. "Not this Angel."

"Please?"

She exhaled a hard sigh. "Fine."

Damian stayed by her side as she moved closer to her Charge and whispered to him. *"Put the pills down, Daniel. Don't kill yourself."*

Daniel looked at the bottle in his hand and shook his head.

"See," Damian said. "It's working."

"You don't want to do this. You want to live."

Daniel set the whiskey on the coffee table. "I don't want to do this. I can't do this anymore." He emptied the contents of the pill bottle into his palm and raised it to his mouth.

"This isn't working, Damian. I'm going in."

"April..."

The tone of his voice was a warning she was about to cross a line, but she didn't care. She was charged with keeping Daniel safe, and his life was in danger. Surely a life-threatening event was good enough reason for what she was about to do.

"Trust me, Damian. Just this once." She closed her eyes and replaced her hot pink top and jeans with a flowing white gown. She thought about throwing on a pair of wings for show, but she figured that was overkill.

He reached for her hand, but she slipped away in time to cross over to the Earthly Realm alone. She half expected him to follow and remove her by force, but he didn't. Maybe he did trust her.

"Hey, Daniel." She sounded more like a ticked off teenager than a Guardian Angel.

Daniel looked up and shot back on the couch, his drunken eyes wide with fear. Little white pills bounced across the hard wood floor as he tried to regain his composure. "Who...who are you?"

"I'm your Guardian Angel, dimwit. Who the hell else would I be?"

Daniel chuckled. "Yeah, right. You're just in my imagination. You're not really here."

She picked up a pillow and chunked it at his head. "Does that feel like your imagination to you?" Walking around the table, she slid onto the sofa.

"We need to talk." Yanking the bottle from his hand, she sat it on the floor, out of his reach. "Oh, God. What's that smell? Did you puke on yourself?"

"Maybe. But so what? I'm not gonna be around much longer anyway. I've got plans." He reached for another pill bottle, but she slapped his hand and knocked the bottle away.

"This is your plan? Listen, Daniel. *God's* got plans for you. Big plans. And they sure as hell don't involve you wallowing in vomit and self-pity. Now get your ass up and get in the shower."

She grabbed his hand and pulled him to his feet. In his

drunken stupor, he stumbled into her, but she caught him under the arm. His breath reeked of stale beer and regurgitated Chinese food, and he smiled as he tried to look down her top.

"For an Angel, you sure have a dirty mouth."

She turned her head to avoid the rancid stench of his breath. "What can I say? I'm new."

The man could hardly stand on his own, much less walk to the bathroom. She supported his weight as best she could, and they stumbled to the bathroom together. Damian still hadn't crossed over, and she was beginning to wonder if he was still there. But when she focused on him, she felt his presence just beyond her plane. What was he thinking about all this?

She leaned Daniel against the wall, peeled his disgustingly wet shirt over his head, and yanked down his pants.

No underwear. Lovely.

She shoved him into the shower and turned on the water. "Wash yourself off. You're a mess."

"Will you help me?"

What had she gotten herself into? She pulled back the curtain to find Daniel clutching the soap dish, with his back against the wall.

"Oh, for Heaven's sake." She tried to ignore his erection as she washed the vomit out of his hair.

His gaze traveled up and down her body. "You're pretty."

"You're drunk."

"So?"

Without warning, he pulled her into the shower and planted his mouth on hers. She fought to pull away, but his grip was too strong. She felt his erection press against her stomach and felt like vomiting herself. She dug her nails into his chest and pushed with all her might.

"Get. Your. Hands. Off. Her."

April nearly fell to the floor when Daniel released her, but Damian caught her around the waist.

"I've got this," he whispered into her ear. "You go get rid of the pills."

"No. He's my Charge. I'm going to finish what I started."

He nearly growled his response. "He's *our* Charge, April. And you obviously need help."

She clenched her fists, and her jaw went rigid. "No. I. Don't."

He released her and took a step back. "Fine. You want to get raped? Go right ahead then."

"He's not going to rape me."

Daniel's sedated mind finally caught up with the conversation. "Who are you?"

Damian went tense as he turned to address the naked man. "I'm her boyfriend. You got a problem with that?"

Her heart threatened to pound through her chest. Did he just say he was her boyfriend? When did that happen? She wasn't about to protest the one thing she desired most, so she went with it.

"Yep. Sorry, Daniel. I'm taken. Now, let's get you to bed."

She shut off the water, and Damian helped her walk him to the bed. Daniel was dripping wet, but she sure wasn't going to towel him off. He lay down, and she pulled the covers over him and turned out the light.

He rose onto his elbows and shot her a drunken grin. "Thanks, Angel."

"Anytime."

Damian picked up the last of the pills and flushed them. April was out of control. She couldn't go around exposing herself like that, and he was about to tell her just that when he looked into her gleaming eyes and beaming smile.

"What?" His clipped tone should have put her off, but it didn't. Instead, her smile widened.

"So, you're my boyfriend, huh?"

His heart nearly stopped. "What are you talking about?"

"In the bathroom, you told Daniel you were my boyfriend."

Damn. He didn't mean to say that. The words slipped out in all the excitement. "I just told him that to get him off you." He shrugged and looked at his shoes.

"Oh."

"And speaking of that. What in Heaven's name did you think you were doing? You can't just reveal yourself to your Charge when he's two years out."

She crossed her arms and widened her stance, just as stubborn as ever. "Why not? Is it against the rules?"

"Well, no. But you just don't do that, April."

"No, Damian. *You* don't do that. *I* do. You can't expect everyone to do everything your way all the time. Besides, it worked, didn't it? He's sound asleep and still alive."

"I'm still your Guardian. And I'm your trainer. You need to learn to do things my way."

"Is that so? Or is it that I did something you'd never thought of, and you can't stand me being right?" She grabbed a bottle of liquor and poured it down the sink. "And should we even be talking about this here in Daniel's house?"

Damian poured the last of the whiskey down the drain and glared at her. She didn't get it. And he wasn't going to spoon feed her for the next two years. Maybe she needed a different trainer, because he sure didn't need all this drama.

"You know what? You're right. We shouldn't be talking about this here. We shouldn't be talking about it at all. Goodbye, April."

CHAPTER 16

April stood there dumbfounded. *Goodbye, April?* What was that supposed to mean? Goodbye forever? Because it sounded so final.

Even though he was clearly wrong, she couldn't leave it like that. She couldn't lose him. She focused on him, and Jumped home.

He sat on the sofa with his head in his hands, gently rocking back and forth. April's heart jumped into her throat. He was in pain, and she'd caused it. The need to wrap her arms around him and hold him close over-whelmed her. But she knew he wouldn't accept her comfort. Maybe he'd at least talk to her.

She tiptoed around the sofa and sat down next to him. He didn't move.

"I'm sorry, Damian. I didn't mean to upset you."

"Forget about it."

She sighed as she tried to think of something else to say. "In the meadow, earlier today. You were about to tell me something. What was it?"

"I don't even remember." He rose from the couch and looked down at her. "Look, I just want to be alone right now, okay? Will you just...leave me alone?"

She didn't try to hide the pained expression she knew her face held. And when a tear slid down her cheek, she didn't bother to wipe it away.

Damian's face held no emotion as he turned and strode out the door.

Good job, April. Real smooth. Could she screw this up any worse?

She picked up her book and tried to finish *Romeo and Juliet*, but she couldn't focus. It'd only been half an hour since Damian left, but she couldn't get him out of her mind. She needed a distraction. Something to keep her busy. Were there any Angels out at the lagoon this late in the evening? She hoped not. A moonlit swim would do wonders for her soul.

She strolled down the path, enjoying the warm night air and the fragrance of the blooms. The stars in the sky twinkled brighter than she'd ever seen, casting a silvery glow on the dew kissed grass.

She reached the lagoon and breathed a sigh of relief. She was alone. Slipping off her shoes, she tested the water. Perfect. With a giggle, she changed into the swimsuit she'd always wanted: a white halter one-piece with a plunging neckline. A golden ring held the straps of fabric together at her navel, and the high-cut bottom portion made her legs look incredible. She'd tried the suit on at the store several times, but even she couldn't justify spending three hundred dollars on a bathing suit. Now she didn't have to.

She dove into the water and came up near the middle

of the lagoon. The cascading waterfalls created a fine mist in the air, and she floated on her back, admiring them. She'd never seen a body of water so beautiful.

When she was young, she and her friends would go down to the neighboring town to swim at a place they called The Ropes. It was a popular hangout for the Felicity teens. Probably still was. It was nothing more than an old, ratty rope hanging from a tree over the bayou. But it was their own little slice of Heaven. A place they could go to escape the pressures of school and family.

She smiled as she thought of the times she jumped off the bridge that crossed the bayou. What a rush that was. It'd been a long time since she'd had a *good* adrenaline rush like that.

She backstroked farther into the lagoon. She missed those days of having no responsibilities. Of freedom. Of course, she had more freedom now that she was a Guardian than she did as a human. She wasn't chained to the dream of getting married and having babies. She didn't need that anymore. She just needed to be herself. But who was she, exactly?

She swam closer to the main waterfall and peered up at the cliff above. It was higher than the bridge she used to jump from, but she could probably make it. After all, she was made of pure energy. It wasn't like she could drown.

She pushed herself onto the bank and climbed the rocky hill that led to a smooth platform above the waterfall. She could've Jumped there, be she didn't want to miss the building anticipation tightening her stomach. When she stood at the top of the hill, the breeze bit at her skin, making goose bumps rise on her flesh.

She stepped to the edge and looked down. Her heart raced, and the sharp sting of adrenaline flushed her system as she dove in headfirst. The lagoon bathed her in warmth, and she swam underwater for what seemed like half an hour. Who knew she didn't need to breathe?

When she finally swam to the surface, she was inches away from the waterfall. An opening in the rocks behind it appeared to lead into an expansive cave. She paddled to the side to get a closer look and discovered it was indeed a cave. Her sense of adventure sparked, and curiosity overcame her. She had to explore. She took a deep breath and swam under the falling water.

When she emerged on the other side, she gasped at the beauty before her. Crystals lined the walls of the cave, glowing dimly in an array of color, though there was no other light for them to reflect.

She pushed up onto a ledge and rose to her feet to examine the extraordinary stones. *Beautiful.* She slid her hand along the wall as she walked on the rocks. The smooth crystals radiated warmth, and her fingers tingled as they glided over them. As she ventured farther into the cave, the beauty of her surroundings quelled her normal fear of tight spaces. Until she lost her footing and tumbled into the water.

Instinctively, she held her breath in anticipation of going under, but a pair of strong arms broke her fall. Damian's arms. Pain still filled his eyes, and she jerked out of his grasp as quickly as she could.

"I thought I asked you to leave me alone." He sounded tired. Defeated.

"I'm sorry. I didn't see the *Do Not Disturb* sign on the waterfall."

He grunted at her joke and stared at her. His gaze traveled to her lips and lingered there. Something sparked in his eyes, and it wasn't anger. His tongue slipped out to moisten his lips as he drifted closer to her in the water.

She pressed her back against the ledge, her feet slipping on the smooth stones beneath the surface. She had no idea what was on his mind, but she was tired of his games. He had her head spinning in circles like a dog chasing its own tail.

"Why do you hate me so much, Damian? What did I ever do to you to make you despise me?"

His eyes narrowed. "Is that what you think? You think I hate you?" He closed the small gap between them, but she was already pinned against the wall. She had nowhere to go.

"Why else would you treat me the way you do?"

He inched closer, his heavy gaze filled with lust, and her heart pounded in her chest. A strange energy danced between them as her Angelic connection to him pulsed, filling her body with warmth and need. His need.

"Does this feel like hate to you?" He pressed his body against her and took her mouth in an urgent kiss. She gasped and slid her arms around his neck. His hard muscles and bare skin felt so good against hers, her common sense flew out the window. She twisted her fingers in his hair and slipped her tongue between his lips.

His arousal was evident pressed against her stomach, and her head spun as he slid his hands over her body to cup her breasts.

"Push me away, April." His breath was hot against her neck as he nuzzled into her and nipped at her earlobe. "Tell me to stop."

"No." She barely got a whisper out before he crushed his mouth to hers. His blistering kiss set fire to her soul, igniting more passion than she'd ever felt before. She had to pull away to catch her breath.

His pupils were dilated, dark with desire, and his husky voice rasped thick with need. "Tell me you don't want me, and I'll leave you alone."

"No, Damian. I do want you. I want you so bad."

He groaned and kissed her again, with a deep, primal need. She couldn't control herself. When he tried to pull away, she wrapped her legs around his waist and slid her hands to his face.

"I need you, Damian." She needed him like she'd needed no other. She couldn't imagine wanting another man. Her womb tightened, and her skin tingled at his touch.

"Oh, April."

She ran her hands down his chest and across his rippled abs. When she slipped her finger into the waistband of his shorts, he sucked in a sharp breath.

"Not here." He held her tight, and in an instant, they were home in her bed.

Damian breathed in a shaky breath and gazed into her emerald eyes. This was the moment he'd dreamed about. Her soft, supple body beneath him called to every masculine urge inside him. All he could think about was being inside her. Pleasing her.

A soft smile curved her lips as she slid her arms behind his shoulders. "Make love to me, Damian."

He shivered at her request. Of course he'd make love to her. But he was going to do it slowly. To let her know just how special she was to him. He placed a tender kiss on her forehead. Then one on her cheek, her lips, her chin. The scent of her skin intoxicated him as he trailed kisses down her neck, across her collarbone, and down into the plunging neckline of her swimsuit. He could've kissed her all night. Her velvet skin was so warm against his lips. Her touch—her taste—sent him soaring on a natural high. He was in Heaven.

When he'd kissed as far as the clothing would allow, he peeled the wet fabric from her body and tossed it on the floor. Good Lord, she was gorgeous. He could do nothing but stare as his eyes soaked in her beauty.

He trailed his fingers along her curves, and goose bumps rose on her porcelain skin. He cupped her firm, round breasts in his hands and teased her nipples with his thumbs. They hardened like little pink pearls at his touch.

His gaze took in her stunning body, but her eyes captivated him. Sparkling emeralds as deep as the sea, so full of love. "You're so beautiful."

Her lips curved into a perfect pink bow as she slid her hands down his back and tried to work his shorts over his hips.

"Let me help you with that." He closed his eyes, and the garment disintegrated.

"Well, that's convenient."

He chuckled and continued his quest to kiss every inch of her perfect body. She moaned as he took a breast into his mouth and circled his tongue around her nipple. She kneaded his back as he worked his way down, trailing kisses to her navel. She spread her legs, and he nestled between them, gliding his tongue along her inner thigh.

When he reached her center, he lapped at her, and a tiny gasp escaped her throat. Dear lord, he loved everything about this woman. The sounds she made. The way she moved. Her scent. The feel of her thighs against his shoulders. Her body tensed with every flick of his tongue, and when he slipped his fingers inside her, she arched her back to take them deeper. She was so wet and tight, it took all his self-control to not take her right then and there. But she deserved more. She was a gem he wanted to treasure.

He focused on his mission, working her in circles with his tongue. Her hips bucked when she reached her climax, and when she cried out, he held her still, relentlessly giving her the pleasure she needed. She tried to pull away, but he gently held her, slowing his pace until her breathing calmed, her tense muscles relaxed. As she breathed a sigh of satisfaction, he went back to work, making love to her with his tongue until she came again.

"Damian, please. I need you inside me."

He climbed on top of her, and she took his length in her hand, guiding him to her center. Her wet warmth closed around him as he pushed halfway inside her. She felt so good he had to hold his breath before he lost it. But when she wrapped her legs around him, pulling him farther inside, he gave up the fight.

With one long thrust, he plunged into her, and she

moaned. He held her face in his hands and kissed her as they made love. She was warm and sweet, and they fit together as if their bodies were made for each other. They belonged together.

He couldn't hold back any longer. He thrust his hips faster and faster as she arched her back, sending him deeper inside. She tightened around him when she climaxed again, and he found his own release soon after. His orgasm ripped through his soul, tearing it to shreds and molding it back together again—stronger than it was before. He was whole again.

Breathless, he collapsed on top of her and nuzzled into her neck.

April's heart overflowed with emotion—with love that grew stronger with every beat. She tried to steady her rapid breaths. There was no going back now. He belonged to her, and nothing could keep her away from him.

A soft moan of protest escaped her throat when he pulled out and rolled onto his side, but he pulled her body to his and tenderly kissed her lips. Gazing into her eyes, he brushed the hair away from her face.

"April, I..." He let out a heavy sigh and rested his hand on her shoulder.

"What is it?"

"I...I really enjoyed that."

Heat rose to her cheeks, and she grinned. "Me too."

"I need to tell you something. It's something I want you to know. About me."

Her heart raced in anticipation. He'd never willingly offered her information about himself. What could it be? She had a million questions bouncing in her mind, and she bit her bottom lip to keep from spouting them out.

"Okay. Shoot." She tried to be nonchalant about it, but his serious expression squelched her humor.

"I had a wife once. A long time ago."

A pang shot through her chest. "Juliet."

"Yeah." Though his gaze fell on April, he looked right through her. Reliving the undoubtedly painful memories of his past.

He seemed to be a thousand miles away. Distant, though they'd never been closer together. She reached up to caress his cheek and bring him back to her. "It's okay. You can talk to me."

He sighed and focused on her once more. "I'm sorry. I don't talk about this with anyone. I *haven't* talked about it since it happened."

"You don't have to tell me if it makes you uncomfortable."

"No, no. I want to. You need to know. See, Juliet was my wife, and I loved her more than anything in the world. I *thought* she felt the same about me. She was the Guardian of a woman. Catherine was her name, I think. Catherine was married, and she and Juliet became good friends.

"She visited their home all the time, and I thought it was nice. She didn't have many close friends in this realm, and I was happy Catherine would be crossing over. But when Catherine turned thirty and ascended, everything changed."

His gaze drifted behind her as he pulled away and started to roll onto his back, but she grasped his hand and clutched it to her chest. "Stay here. With me."

He inhaled an unsteady breath and nodded. "Juliet kept crossing over to spend time with Catherine's husband. Comforting him, according to her. I should've been suspicious at that point; Catherine's husband had a Keeper to comfort him. But I was too blind to see the warning signs. A few weeks later, Juliet Fell to be with him."

"Oh, Damian. That's awful. I'm so sorry you had to go through that."

He squeezed his eyes shut and shook his head. "It gets worse. She was pregnant. We were going to have a baby, and she *Fell*." Tears of pain filled his eyes, spilling over onto his cheeks. "The baby Fell with her." His voice came out a raspy whisper. "He didn't survive."

Tears welled in her own eyes, and she wrapped her arms around him, pulling him close. The agony he must have been going through all these years. Her core ached with his pain. She couldn't imagine the torment he felt to lay out his emotions like that. Words could never soothe his pain, so she said the only thing she could.

"I'm so sorry."

"She left me, April. She left me, and she killed my child." He snuggled into her embrace, and she held him as her heart broke for him.

No wonder he always seemed to be on an emotional roller coaster. Juliet had taken so much from him. She'd made a hole in his heart April was determined to fill. This man had been there for her her entire life. Now it was her turn to be there for him. To take care of him. He was so still, she thought he'd fallen asleep. But he finally lifted his head and looked into her eyes.

"I'm okay. Thanks for listening. I just wanted you to know that, so you might understand why I acted the way I did. It's no excuse, but it is the reason." He trailed his fingers down her cheek and took her hand in his. "I'm scared. I'm afraid to get close to you, because I can't go through that again. I can't lose you."

"I'm not going anywhere. I promise." Her heart filled with so much joy she thought it would explode in her chest. Damian wanted her, and nothing else in the world mattered.

He smiled and brushed her lips with his. "Good. I… uh." A rosy blush crept up his cheeks. "I haven't been with another woman since."

"You haven't?"

"It's been more than six hundred years."

"Not even to…"

"You're the first."

Her heart flip flopped in her breast. Surely he'd had plenty of opportunity; the man was gorgeous. But he'd built a fortress around his heart to guard himself from the pain. And she had broken down his walls. He'd certainly been a tough nut to crack, but she had peeled away his rough exterior and found the sweetness in the center. A sweetness she wanted to savor for the rest of her life.

She put on her best seductive smile and climbed on top of him, admiring his perfectly cut muscles that looked as if they were carved from stone. She ran her hands up the ripples of his abs and across his muscular shoulders.

Bending down to nuzzle his neck, she nipped his earlobe before whispering in his ear. "Well, then. Let me show you what you've been missing."

She inhaled deeply as she trailed her tongue down his chest, stopping to admire the halo and crescent moon that glowed softly over his heart. The image felt smooth as she traced her finger over the pale blue design, and it pulsed dimly in reaction to her touch. "I didn't have this mark when I was alive."

He ran his fingertips across her shoulder where her own crescent moon lay. "Not on your Earthly body, but it's always been in your soul."

His gaze caught hers, deep with desire, and she lowered her head to press her lips against his mark. She could feel his heart pounding through his chest as she continued kissing her way down his body, stopping just below his navel. When she gripped his length, he let out a hiss, his hardness growing in her hand. He fisted the sheets and moaned as she stroked his shaft. She showered him in pleasure and relished every second of it. He was the one; she was sure of it. And she wanted nothing more than to make him happy.

Moisture beaded on his tip, and when she flicked out her tongue to taste him, he gasped. She reveled in the way his body reacted to her touch, the ease at which she could please him. When she took him in her mouth, he moaned. His hips rocked to her rhythm as she pushed him closer to the edge. His sighs of pleasure enthralled her, making warmth pool in her core. She released him, and he groaned as she trailed her tongue up his body.

"I need to be inside you. Right now." His deep masculine voice was rough, raw.

His urgency aroused her, and she couldn't deny him. She raised her hips, guided him with her hand, and shuddered as he filled her. Leaning down, she pressed her lips against his forehead and held his gaze as she rocked her hips. Faces close, fingers entwined, they moved to the raw rhythm of love as her climax knotted inside her.

He sat up and crushed his mouth to hers as she slid up and down on his thick cock. He filled her fully, and electricity buzzed and tightened her womb. She cried out when her orgasm ripped through her body, just as he found his own release.

They fell to the bed together, panting, and he traced his fingers across her back.

"You're incredible, April."

"You're not so bad yourself."

She slid to her side and draped a leg across him. *This* was what love felt like. She wanted to tell him she was his forever. That she didn't know love until this moment, and he was the only one for her.

But she'd wait. She'd rushed into relationships far too many times, and the guy would only say the words because she did. When Damian told her he loved her, she wanted it to be for real.

CHAPTER 17

$\mathcal{I}$n the warmth of April's embrace, Damian slept more soundly than he ever had. Though the sunlight filtering in through the sheer lavender drapes roused him from his Slumber, April still slept peacefully on his shoulder.

He watched her hand on his chest, rising and falling with each breath he took. She was stunning; her lips curved into a slight smile, and her complexion glowed like an Angel.

A wave of possessiveness filled him. This was it. He was going to tell her he loved her. Ask her to be his forever. As soon as she woke up.

Anticipation built in his limbs, and he couldn't stay still any longer. He carefully slipped out of April's embrace, trying not to wake her. But his elbow knocked the bedside table, and something heavy and metal crashed to the floor.

April woke with a start and smiled at him. "Oh! Hi."

He couldn't help but smile back at her sleepy expression. "Good morning."

"Mmm...where are you going?"

"Nowhere. I knocked something over; let me pick it up." He leaned over the side of the bed to find the culpable object and froze. He'd forgotten about April's token from her visit to Jared. He swung his legs over the side of the bed and picked up the frame. As he stared at the photo of the supposedly happy couple, he realized her heart wasn't free for her to give.

How could he be so stupid? Making love to her was reckless, and he deserved the heartache that would come from it. He should've known better.

April slid her arms around his chest and kissed the back of his neck. How could she do this with him when she was still in love with Jared?

"How long ago was this taken?"

She rested her chin on his shoulder and slid her hands down to his thighs. "About seven months ago, I guess. In the summer. But, it's not what you think."

"Really?" He laid the picture on the table. "What is it then? Why'd you bring this into our home?"

Our home. That's how he thought of it. He had since the day she moved in. But now he knew his vision of them sharing a life together would never be. Sorrow pressed against his chest like a weight.

She sighed and sat beside him, wrapping her arms around his shoulders. "I took it because I needed a reminder that—"

"A reminder? Why on Earth would you want to remember a sorry excuse for a man like that?"

"No. Not to remember him. I wanted…"

Damian shot off the bed and stormed to the middle of the room. Dressed in his usual jeans and white T-shirt, he turned to her and said, "You know what? It doesn't matter. None of this matters. How can you be with me like this when you're still in love with him?"

She clutched the blanket to her chest and rose onto her knees. "I don't love him. I don't think I ever did. But if you want to talk about someone who can't let go of the past, how about *you*? I held you last night while you cried over a loss you experienced how many years ago?"

"Six hundred and fifty-three."

"Do you hear yourself, Damian? In nearly seven hundred years you haven't worked through the pain. How can you be with me when you're still hung up on her?"

He took a deep breath and closed his eyes. How dare she compare her shallow relationship to the years of torture he'd endured? He'd lost a child, and he'd never forgive Juliet for that. He'd never forgive himself.

"This was a mistake. We never should have done this."

She stumbled off the bed, still clutching the blanket to her chest. "Damian, wait. What we did last night was…"

"An unfortunate accident. It won't happen again."

When the tears spilled down her cheeks, he couldn't bear to look at her. He had to get out of there fast, so he Jumped to his hill to wallow in his own self-pity.

The next two days went by in a fog; Damian ignored her completely. She checked in on Daniel occasionally, but he was as good as could be expected. Who knew the life of a Guardian Angel could be so boring?

Of course, the only reason it was boring was because she missed Damian so badly. That man could be so stubborn. She'd tried again and again to tell him she wasn't in love with Jared, but he wouldn't listen. And now he wouldn't talk to her at all. She almost wished something would happen with their Charge, so he'd be forced to speak to her.

At least she'd gotten to know more of the Angels. She'd spent a good portion of the day hanging out with them at the lagoon. She lay on her stomach on a rock, watching the waterfall where her encounter with Damian occurred. What she wouldn't have given to be in that cave with him right then.

"Come on, April. We're going to play water volleyball." Ella squealed when a man goosed her from behind. "Come have some fun."

"That's okay. I'll have fun watching."

Ella climbed onto the rock and sat next to April, her wet hair raining droplets on them both. "I'm worried about you, sister. What's going on?"

April shrugged and rested her chin on the rock. "I just miss him."

"He's still not talking to you?"

"Not at all."

"Well, there's no sense in making yourself miserable. He can't ignore you forever, and you might as well have a little fun while he's being hardheaded."

April turned her head toward her friend and rested her

cheek on her hand. "I'm okay. Really. Go play volleyball and have some fun for me."

"Suit yourself, girl. But the invitation's open whenever you decide to join us."

"Thanks, Ella."

She tried to talk herself into getting out there and playing, but her mind kept drifting back to the cave. To their night in her bedroom. The way his chiseled body felt pressed against hers. Ella was right; he couldn't ignore her forever. And when he finally decided to listen, she'd tell him just how she felt.

When the sun began to set, the game ended and most of the Angels ventured back to their houses. She said goodbye to Ella and strolled back home. The evening air caressed her skin, reminding her of Damian's gentle touch. Roses bloomed on a nearby bush, their romantic fragrance filling the air.

The whole situation was ridiculous. A simple misunderstanding. If he would just listen to her, they could work things out. And she was going to make him listen tonight.

She marched home with purpose now. He was there in his bedroom; she could sense him. She walked into the living room and changed into a slinky, white satin dress. If she couldn't appeal to his mind, maybe his body would listen.

She tiptoed across the room and hesitated by his door. Could she handle the rejection if he still refused her? It couldn't be any worse than what she was going through now. She tapped on the door and waited for him to answer.

Nothing.

She knocked again and waited. Still nothing. She knocked a third time, and her persistence paid off. With an annoyed look on his face, Damian opened the door, but his breath caught when he saw her. His eyes traveled up and down her body, and he gulped.

"We need to talk."

Without saying a word, he pushed the door open, allowing her to step inside. She'd expected a bare, white space; his bedroom was anything but. Hunter green walls encircled dark mahogany furniture and a king-size bed. Varying hues of green made up the duvet and matching curtains. A large mirror with a heavy wooden frame hung on one wall, and a painting of the meadow hung above the headboard.

She spun around to meet his gaze, expecting to see anger and resentment in his eyes. Instead she saw hurt, confusion, frustration.

"Listen, Damian. This is all a misunderstanding. I'm not in love with Jared. I'm..." Adrenaline spiked in her blood, and she gasped. "Oh, no. Daniel."

"I feel it too. Let's go."

They jumped to The In-Between, to the parking lot of a seedy bar. Angels gathered around a group of men beating the tar out of Daniel. A frail, blonde woman stood off to the side, screaming at the men to stop.

"What's going on?" Damian called to a Keeper.

"We have to help him." April didn't wait for an answer. She crossed over behind the crowd and tore into the man holding Daniel. She knocked his legs out from under him, and he hit the ground cursing. She pushed Daniel out of the way, but he froze, staring at April in wonder.

"It's you. I thought I dreamed you."

"Well, you didn't. And now I'm here to tell you to get the hell out of this place. Run!" She gave him another push, and he grabbed the blonde woman's hand and took off. Her smile only lasted a second. A man grabbed her from behind and threw her to the ground.

"Oh. Look, guys. A little *girl* wants to fight." He spat at her and knelt down, pressing her shoulders into the ground. "Or maybe you're here for something else. That's a pretty dress." His breath reeked of beer and cigarettes. What was it about drunken men thinking they could force themselves on her?

"Leave Daniel alone," she said through clenched teeth.

"Me? He's the one who came in here accusing me of murder. I didn't kill his wife. That bitch that was with him did."

Before April had time to formulate a response, Damian tackled the man. The other men stared with open mouths and wide eyes. Damian had appeared to come out of nowhere. He grabbed the assaulter by the collar of his shirt and relentlessly pounded the guy's face until April grabbed his arm.

"That's enough, Damian."

He released his hold on the man's shirt and backed away. The guy and all of his buddies ran off, spouting curses at them as they fled.

"Are you hurt?" He brushed the hair out of her face and checked her skin for bruises. The worry in his eyes turned to relief when he found no injuries.

"I'm fine. What about you?"

"I'm good. C'mon. Let's get out of here." He took her

hand, and they crossed back to The In-Between.

The woman's Keeper was waiting for them.

April didn't bother with introductions; she pelted the Angel with questions. "Is what he said true? Did that woman kill Daniel's wife?"

"I'm afraid so."

"Who is she?"

The Angel sighed and looked at her feet. "Her name is Jenny. She's his wife's sister. I tried to stop her."

Damian put his hand on the Keeper's shoulder. "It's okay. You tried your best."

"Thank you. I'm trying to convince her to confess, but she's stubborn."

"Okay. We'll take it from here." And April knew just how she'd handle it.

The Angel smiled sadly and disappeared.

"He has to know the truth. I'm going to tell him."

"No, you're not, April. It's not our place to tell him. Don't you think you've overstepped your boundaries enough with this guy?"

"My boundaries? I'm sorry. I didn't realize saving someone's life was against the rules."

Damian raked his hand through his hair and blew out an exasperated breath. "C'mon. You know what I'm talking about. Saving his life is one thing. But charging in with no plan, without knowing all the facts? That's reckless, and it's going to get you killed again."

She put her hands on her hips. "So what? If it's for his benefit, who cares if I die? I'll come back to life."

"You'd go through all that pain? Sacrifice yourself again and again to help your Charge?"

"Of course I would." Without a second a thought. Wasn't that what Guardian Angels did? Wasn't that her purpose?

He smiled and stared at her for a moment. "Okay, just promise you won't tell him tonight. Go home and sleep on it. And if you still want to tell him tomorrow, I won't try to stop you."

"That's a compromise I can live with. But I do want to check on him. Wanna come?"

His smile widened, and he reached for her hand. "Yeah. I do."

Daniel sat on the sofa in his living room with Jenny's arms wrapped around him. Damian's blood boiled. "How could someone kill her own sister? It's despicable."

"That it is." April clutched his arm and shook her head.

"Why do you think she did it?"

"Isn't it obvious? Look at them. She's in love with him. Or at least infatuated."

Damian's gut wrenched, and his knees went weak. Love drove her to murder, and that hit too close to home. He couldn't stand to look at the woman whose actions so closely mirrored Juliet's.

He forced a whisper over the lump in his throat. "I have to leave."

"Are you okay? Damian, what's wrong?" She placed her palm on his cheek and looked up at him with worry in her eyes.

"I need to go."

"Okay, let's go." She laced her fingers through his and Jumped to their living room.

He clenched his fists as he paced the room, trying to gain control of his emotions. He'd seen plenty of loathsome people in his life, hadn't he? This shouldn't have been any different.

But it was.

"Damian. Come talk to me. Please don't shut me out." She patted the space next to her on the sofa. Her emerald eyes held concern, compassion. For *him*. Whether she was in love with Jared or not, she *cared* about Damian.

He sank onto the couch and rested his elbows on his knees as she wrapped her arms around him, and he was foolish enough to find comfort in her embrace. When she laid her head on his shoulder and rubbed his back, his tension drained away.

"Love drove her to murder her sister. Love for a man she couldn't have."

She inhaled sharply and raised her head. "Ah, like Juliet."

"Yeah." He didn't realize he was wringing his hands until she stilled them.

"Well, if it's too difficult for you, maybe we should ask Mira for another Charge. Do you think she'd give us one?"

"You...you'd do that for me? You're so committed to Daniel, though."

She ran her fingers through his hair and kissed his cheek. "I'd do anything for you, Damian."

He looked into her eyes, and he knew it was true. In spite of all the hell he'd given her, she'd sacrifice everything to ease his pain. Liquid warmth bloomed in his heart and radiated through his limbs. With April by his side, he was capable of anything. It was time to let it go of the past.

"No. I'll work through it. I would never expect you to abandon a Charge. Especially over a pain I should've dealt with a long time ago. I can do this."

She reached for his hand and smiled. "We'll do it together."

"Thank you, April. I think I'm going to go to bed now." He stood and made his way to the bedroom door.

"Do you want me to stay with you?"

Yes. "No. I'll be fine. I've got some thinking to do. See you in the morning."

The door clicked shut, and he pressed his forehead against it. What the hell was he doing? April was the best thing that ever happened to him. He'd never been happier than when he was with her, and if he didn't get his act together, he'd be throwing it all away. She'd get over Jared eventually. And if there was one thing he'd learned in his thousands of years of existence, it was that he needed to have patience. He had all the time in the world to wait for her.

But could he let go of his own demons? He shuffled to his bedside table and pulled a crumpled sketch out of the drawer. Juliet stared back at him with her crystal-blue eyes and long, golden hair. With her body turned sideways, she rested her hand on the tiny bump of her belly. He stroked his thumb across her stomach and shook his head.

Could he ever forgive her? Could he forgive himself?

"Ah, Juliet. It's time for me to move on." He folded the picture and laid it back in the drawer.

CHAPTER 18

When April awoke, Damian was nowhere to be found. She considered searching for him in her mind, but thought better of it. His emotions were so intense the night before, she figured she'd give him some time to work through it on his own. At least he was speaking to her again.

She dressed in faded denim jeans and a pale green top she'd created in her mind. Designer clothes had lost their appeal, since she could have anything she wanted. In fact, material things in general no longer interested her. She chuckled. *Who would've thought?*

She looked at her beaming smile in the mirror and felt the first twinge of excitement. It was going to be a great day. She could sense it in her soul.

Ella and some of her friends were hanging out by the lagoon, and she'd invited April to come. Of course, she had declined. But she was in such a good mood, she decided to join them anyway.

"April! You came!" Ella embraced her and bounced

with excitement. She grasped April's hand and pulled her toward the crowd. "Come meet everyone. This is John, Randy, Cynthia, and Lindsey."

"Hi. I'm April." She waved at the Angels who beamed back at her.

John wrapped his arms around Lindsey and kissed the top of her head. Envy surged through April's heart, but she pushed it aside. She was determined to stop longing for Damian's love. He would come back to her when he was ready.

"So, April," John said, "we've been debating. What's the best Pixar movie of all time?"

She looked at him incredulously. "Seriously? Angels watch movies?"

Ella giggled. "Sure we do. It's one of my favorite ways to spend time with my Charges."

"Yeah," John added. "We don't float on clouds and play harps all day, like on TV." He shot April a teasing grin, and Lindsey elbowed him in the stomach.

"Be nice. She's new. Sorry about that, April. Sometimes John forgets to turn on his social filter."

John blushed. "What? She knew I was kidding. Didn't you?"

"Uh, yeah. Wow." She scratched her head and looked at their beaming faces. This was exactly what she needed to get her mind off her tormented love life. Friends. "Well, I guess I'd have to say *Up* is my favorite."

"In your face, Randy!" John smiled triumphantly at his friend.

"Whatever, man. *Toy Story* beats *Up* any day."

April laughed. "I guess we'll have to agree to disagree."

As the Angels continued their debate, Ella clutched April's arm and pulled her aside. "So, how are things?"

She glanced at the Angels who were engrossed in conversation. "Better. We're talking again."

"That's awesome! You seem like you're a lot happier today."

"Yeah, I don't know what it is. I woke up in a good mood, and I have this feeling it's going to be a great day."

"That's a good feeling to have."

"Sure is."

Ella's eyes widened as she looked over April's shoulder and grinned. "I think I know why your day's going to be so great."

"Oh, yeah? You can see the future now?" April giggled and followed Ella's gaze.

Damian strolled toward her through the grass, wearing his usual faded jeans and white shirt. The sun shone behind him, creating an ethereal glow. In his hand, he carried a bouquet of lavender tulips, and he offered them to her as he approached.

"Thank you, Damian. Tulips are my favorite."

He grinned. "I know."

"I'll see you later, April." Ella gave her a quick hug and scurried away.

She looked at him, and heat rose in her cheeks. He seemed different, somehow. Peaceful. Her stomach did flip-flops when he smiled.

"So, uh... You want to go grab a bite to eat? I know a great place to get Italian."

"But I thought that was against the rules."

He raised one shoulder on a dismissive shrug. "I've never been one for rules. What do you say?"

A smile stretched across her face. "Well, that depends. Are you asking me out on a date?"

He put his hands in his pockets and stared at his shoes. When he raised his gaze to hers, his hazel eyes sparkled. "Yeah. I guess I am."

Her heart sprinted in her chest. "Do I need to change before we go?"

"No. You're beautiful just the way you are." He reached for her hand, and they strolled down the path to their home. "Let's drop your flowers off in the house, and then we can go."

He opened the door for her, and she created a vase on the table, placing the bouquet inside. "Where are we going?"

"It's a surprise." He pulled her to his chest, and she inhaled his intoxicating scent. His mouth quirked into a crooked grin as his strong arms tightened around her, and they Jumped.

They arrived in a narrow alley with a stone path. Ivy clung to russet clay brick, twining its way up the three story buildings. Quaint windows with brown shutters and window boxes scattered about the walls gave the passage a homey feel. A lone woman tending to her flowers looked down at them and smiled.

"Where are we?"

"You'll see."

He laced his fingers through hers and led her into the heart of a bustling village. Olive-skinned people darted about, shopping, working, strolling with friends. Stone and stucco buildings lined the streets, and a group of girls played jump rope on the corner. She'd seen the familiar, picturesque view so many times in paintings and movies, but she never dreamed she'd get to visit in person.

"Italy?"

"There's no better place for Italian food than straight from the source." He ushered her into a cozy little café on the corner.

The stone floors and dim lighting were reminiscent of a time long forgotten. Couples chatted over coffee, businessmen made deals over lunch. The modern patrons were a harsh contrast to the tranquility the town possessed.

They found a small table in the back of the room, away from the hustle of the midday crowd. He pulled out her chair and gracefully slid it beneath her as she sat. Then, he slipped around the table to his chair and picked up a menu.

She held the menu in her hands, afraid to open it. "I'm sure this is written in Italian. Can you read it?"

He grinned. "Yes. So can you. Give it a try."

How could she possibly read it? She didn't know a lick of Italian. If it was Spanish, she might be able to fumble her way through, but Italian? Yeah, right. To humor him, she unfolded the paper and looked at the words.

Everything made sense. Her mouth hung open as the shock registered in her brain. She could read Italian. "Why do I understand this? I don't know Italian."

"Sure you do. You know whatever language you need to know, whenever you need it."

"Wow. That's pretty cool." *Absolutely incredible!* This Angel gig never ceased to amaze her.

The server arrived to take their orders then hurried off to the kitchen. Damian fiddled with his napkin; then he looked at her and smiled.

"Well, what do you think?" His grin held all the excitement of a child on Christmas morning.

"This is amazing, Damian. This building alone is so rich in history. I've always wanted to travel the world. You know, to see all the places I taught my kids about. I never thought it would actually happen." Excitement bubbled inside her. Not just because she was in Italy, but because she was there with *him.*

"I know." He reached for her hand across the table, and her body buzzed with need.

"What else do you know about me?"

"Hmm...I know you're stubborn, just like your mom. You're adventurous. You were always up for whatever hare-brained idea your friends threw at you, which got you into trouble a few times. Your favorite ice cream is mocha chocolate chip. Starbucks is one of your all-time favorite restaurants, though it's not really a restaurant. And you've seen *Steel Magnolias* at least fifteen times, and it still makes you cry."

She was speechless. This man knew her better than she knew herself. No one had ever taken the time to truly understand her. But he did. She had to swallow the lump in her throat to speak.

"You...know everything about me."

"*Almost* everything." He dipped his head and flashed a sheepish smile. "Is that creepy?"

"It probably should be, but it isn't." She linked her

fingers with his and traced his palm with her thumb. "You know all my flaws. All my insecurities."

"Yes."

"Yet, here you are on a date with me, holding my hand."

The corner of his mouth pulled into a crooked grin. "Here I am."

Her heart swelled with joy. He did know everything about her, and he *still* liked her. She had to tell him how she felt. How she wanted to be his and his alone. That she wanted to love him forever.

"Damian, I..."

The server brought their plates to the table and rattled off their orders in Italian. He set their plates down and stood there, staring at them expectantly.

She tried to hide her frustration with a smile. They were always getting interrupted. "*No, grazie. Siamo a posto così.*" She put her hand to her mouth and gasped. Did that language really just cross her lips?

Amazing.

She turned back to Damian, but the moment was gone. The overwhelming need to lay it all out for him gave way to her practical side. He'd have to let go of his past before he could make a future with her. Besides, she wanted to hear him say it first.

Sitting across the table from the most beautiful Angel in the Realm was like a dream. He knew about her desire to travel, and bringing her here was the perfect setting for their first official date.

Her smile brightened the entire room, and her eyes sparkled as she admired the architecture. "When was this place built? It's incredible."

"Around the twelfth century. It's beautiful, isn't it? And it really hasn't changed much since then."

"You were here when this was built?"

He shrugged. "Sure. I told you, I'm old as dirt."

She giggled until she was gasping for air. Her laugh was like beautiful melody in his ears.

"Wow. I'm on a date with a geezer. How gross."

"Well, maybe I shouldn't be robbing the cradle. Isn't there a law about that?" He winked, and they both laughed.

"I am not a child, mister. I'm more woman than you could handle."

"Mmm... We'll see about that. You ready to get out of here? See the sights?"

"I'd love to."

He savored one last bite of his meal, and then led her out into the street. They ambled, hand in hand, through a courtyard and down three blocks of cobblestone. The Leaning Tower of Pisa stood just across the street, and he paused to watch her reaction.

But she wasn't looking at the tower; she was gazing up at him. Her eyes were greener than the Italian countryside, and he forgot all about the sights of the city. He forgot about everything else in the world when he leaned down to kiss her. Her lips were so soft, her taste so sweet, his head spun. At that moment, the only thing that mattered was having April in his arms.

She slid her hands over his shoulders and pulled him closer. He could have drowned in her essence right there on the sidewalk. The need to be with her surged through his body, and he had to pull away before he took her to his bedroom and made love to her all day.

He tucked a piece of hair behind her ear and tried to find his voice. But what could he say?

Her expression was one of anticipation. Longing. She looked at him like she wanted him. "That was...nice."

"Yeah, it was."

She wrapped her arms around his waist and rested her head on his chest. "We should do it more often."

"Sounds good to me."

She took a deep, satisfied breath as her gaze traveled to the building in front of her. "Oh my gosh! It's the Leaning Tower of Pisa."

He chuckled. "Yeah. That's what I brought you here to see. Want to get a closer look?"

"Uh, yeah."

They darted across the busy street and walked up the path to the tower. She put her hand over her heart as she admired the structure. "It's amazing that the foundation shifted so much for it to lean like that. But it still stands. They just don't make 'em like that anymore." She grinned and tousled his hair. "But I bet you remember when it stood straight."

Heat rushed to his cheeks, though he didn't know why he was embarrassed. He shrugged and kicked at the dirt with his foot. "Yeah. I guess I remember. But it's no big deal. A thousand years from now, we'll be looking at present day skyscrapers and saying, 'Remember when.'"

"True. But I bet skyscrapers won't be around a thousand years from now."

"Wanna put money on it?"

She flashed a mischievous grin. "Okay. I'll give you a trillion dollars if they're still standing in a thousand years."

"You're on." Having April by his side for the next thousand years was exactly what he wanted. What he craved.

"But that means you'll still have to be speaking to me. No more games."

He pulled her into his arms and pressed a kiss to her forehead, her nose, her lips. "You don't have to worry about that."

They spent the rest of the afternoon lazily roaming the city. They strolled along the riverbank and settled on a patch of grass in a secluded spot to watch the sunset. If only Angels had the ability to freeze time; he could have lived in that moment forever.

With his arms wrapped around her, she snuggled into his side and sighed. "Thank you for this. The whole day, you, everything. It was perfect."

He closed his eyes and inhaled her sweet scent. The day really was perfect. *She* was perfect, and he didn't want it to end.

She lifted her head and placed a soft kiss on his cheek. "The sunset sure is beautiful."

"Not as beautiful as you."

~

April couldn't resist those luscious lips that whispered so close to her skin. She lifted her face to his, and he leaned toward her. Their lips didn't touch, but his breath warmed her skin as the tension built before the kiss. Still, he waited. He wanted her to come to him, and she was more than happy to oblige.

She teased him first with a gentle brush of the lips. When he opened for her, she lapped at him and caught his bottom lip between her teeth. When the first moan escaped his chest, she couldn't hold back any more. Straddling his lap, she pressed her body to his and took his mouth in a fervent kiss as she pushed him to the ground.

Passion ignited between them as the heat from his body warmed hers. She linked her fingers with his and pushed his hands up over his head. She ran her hands down his muscular arms and gripped his shoulders as her pelvis grinded against his.

Her hand slid beneath his shirt while her tongue trailed down his neck and up to his ear. "Take me home, Damian. I want to make love to you."

The only response he gave her was a masculine grunt, and when she blinked, she was lying on top of him in his bed. His hands kneaded her back, and he nibbled on her neck, sending warm shivers up and down her spine. Nestled in the protective cage of Damian's arms, she felt safe and adored, and she wanted to give herself to him completely.

"I need you, Damian."

He groaned and rolled on top of her, dissolving his clothes as his hands explored her body. His passion drunk eyes were deep and heavy, and he struggled to tug her shirt over her head. "You aren't making this easy on me."

She bit her bottom lip and closed her eyes. The warmth of his skin enveloped her as her clothing melted away.

"That's better." He kissed her with urgency, as if he was afraid she'd slip away at any moment. But she wasn't going anywhere. She belonged to him. Every part of her. Body, mind, and soul.

She gasped as he filled her, clung to him as they made love. His gentle rhythm quickened, sending electricity pulsing through her soul. Her orgasm overtook her, and she trembled beneath him as he shuddered, consumed by his own release.

Rising onto his elbows, he trailed his fingertips down her cheek and across her lips. "Oh, April...aw hell." He dropped his head on the pillow beside her and blew out an exasperated breath. "He's really got bad timing."

Their Charge's adrenaline pulse through her core, too. "Daniel's suicidal again."

"Come on. But this time, will you *try* to help him from The In-Between?"

She grinned and ran a finger down his back. "No promises."

They arrived in Daniel's apartment without a second to spare. He sat on the sofa with a gun pointed at his temple. His finger trembled on the trigger, and he squeezed his eyes shut.

She clutched Damian's arm as she formulated a plan in her mind. "Where the hell'd he get a gun?"

"I don't know, but we need to start paying more attention to him. What are you going to do?"

Did she have a choice? The guy was about to blow his head off. "I'm going in."

"April, let's think about this first."

Daniel exhaled and lowered the gun.

"Please try whispering to him first."

She fisted her hands at her sides. "Whispering doesn't work with him."

Damian shot her an imploring look, and she sighed.

"Daniel, please put the gun down. The pain will lessen. Your life is worth living."

"Life's not worth living." He pressed the gun into his temple.

"That's it." She Jumped to his apartment and ripped the gun from his hand.

Rubbing his hand on his forehead, he let his head drop back on the couch. "Go away."

"Sorry, Daniel. No can do." She plopped down next to him on the sofa. At least he didn't reek of vomit this time. "What are you doing with your life, buddy? You've gotta get it together."

"Ha. Right."

"Seriously. God really does have big plans for you, but you have to stay alive."

He leaned forward, resting his elbows on his knees and dropped his head into his hands. "What do you know about God?"

"Uh, hello? Guardian *Angel*?"

"Okay then. If God has such big plans for me, why'd he take my wife away? She was everything to me."

She rubbed her hand across his back. "God didn't take your wife away; she was murdered."

"They didn't even catch the bastard. No one knows who did it."

Tears streamed down his cheeks, turning into heavy sobs, and she couldn't stand seeing him in that much pain. He needed closure, and she had to give it to him.

"I know who did it."

His head whipped up, and he glared at her. "Who? Tell me who." He grabbed her by the shoulders and shook her. "Tell me!"

"If you'll let me go, I might." She felt Damian's presence growing closer. He was on the verge of crossing over, but she needed to do this on her own. She went utterly still and stared into his eyes, lowering her voice to an almost inaudible level. "Let me go."

Daniel released her. "I'm sorry. Please, Angel. You have to tell me."

"Okay. First of all, I have a name. It's April. And second, I'll only tell you if you promise not to do anything stupid."

He bit his bottom lip and cut his gaze to the left. "All right, I promise."

"*April...*" She heard Damian's warning like a voice in her head, calling her back to her senses. But she knew her Charge wouldn't make it to thirty in his current condition.

"He needs closure, Damian."

"Who's Damian? Who are you talking to?" Daniel jumped to his feet and paced the small living room. Tension built in his muscles, and he clenched his trembling hands into fists. "Dammit, April. I need to know!"

She crossed the room to stand in front of him and leveled her gaze on his. "Her sister killed her."

He froze.

"Jenny? No...that's ridiculous. She'd never hurt her own sister. And she's been helping me get through this. She even planned the funeral. No, I don't believe you."

She gave him the most sincere look she could muster. "I wouldn't lie to you. It's my job to protect you."

His bottom lip trembled and his brow furrowed. "Protect me from what?"

"Well, yourself apparently. Look, I wasn't supposed to tell you anything. It's not my place, yada, yada, yada. But I thought you needed to know. So you can move on with your life. Great things will be happening to you in two short years, and you need to be around to experience it."

He raked his fingers through his hair and shook his head. "Jenny. But, why?"

"Because she wanted to be with you. She's not right in the mind. She needs help. Now you can call the police, and they can help her."

His jaw went rigid as he glared at her with steely eyes. "No...no police. She deserves to burn in Hell. Give me my gun."

She took a step back. "No."

"Give it to me!" He lunged toward her, but she moved just out of his grasp.

For the first time since becoming a Guardian, April was scared. But not for herself. If he managed to get the gun from her, it would all be over. He'd either blow his own head off or put a bullet in Jenny's.

"I know you're angry. I understand what you must be feeling."

He stalked toward her with his jaw clenched so tight the veins in his neck protruded. "Do you? Have you *ever* been betrayed like this?"

She took another step back and found herself against the wall. "My boyfriend cheated on me for five months."

He spat out a sour laugh. "You're comparing a cheating boyfriend to a murderer? You have no idea what I'm feeling right now."

"Maybe not, but I do."

Daniel spun around at the sound of Damian's voice behind him, and April shoved the gun into the back waistband of her pants.

"Who? You're her boyfriend."

"I hope to be, someday. If she'll have me. But I know what it's like to lose someone you love to murder. To have the one person in the world you trust the most betray you."

The sorrow in Damian's eyes tore at her heart, and she couldn't let him go through those painful memories again. She rushed to his side and threw her arms around him.

"You don't have to do this. Just let me..."

"No. You said he needs to find closure? Well, so do I."

Daniel's hands trembled as he wiped the tears from his eyes and pressed his back against the wall.

Damian looked at him and sucked in a deep breath. He held on to April like she was the only thing holding him together. She thought he might fall apart if she let him go.

"My...wife. Ex-wife since I denounced her the day it

happened. She murdered our unborn child to be with another man."

Silence pressed down like a weight in the room, and for a moment, she thought Damian would buckle to the ground. Instead, he straightened his spine and relaxed his shoulders.

"Getting even...killing Jenny. It's not going to bring your wife back. And neither is hating her for the rest of your life. Trust me. The only person you'll be hurting is yourself."

Daniel shook his head. "But she needs to be punished."

"She does, yes. But it's not your place to deliver it. God will judge her actions one day. But for now, leave the punishment up to the law."

Had Damian really forgiven Juliet? Was he ready to let go? The anger in his eyes had relented to compassion. His hands no longer clenched into fists. April rose up on her toes and kissed his cheek.

"I'm proud of you," she whispered. And he smiled.

"So, Daniel. What are you going to do?" She stepped toward him and squeezed his hand. "Will you leave it up to the law?"

He stared straight ahead, his face expressionless. The moments stretched into minutes as April waited for his answer. He closed his eyes for a long blink, and then he looked into her eyes.

"Okay...okay. I'll turn her in to the cops. But I want to talk to her first. I'll take a recorder so I can tape her confession."

"I don't think that's a good idea. You're too volatile right now."

He pulled his hand from her grasp and crossed his arms. "I need closure. I need to hear it from her."

She looked to Damian, who nodded his head.

"All right. But the gun stays with me."

"Yeah. Fine. Whatever." He pulled his phone out of his pocket and dialed Jenny's number. "Hey, Jen. Can you meet me at O'Sullivan's? I want to talk to you about something. Yeah. Twenty minutes? Great."

He shoved the phone in his pocket and paced. His rigid posture and staccato movements revealed his anger, and April wondered if she made the right decision.

"Are you sure you want to do this? Maybe you should wait a few days, until you calm down."

"No." He shrugged and shook his head. "I'll be fine. It's a public place. Nothing's gonna happen."

"Right. We'll stay out of sight, but we'll be there if you need us."

Daniel nodded, and with an air of determination, he marched out the door.

"This was a bad idea, wasn't it?" April looked at Damian like a child who'd been caught in a lie. She knew she was in trouble, but her determination to help her Charge made it impossible for him to be upset with her.

"Possibly. But you were right. He does need closure, and we'll help him get it any way we can." It would take time, but she'd learn what methods worked for keeping Charges safe. The most important aspect of being a Guardian was dedication, and she showed plenty of that in every move she made.

She grinned and poked him in the ribs. "Did you just admit I was right about something? Is that what I heard?"

"Yeah." He pulled her to his chest and kissed the top of her head. "But don't get used to it."

When they reached O'Sullivan's, a small, rundown bar on the outskirts of downtown Chicago, they found Jenny's Keeper waiting for them in The In-Between. The dimly lit side parking lot was empty, and an eerie silence filled the air. April clung to his side, and her racing heart thrummed against his ribs.

"Where's Jenny?" he asked.

The Keeper drifted toward them, sadness filling her eyes. "She's on her way. You told him, didn't you?"

"Yes. We felt that—"

April squeezed his hand. "It was my idea. If anything goes wrong, I take full responsibility."

"We both do."

"I don't think this will end well," the Keeper said. "She's distraught and conflicted about her actions."

"As she should be," he replied.

A light-colored Toyota Camry pulled into the lot. Daniel cut the lights, and with the engine still running, he got out and leaned against the door. His relaxed posture appeared casual, like he was waiting to meet an old friend. But the scowl on his face revealed his inner torment.

April moved closer to her Charge, pulling Damian along with her. "What do you think's going through his mind right now?"

"Hurt, anger, disbelief."

April furrowed her brow and cocked her head to the side. "Disbelief?"

"I didn't want to accept it. I couldn't believe my wife would commit such a horrendous act."

"Did you want to kill her?"

He inhaled deeply. Did he want to kill her? Maybe at the height of his distress, when his emotions were so out of control he didn't trust himself to be around anyone. The thought may have flitted through his mind at some point, but Damian wasn't a killer. That he'd held on to his anger and resentment for so long was regrettable enough.

"No. As angry as I was for all those years, I couldn't have killed her. I could never take the life of another person, no matter how heinous their crimes."

"That's good to know."

Her accepting smile warmed his heart. Even in the midst of a possible disaster with their Charge, her beautiful soul reminded him just how much he loved her.

A dark Lexus parked next to Daniel's car, and Jenny hastened around to face him. She stopped ten feet away and smiled. Her eyes held excitement and fear, like she didn't know whether to rush into his arms or run away. The Keeper stood behind her, wrapping her in as much compassion as she could offer to the murderer.

"Hi, Daniel. I hope I didn't keep you waiting too long."

Daniel pushed from the car and took two steps toward her, his expression blank. "I know what you did."

Her eyes grew wide, and her gaze darted about the empty parking lot. "What I did? I...I don't know what you're talking about."

"Don't play games with me, Jenny. You killed my wife." He took another step toward her and clenched his fists.

April winced and moved toward him. *Calm down, Daniel. You promised not to do anything stupid.*

"That's ridiculous." Jenny's voice pitched an octave higher. "Who told you that?"

The corner of his mouth pulled up into a wicked grin. "My Guardian Angel."

Jenny balked. "Do you hear yourself, Daniel? You need help. Maybe you should see a therapist."

"No. You're the one who needs help. You killed your own sister. Admit it."

"Tell him, Jenny. He knows the truth," the Keeper whispered.

"No! I would never."

"Why'd you do it? Tell me!"

Tears streamed down her cheeks as she pleaded with him. "I...only did it so we could be together. I love you, Daniel."

He covered his ears. "No....you don't love me. You're sick. You're obsessed."

"No, I *do* love you. I always have. We're supposed to be together. Don't you see? With her out of the way, we can finally love each other like we were meant to. I did it for us."

He clenched his jaw, and the corner of his lip pulled up into a snarl. "I don't love you. And I will *never* be with you."

"No. Don't do this, Daniel. We can work it out." She held out her hand and took a tentative step toward him.

"No. I'm calling the police. You belong in prison."

Jenny blew out a defeated sigh and reached into her handbag. "You're right, Daniel. You're right." She dug through her purse as if she was looking for her keys, but instead, she pulled out a handgun. Her Keeper frantically whispered her disapproval.

April rocked onto the balls of her feet; she was going to Jump. Damian took her hand and squeezed it gently.

"Not yet. Give her Keeper a chance."

With trembling hands, Jenny pointed the gun at Daniel. He didn't move. He simply lifted his head and stared at her with cocky confidence.

"I didn't want it to come to this." Jenny's voice trembled like her hand. "But if you won't be with me, then you won't be with anyone."

He straightened his posture and glared into her eyes. "You wanna kill me? Go ahead. I've got nothing left to live for."

Jenny's finger twitched on the trigger, and April leaped into the scene, knocking the pistol from her hands. The gun skidded across the parking lot and landed at Daniel's feet while Jenny collapsed to the ground in sobs.

Daniel hesitated, then picked up the weapon. He raised it level with Jenny's head, and without as much as a tremor, his finger rested on the trigger.

"Put the gun down." April stepped between them with her hands raised in surrender. "Let's think about this, okay?"

He looked at her and jerked his head to the side. "Move."

Damian's heart slammed into his throat. The scene was all too familiar. He couldn't stand by and watch her be killed again. His stomach wrenched at the thought of her going through all that pain.

"Come on. You don't want to do this." April took another step toward him. "Remember what we talked about? Killing Jenny won't bring your wife back. Give me the gun, Daniel."

His hand shook. His body trembled, but he didn't give up the weapon.

"I love you, Daniel," Jenny cried from her heap on the ground.

"Shut up!" His hand steadied. Determination filled his eyes. "Move, Angel."

Without a second thought, Damian flew at Daniel and grabbed the gun. But Daniel's grip was too tight. They wrestled, and though Damian's strength was overwhelming, Daniel pulled the trigger.

Jenny's scream ripped through the parking lot, and the metallic smell of fresh blood flooded Damian's senses. Daniel dropped to his knees, shock making him speechless. Jenny's cries blasted in Damian's ears, and his stomach dropped.

April was silent. Dead. Again.

He spun around and found her lying lifeless in a pool of bright red blood. The bullet went straight through her head, blowing a hole the size of a baseball out the back. He scooped her into his arms and turned to Daniel.

"Oh my God. I killed my Angel." Daniel's voice was barely a whisper.

"We both did," Damian said with a growl. How could he have let this happen?

Sirens blared in the distance. He had to get out of there. With a wave of his hand he scrubbed his and April's existence from Jenny's mind before turning to Daniel. He could remove them from Daniel's memory too. It would be as if they never existed to him. Her blood and all traces of her Earthly body would disappear as soon as he Jumped to the Angelic Realm. But he was April's Charge. And though Damian didn't agree with her methods, he wouldn't force his own way on her. He'd leave Daniel's memory intact.

As the police cruiser neared the building, he moved toward Daniel.

"You saw nothing."

CHAPTER 20

Two days passed with April in Slumber and Damian by her side. He ignored the questioning glances and judgmental stares of the other Angels, refusing to speak to anyone but Mira. And then only if he had to.

Halfway into the third day, Mira approached him again. "Are you ready to talk about what happened, brother? It will help to get it off your chest."

"No." Nothing would take away the guilt that consumed him. April died three times because of him. She'd never forgive him.

"Would you like to talk about something else, then? Pass the time while you wait?"

He shrugged, never taking his eyes off April's face. The wound had healed, and Mira cleaned her up. But she'd still felt all the pain of the bullet ripping through her head. Excruciating, life-ending pain.

Mira pulled up a stool and sat next to him. "She's beautiful, isn't she?"

He nodded.

"Aside from this incident, how are the two of you doing? Are you getting along?"

"We were on a date when all this started."

Mira grinned and rubbed his back. "And how was that going?"

He inhaled deeply and blew it out; then he took April's hand in his. "I think it was going well. She seemed happy."

"Were you?"

"Happier than I've been in a thousand years."

"Does she know?"

"She knows everything."

Mira patted his shoulder. "I'll leave you to your thoughts."

"Hey, Mira? How much longer do you think she'll Slumber?"

"At least another twenty four hours. Do you need a break?"

"There's something I need to take care of. Will you stay with her? And call me if she starts to wake up?"

"Of course. Paul will want to talk to you both when she awakens."

"Yeah, I know." He wasn't looking forward to *that* conversation. He'd been in enough trouble already. And while he'd always conceded, or pretended to, he wasn't about to let Paul take April away. He'd fight to the death for her, if Angels could die. "I'll be right back."

He arrived in Daniel's office on the twenty-third floor of the Sears Tower. Daniel sat in a large, leather chair and stared blankly out the window. Damian pushed the office door shut and moved toward the desk.

"Have you come to take me to Hell? Lord knows that's where I belong."

Damian chuckled and sat on the edge of the desk. "You're not going to Hell. And I'm not here to punish you, either. We don't work that way. Can you tell me what happened after I left?"

He never dragged his gaze away from the window. "The cops came. Jenny confessed, and they arrested her. They questioned me. Filed a report. Went home."

Damian nodded and followed Daniel's gaze. They sat silently, staring out the window as Damian played the event over in his head. He'd never forgive himself for causing April pain, but Daniel shouldn't have to suffer for it.

"April's not dead."

His head whipped around and his eyes grew wide. "What? She survived?"

"Angels can't die. She's sleeping right now. But in a day or two, she'll be fine."

Daniel smiled for the first time since Damian met him. "So, she's alive? She'll still be my Guardian Angel?"

"Yeah. And you're lucky, man. She's a special girl."

He crossed his arms and leaned back in his chair. "Then why are you here, instead of with her?"

"Pardon?"

"I saw the way you two looked at each other...like my wife used to look at me. Passion like that happens once in a lifetime. Don't let her get away."

Damian rose from the desk and slapped Daniel on the

shoulder. "Thanks, buddy. That's good advice. Take care of yourself, okay? April wasn't kidding when she said God has big plans for you."

They shook hands, and Damian rushed back to the woman he loved.

Her head seared like a scorching branding iron had pierced her skull. It throbbed as if it would explode. The intense pain made her stomach churn, and for the first time, she was glad Angels didn't eat. If she could just hold on a little longer, she knew the tranquil float through the midnight sky would squelch the flames.

She felt Damian's presence. Felt him watching over her. And when he left, she panicked. But she was paralyzed. Her body felt like lead pressing against the sheet, and she screamed inside. A five-ton anvil pressed into her chest as anguish pulsed through her limbs. The pain was unbearable, and Damian had left her.

As she fought her way through the agony, she felt a break in the storm. The fire in her head cooled, and the throbbing slowed to a manageable level. The starry sky was only moments away, but she didn't want to go there without him. Why did he leave her? Was he that angry?

She couldn't fight the pull of the light, though she'd rather Slumber forever than live a day without Damian. She was about to give up hope when she felt him squeeze her hand.

"She's coming back. I can feel her waking up." Damian's voice danced in her ears.

"Keep talking," she wanted to say, but her voice wouldn't come. She heard footsteps around her, and then a male voice she didn't recognize spoke.

"This is the second time she's been killed since becoming a Guardian. Perhaps Keeper would be a better fit for her."

No! No, I can do this.

"No, Paul. She's meant to be a Guardian. She bears the mark."

Paul. The leader of the Angels. Surely Damian's own brother wouldn't do this to her.

"But she was killed by recklessly entering a scene which was beyond her control."

"She had it under control. I'm the reason she died. I'm the one who jumped in recklessly. And because of my mistake, she was shot. If you're going to punish someone, it should be me."

"No." She found her voice, though it was barely a whisper.

"April?"

She tentatively opened her eyes and winced at the pounding in her temples. She pushed into a sitting position and nearly passed out from the pain, but she couldn't let Damian take the blame.

"It's not his fault. He didn't want me to get involved in the first place. He was only trying to protect me."

He wrapped his arms around her and rested his head on hers. "I'm so glad you're back," he whispered. "She's meant to be a Guardian, Paul."

"Then perhaps she needs a new trainer. Someone who is not so...involved with her. You don't belong out there,

Damian. It's time you took your rightful place as leader. And she needs some time away from you."

Her blood ran cold. "No! Damian's been with me my entire life. You can't take him away from me now. Punish me. Do whatever you have to. To me. I'm the one to blame for everything." Her head spun, and she clung to his chest. She couldn't lose him. Whether he was meant to be a leader or not, he belonged with her.

Mira reached out to Paul and squeezed his hand. He looked at her and nodded.

"Very well. Take her home and tend to her, but our conversation is not finished, brother. We have other things to discuss."

Damian nodded and scooped her up in his arms. The strength of his embrace made her feel safe, secure. And the relief that he wasn't being taken from her just yet eased the throbbing in her head. When he grinned his crooked grin, she couldn't help but steal a kiss. She didn't care who saw them. She was in love with Damian, and she wanted the world to know.

Just as soon as she told *him*.

"Come on, baby. Let's go home." He carried her out of the sanctuary and up the path to their house. And when he carried her across the threshold, her heart did a little flip.

He lowered her onto the sofa and pulled her into his lap. Brushing the hair out of her face, he trailed his fingers down her cheek. Her skin tingled beneath his touch, and she snuggled into his embrace.

"How's your head?"

"Better. Thank you for standing up for me in there. It was sweet."

He kissed her forehead and nuzzled her neck. "It was the truth."

"You don't really blame yourself for me getting shot, do you?"

"Of course I do."

"But I don't. It happened because of a combination of things. It was no one's fault. It was an accident." She took his face in her hands and peered into his eyes. "Please don't beat yourself up over this. I'm fine."

She brushed her lips against his and lingered by his mouth for more.

"I'll try not to." His whisper tickled her lips before he took her mouth in a tender kiss.

As he pulled away, a sickening feeling twisted in her gut. "Is Paul really going to take Daniel away from me? Is he going to take *you* away?"

His gaze fell to their hands joined in her lap. "I don't know. I can't stop him from reassigning your Charge, but I won't lose you. I don't think I'd make it without you in my life."

She pulled away from his embrace and looked into his eyes. "Why can't you stop him? He said you're supposed to be the leader. So, be the leader and stop him."

He inhaled and rubbed his brow. "It's not that simple. I'd be giving up everything. No more Charges. That means *you* wouldn't be my Charge. The connection we share would be gone."

"Oh." That sure wasn't worth it, then. She didn't want to

lose either one. But if she had to choose, she'd hold on to Damian. She couldn't imagine losing the deep connection she shared with him. The ability to find him by simply focusing on his face. Losing that would be like losing a piece of herself. "Well, will you try talking to him? Surely he's open to reason."

Damian chuckled. "I'll try. But he doesn't think you're ready to be a Guardian, since you keep getting killed and all. And he definitely doesn't think I'm the right trainer for you."

"We have to convince him he's wrong. Damian, I can't do this without you...and I can't leave Daniel alone."

"I know, baby. I'll do everything I can."

She kissed him on the cheek and rose to her feet. "I know you will. But I need to talk to Daniel. If I'm going to lose him, I at least want to say good-bye.

Damian trudged through the meadow to Paul's house. He could've just as easily called to his brother in his mind, but he needed the long walk in the fresh air to clear his head. Paul was set on April being a Keeper, but Damian knew she was meant to be a Guardian. She had all the drive and commitment of an Angel who was born a Guardian. It was he who kept screwing up.

Her tough love method of working with Daniel seemed to be working for her. And while it wasn't the way he'd have gone about it, she'd made the right decisions. He trusted her to do what was right.

He knocked on Paul's door, and it swung open. Paul motioned for him to step inside, and he reluctantly crossed the threshold. Mira stood by the window watering her plants, and she put down the watering can to greet him.

"How is she?" Mira asked.

"She's better. Her head still hurts, but she'll be okay."

"And how are you?"

He stared blankly back at her. He wasn't about to disclose his feelings to them when he hadn't even talked to April. Especially not to Paul.

He cut his gaze over to his brother and raised his chin. "She's still mine."

Paul linked his hands behind his back and returned Damian's stubborn gaze. "For now. She'll be transferred to a Keeper tomorrow. Then, you'll be free to join us where you belong."

He sucked in a sharp breath, and dread squeezed his heart. He couldn't lose her. He wouldn't. "No. She's meant to be a Guardian. Mira, tell him."

She sighed and looked at him with sympathetic eyes. "She has been killed twice in a matter of days."

His stomach dropped to his knees. Not Mira too. This couldn't be happening. She knew how much he cared about April. His hands trembled, and he clenched them into fists.

"I'm the reason she was killed. I didn't trust her to handle the situation, but I do now. She can do it. She's supposed to be a Guardian. She's saved her Charge's life multiple times. She's dedicated to him. Committed."

Paul took a step toward him and placed his hand on his shoulder. "But has she ever saved him without your intervention? I'm not sure she can do it on her own."

"She can. You can't take her away from me. I won't let it happen." Sweat beaded on his brow, and his stomach churned.

"Oh, dear," Mira said. "We've got one waking up. Please be nice to each other." She kissed Paul on the cheek and disappeared.

Paul furrowed his brow and tilted his head to the side. "She's just your Charge, brother. You've let go of countless others without a fight. Why do you want to hold on to her so badly?"

Damian took a deep breath and closed his eyes for a long blink. When he opened them, he leveled his gaze on Paul. He was going to have to say it.

"Because I'm in love with her."

Paul's eyes widened as he smiled and stepped back. "Well, that makes a difference then, doesn't it? It's quite the predicament now." He linked his hands behind his back and paced to the window.

"Look, just give her a chance. Let her work with her Charge alone, and I won't interfere. Let her prove it to you. She's ready, Paul. I know she is."

Paul rested his arm against the window and lay his forehead on it as he inhaled deeply and sighed. "This decision shouldn't be mine to make. This is *your* position. I've been picking up the slack for you for nearly seven hundred years."

Damian cringed. He knew he'd let both Paul and Mira down, but the mental state he'd been in wouldn't allow him to lead. He was supposed to be the decision maker—the one assigning Charges and making sure everyone followed the rules. It's what he was made to do. But he couldn't even follow the rules himself.

"The choices I've made have led me to where I am today. It was a long, hard journey, but April's worth every painstaking moment of it. Please, brother. I'm begging you."

Paul sighed and turned to face him. "I don't know. The Charge's safety comes first. Giving her a chance to prove herself may result in his death."

Damian started to argue, but the first twinge of adrenaline shot through his veins. Daniel's excitement, then April's panic. Her pulse pounded in his head. She needed him.

"You don't have a choice, Paul. It's happening now." He grabbed his brother by the arm and Jumped.

~

"Hey, Daniel." April appeared in the passenger seat of his car and buckled her seat belt.

He swerved, ran up on a curb, and knocked over a trash can. The car came to a screeching halt inches from a pedestrian. "Jesus, Angel! Don't do that!"

Daniel waved to the almost victim, threw it in reverse, and backed out. "Are you trying to kill me now?" He pulled into a parking space.

"Oops. Sorry." She shrugged and smiled. "How are you?"

He smiled and shook his head. "Better, actually. I'm getting better."

"That's good to hear." They stared at each other in

silence as April tried to figure out how to tell him. It was like breaking up with a boyfriend she really didn't want to leave. She'd have to give him the "it's-not-you, it's-me" speech. There was no avoiding it. She took a deep breath, but to her relief, Daniel spoke first.

"I'm sorry I shot you."

"That's okay. It could've been worse." She rubbed her hand across her forehead. "Good as new."

He gripped the steering wheel and stared at his hands. "I'm still sorry."

"Hey." She rested her hand on his shoulder. "I don't blame you or anyone else. Accidents happen. Okay?"

He nodded, took a deep breath and looked at her. "Yeah. Thanks. And thanks for saving my life. I must have the best Guardian Angel in the world."

"Ah, yeah. About that." Good Lord, she didn't want to do this. She'd gotten through to Daniel, and she knew she could help with the transition to the Angelic Realm. It killed her to lose her Charge.

"Apparently, the big guys up there don't think I'm doing such a good job with you. They don't think I'm cut out to be a Guardian."

"Seriously? But you've saved me so many times already."

"Yep. But Damian's helped every time. They don't think I can handle it on my own, so they want to give you a new Guardian."

"Would it be Damian?"

"No. They want to separate the two of us. Supposedly we aren't good for each other."

"Aren't good? That's insane! Have you noticed the way he looks at you? He's in love with you."

Heat flushed her cheeks, and her pulse quickened. She couldn't stop the smile from spreading across her face. Even though it wasn't Damian saying the words, hearing them from someone else still thrilled her. If Daniel thought Damian loved her, maybe he really did.

But Paul was set on taking it all away.

"I'm in love with him too."

"Well, we can't let it happen then. What do we need to do to stop them?"

She shrugged and clasped her hands in her lap. "Damian's trying to talk them out of it right now. But short of me saving your life on my own, I don't think they'll change their minds."

Daniel stared straight ahead, his grip on the steering wheel so tight his knuckles turned white. He chewed on the inside of his cheek and furrowed his brow like he was deep in thought. Too deep.

He threw the car into drive and peeled out of the parking lot. With tires screeching and horns honking, he wove in and out of traffic like a mad man. He floored it, and with a look of determination and hysteria, he sped toward the riverbank.

April's heart raced as she gripped the sides of her seat. Though she couldn't die, the thought of living through yet another death paralyzed her.

"What are you doing, Daniel? Slow down!"

The corner of his mouth curved into a conspiratorial grin. "It's okay. I have a plan." He swerved to miss a delivery truck pulling out on the road, and she squealed.

"If your plan is to get us both killed, you're doing great. What the hell is your plan?"

"You have to save me on your own, right? Well, Damian's not here to help you."

He lowered his head and focused on his target—a bridge crossing the river ahead.

"He'll be here any second. He can feel my panic, Daniel. It won't work."

He raised one shoulder and grinned. "So tell him to go away, because we're going in."

Her eyes grew wide as she braced herself for the fall. The car crashed through the railing and plunged into the deep river below. The impact threw her forward, the seatbelt cutting into her collar bone as it stopped her from smashing through the windshield. Icy water poured in through the door jambs, filling the car as it submerged.

Damian arrived on the bridge in time to watch the car sink into the murky water, with April and Daniel inside. He jumped into the river and pulled Paul in with him. It took every ounce of willpower he could muster to stay in The In-Between and let April handle the problem. Every fiber of his being wanted to rush in and save her, but she had to prove to Paul she could get out of it on her own.

His emotions tipped toward panic as he waited to see April emerge from the wreckage. She could do it. He knew she could, but his Guardian instincts begged him to step in.

Paul remained calm. "Why did he drive off a bridge?"

"He's suicidal. She's saved him from suicide twice already." He couldn't pull his gaze away from the car. She struggled with her seatbelt inside, while Daniel calmly watched her.

"You need to step in, brother. Help her save him."

"No. She can do it."

"You're willing to let another Charge die to prove a point?"

"He's not going to die."

April released her seatbelt, and within seconds she had Daniel out of his. Damian held his breath as she pounded her foot against the window. Would she be strong enough to break the glass?

She banged and banged against the pane until her foot finally smashed through. She was going to make it.

Shoving Daniel through the window, she linked her left arm around his chest. Using her right arm to paddle, she made her way to the surface and came up gasping for air. She lugged her Charge to the riverbank and pulled him up onto the dirt.

Daniel was unconscious, and April started CPR immediately. When he took his first breath and river water spewed from his mouth, Damian raised his chin and turned to Paul.

The Angel stared at the couple on the bank. "You've made your point." He crossed his arms over his chest and disappeared.

Damian chuckled and crossed over to stand next to April as she berated her Charge.

She fell back on her rump and attempted to wipe the dirt off her knees. Her tangled hair dripped down her back, creating little droplets of mud around her. She wiped the back of her hand across her forehead, leaving an adorable streak of grime on her skin.

"Are you insane? You just about killed us both!"

Daniel sat up and smiled. "But you saved me. All by yourself."

"I..." She paused, a flicker of realization dancing in her eyes.

Damian knelt beside her and put his hand on her shoulder. "You did. And Paul saw you, too."

Sirens blared on the bridge above, and shouts echoed off the water.

"We have to go, April." Damian helped her to her feet and took her hand in his.

"Well, Daniel. This might be the last time I see you. So if it is, I hope you have a good life."

"Oh, you'll be seeing me again. I can feel it." He waved good-bye, and they Jumped home.

CHAPTER 21

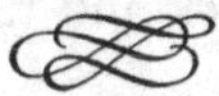

April caught a glimpse of herself in the mirror and gasped. She was filthy, and Damian saw her that way. How embarrassing. She closed her eyes and quickly cleaned herself up before she slipped into a knee-length lavender chiffon dress.

"Sorry you had to see me all dirty like that."

He grinned and pulled her into his arms. "Are you kidding? You looked so sexy, I could've taken you right there on the riverbank."

She slipped her hands up his chest and linked them behind his neck. "And now?"

"Mmm...now's good for me." He pressed his hand on the small of her back, pulling her body to his. When his lips brushed hers, electricity shot through her veins, and her body warmed with desire.

He pulled away and tucked a piece of hair behind her ear. "I've been wanting to talk to you about something."

"Me too."

"It's just that, well, we've gotten really close, and I..."

A knock on the door stopped him midsentence. He sighed and closed his eyes. "That'll be Paul. He's a bit impatient. I'm sorry, April. I need to go talk to him, but it shouldn't take long."

"It's okay. There's something I need to take care of anyway." She stepped back and turned her lavender gown into one of gleaming white.

"You're going to see him again." The look of disappointment on his face almost crushed her, but this was something she had to do. For both of them.

"Yes. But it's not for the reason you think. You can come with me if you want." She reached for his hand, but he shoved them in his pockets.

"No. Just do whatever you need to do and come back to me, okay?"

"Always."

She watched him walk out the door, and when it clicked shut, she Jumped to Jared's bedroom. When she appeared at the foot of his bed, he screamed.

"Ahhh! You're not really here." He pulled the covers up to his chin and squeezed his eyes shut. "When I open my eyes, you'll be gone. Please be gone."

He opened his eyes into small slits and squeezed them shut again. "It's just my imagination. She can't be here. She's dead."

He opened one eye, and then the other. "You're still here."

She grinned. "Yes, I am."

"Am I dreaming?"

"Nope. You're wide awake as far as I can see." She

strolled around to the side of the bed, and Jared inched away.

"Please don't hurt me."

What happened to his confident, overbearing attitude? For once, she was in control. He couldn't hurt her anymore. "Relax, Jared. I'm not here to hurt you. I just want to talk."

He stared at her with wide eyes, every muscle in his body tense.

She sighed and sat on the edge of the bed. "Look, I know you were cheating on me. You did it for five months, and I didn't have a clue."

He swallowed, and his gaze darted about the room. "I...I'm sorry."

"I am too. I'm sorry I was so wrapped up in getting married that I didn't see the big picture. We weren't right for each other. You knew that. You could have told me, rather than sneaking around behind my back, but whatever."

His shoulders relaxed, and he let go of the covers. "What do you want from me?"

"Nothing. No apology, no explanations. Nothing. I'm just here to tell you that I forgive you, and I hope one day you'll be able to forgive yourself."

"I—"

"Just think about it. I won't bother you again." She touched his shoulder, and his eyes widened like saucers. He looked at her hand, then into her eyes.

"Good-bye, Jared."

～

When Damian opened the door, he was surprised to find both Paul and Mira waiting for him. He pulled it shut and tried to keep his face expressionless as he approached his siblings.

"Have you thought about my offer, brother?" Paul raised an eyebrow as he regarded him.

"We need you," Mira added.

He blew out a hard breath and raked his fingers through his hair. "I don't know if I'm cut out to be a leader. Heaven knows I'm not perfect. And what about April? What's going to happen to her?"

Paul placed a hand on his shoulder. "None of us are perfect. But you've been out there long enough. You've been a part of the modern world, and your insight would be a perfect addition. There are too many Angels now for Mira and me to handle on our own. What do you say?"

He cast his gaze to the dewy grass as he thought about the suggestion. Where *did* he belong? He'd spent most of his existence on the front lines, fighting off his demons by absorbing himself in his Charges. Anger drove him to exile himself from the love of others, and self-hate kept him away from his true responsibilities.

He took a deep breath and looked Paul in the eyes. It was time to let go.

"I'll do it. But as long as April needs a trainer, I'm with her. She comes first."

His brother shook his head. "We need you now."

"I won't abandon April. And I won't allow you to assign her to another trainer. She's a Guardian, and she belongs with me."

Paul cut his gaze over to Mira, and she smiled and

nodded her head. She stepped toward Damian and took his hands in hers.

"You are her trainer. Do you feel she is prepared to work alone?"

The thought of losing that deep connection with April was unbearable. But she was ready. He knew it deep in his soul, but he didn't want to let her go. He chewed his bottom lip as he tried to force the answer over the lump in his throat.

"You're worried about losing her."

He nodded.

"You know there is a way to get the connection back. To still have her be a part of you."

That's right. But it would only work if she felt the same. He couldn't be her Guardian forever, but maybe there was another way. He took a deep breath and looked Mira in the eyes.

"She's ready. She'll make a great Guardian."

"Welcome back." Paul shook his hand and pulled him into a bear hug. "I've missed you, brother."

As Paul released him, Mira smiled and cupped her hand on the back of his neck. "It is done." The connection to April severed.

What had he done? The connection he lost tore a gaping hole in his heart, and he doubled over with the pain of losing her. He couldn't sense her. Couldn't feel her pulse beating in his blood. Her life force was what kept him going. Without it, he was lost.

"Why does it hurt so bad? I've never felt pain when freeing a Charge."

Mira placed a hand on his shoulder. "April was much more than a Charge. Go find her."

"I don't know where she is."

"She's home."

His head snapped up to meet Mira's gaze. Was she home so soon? Had she gotten the closure he hoped she'd needed? He looked at his door and back at the couple.

"Go to her. She needs you."

He nodded and flew through the door. "April? Where are you?"

No answer.

He darted to her bedroom and called to her.

Still no answer.

He was on the verge of panic, not knowing where she was. He was empty. Hollow without her. He had to make her his, and it had to be tonight. He closed his eyes and worked his magic on their home. Then he caught sight of her out the window.

April sat on the grass with a piece of paper in her hands. His stomach wrenched as the intense need to be with her ripped through his body. This was it. He was going to tell her, and nothing could stop him.

She looked peaceful out there all alone, and he couldn't tear his gaze from her beauty. Her crimson hair sparkled in the starlight, and she looked every bit the Angel she was. She lifted the paper in front of her and tore it down the middle. Then she took a lighter and set one half ablaze.

She was finally letting go of her past.

He was too.

He rushed to his bedroom and took the folded paper

from his bedside table. Then he strode to the meadow and sat down beside her.

"Hey."

"Hey." She leaned over and bumped his shoulder.

"Did you do everything you needed to do?"

"Yeah. You?"

"Uh-huh."

She laid her head on his shoulder and held his hand. "Why can't I feel you anymore? It's like there's a hole in my heart."

"Mmm...yeah. I'm not your Guardian anymore."

"That's what I thought. It hurts. Right here." She pressed her hand to her chest.

Pain pulsed through his own heart. "I know."

"Am I still..."

He kissed the top of her head and inhaled her sweet scent. "You're still a Guardian. Daniel's still your Charge."

He picked up her picture and looked at her image. "You're beautiful. You always have been. Why'd you burn the other half?"

She smiled sadly and took the paper from his hands. "Because I let it go. That's the whole reason I brought the picture here. I tried to tell you that."

"Yeah, I guess you did. But I didn't listen."

"No, you didn't."

He brushed the hair away from her face and kissed her cheek. "I'm listening now."

"I know." She flicked on the lighter and set fire to the scrap.

"Why are you burning yourself?"

She smiled as the last of the paper went up in flames,

and she stomped the embers with her foot. "Because that's the old me. I'm not that person anymore. I don't want to be that person. You've changed me."

He took the folded sketch from his pocket and showed it to her. "This is Juliet. She was four months pregnant in this picture." He stroked his thumb across his unborn child, and April held out the lighter.

He looked at the picture one last time and took the lighter from her hand. Without another thought, he lit it on fire. Flames engulfed his painful past, and sweet freedom burst in his soul. He put his arm around her, and they watched it burn together.

"So, who's my Guardian now?"

"You don't have one."

She looked at him with confusion in her eyes. "Why not?"

"You've graduated. You're a full-fledged Guardian now. You won't have to have me following you around anymore."

"But what if I want you to?" She wrapped her arm around his waist and rested her chin on his shoulder.

He smiled and pressed his lips to her forehead. "I think that can be arranged."

"What's gonna happen to you? Are you in trouble?"

He chuckled. "No. I'm actually going to try my hand at being the leader I'm supposed to be. I'm going to work with Paul and Mira."

"Is that what you want?"

He took a deep, trembling breath. It was now or never. "What I want is to be with you." Lifting her chin with his fingers, he kissed her. Heat rushed through his body as she wrapped her arms around him and slipped her tongue into his mouth. He slid his arms behind her back, pulling her closer. Emotions exploded in his heart, and he couldn't wait anymore. He pulled away so he could look into her eyes.

"I love you, April."

She smiled and brushed her lips against his. "I love you, too."

His heart did backflips. He'd wanted to hear those words cross her lips for so long. All he could do was grin at the beautiful Angel before him. His Angel.

"So, what now?" She ran her finger down his chest, stopping just below his navel.

Her playful tone sent electricity jolting through his core, but he wasn't done talking to her. There was still one more thing he had to do.

"Come inside with me. I want to show you something."

"I thought you'd never ask." She grinned wickedly, and he picked her up and carried her into the house. *Their* house.

With her hands behind his neck, she pulled him into another kiss. He slowly let her legs drop to the floor as he explored her taste with his tongue. She pulled away, and with pure passion in her eyes, she took his hand and turned around.

Then she froze.

"Where's my door? Where's my *bedroom*?" Tears filled her eyes when she turned to face him. "What's going on?"

"Come with me." He led her toward his bedroom

door. "Since I'm not your Guardian anymore, you don't have to live here."

"So I have to make my own place?" A tear rolled down her cheek, and he wiped it away with his thumb.

"You don't *have* to. You can stay with me. If you want to." He opened the door to reveal his own hunter green room draped in lavender. April's duvet covered his bed, and her sheer drapes cascaded over his window.

Her breath caught as she took a step inside. "This is my stuff...in *your* room."

"*Our* room. If you want it to be." He dropped to one knee, and when she turned around, she gasped.

Damian reached for her trembling hand. Her heart raced. Her head spun. Was this really happening?

"April May Carter, I love you more than I've ever loved anything in my life. You are my reason for living. I want you to be the first thing I see when I wake each morning, and I want to fall asleep in your arms every night."

A black velvet box appeared in his hand, and he opened it to reveal a simple golden ring. "I want to love you forever. Will you marry me?"

Her entire body trembled as her heart thudded against her breast. She couldn't speak. She couldn't move. All she could do was look at the beautiful man before her as tears poured down her cheeks.

He took her left hand and slipped the ring on her finger. "It looks good on you. What do you think?"

"Damian, I...yes! Yes, of course I'll marry you!"

He stood and swept her into his arms, stroking her hair and caressing her cheek, wiping the tears away.

"I love you, April."

"I love you, Damian."

He crushed his mouth to hers, and fire shot through her core. He pinned her against the wall with the weight of his body, and his essence filled her heart once more. He was inside her. A part of her. Swirling in her soul.

"I can feel you again."

"You're about to feel a lot more of me." He worked her gown off her shoulders and nuzzled into her neck. He nipped and kissed her sensitive skin from her earlobe to her collarbone. Chill bumps rose on her skin, and her womb tightened with need. But the most miraculous sensation was in her soul.

"I mean in my heart. The hole is gone."

His intoxicated gaze landed on hers, and he grinned. "That's because we've given ourselves over to each other. We'll have this connection forever now."

And forever was exactly what she wanted. She slid her hands under his shirt and pulled it over his head. His sculpted body left her breathless. She'd never get over how beautiful he was.

The corner of his mouth pulled into a grin, and he worked her dress down her hips and let it fall to the floor. He inhaled deeply as his gaze traveled up and down her body, and his hands caressed her curves.

"You are truly the most beautiful creature in the universe."

"And I'm all yours." She popped the button on his jeans and pushed his clothing to the floor. His erection sprang out, and he moaned when she took it in her hand. "To have and to hold and make love to whenever you please."

He lifted her up, and she wrapped her legs around his waist. His hardness pressed into her, making her wet with anticipation. Then, he dropped her on the bed and climbed on top of her.

His tongue brushed against hers, and the taste of him made her head spin. He belonged to her, and a wave of possessiveness washed over her. He was the one; she'd never let him go.

"You're mine," she whispered against his lips.

"Yes, ma'am."

He trailed his tongue from the tip of her chin to the middle of her chest. Then he took a breast in his mouth, teasing her nipple with his tongue. He took the other between his thumb and forefinger, and he gently squeezed. Blissful sensations shot down to her hips, and she spread her legs to let him in.

He moved to tease her other breast, and using his hand as a guide, he rubbed against her, slipping his tip inside only to pull it out again. The anticipation drove her insane, and she lifted her hips to take him in deeper.

He took the hint and plunged inside. She moaned when he filled her, and her fingers dug into his shoulders as his hips began rocking. Tingling electricity throbbed in her womb and wound its way into her core like tendrils of ivy climbing a trellis. It reached her heart and cascaded down her arms and legs until her entire body pulsed with warmth. The feeling was intoxicating. Love and lust coming together in a beautiful union.

His rhythm increased as he gazed into her eyes, and she lost control. Wave after wave of orgasm rocked through her body, and she cried out in ecstasy. His hips pumped relentlessly, sending her over the edge again and again. He gripped her shoulders and buried his face in her hair when he came.

Breathless, she traced her fingers along his back and kissed his neck. When he raised his head, his eyes sparkled with his smile.

"I love you, April."

"I love you too."

"Say it again. I can't get enough of that."

She grinned. "I love you, Damian. I love you, I love you, I love you. And I will *always* love you. Forever."

"Mmm…Sounds like Heaven to me."

With their legs entwined, they lay face-to-face in his bed. *Their* bed. The idea of spending the rest of forever with him made her giddy with excitement. Nothing could bring her down from this high.

"Oh, no!" Except for losing her Charge. She searched for Daniel, opening her mind to feel him. To find him. But he was gone.

"What is it?"

"Daniel's gone. I can't feel him anymore."

"Hmm…If you feel anything like I do right now, your own emotions might be overpowering his."

"No. He's definitely gone. I can't sense him at all. Did Paul take him away from me? I thought you said I was still his Guardian." Panic coursed through her veins. She couldn't lose her Charge. Daniel was *her* responsibility. She was the one who cared about his life. *She* was the one who went through the agony of death to keep him from committing murder.

Damian must have seen the terror in her eyes, because he pulled her into his arms and called for Mira.

"Mira? Mira, we need you. It's an emergency."

"She can hear you?"

"She can hear everyone."

April clutched the blanket to her chest and clung to Damian. When Mira appeared at the foot of the bed, she blushed.

"Oh, my goodness. I'd apologize for intruding, but you called me."

"April can't feel her Charge. Did Paul take him away?"

She looked at April and smiled warmly. "No worries, dear. It's only temporary. But, this." She gestured to the couple. "Do my eyes deceive me? Has Damian fallen in love with his Charge?"

His cheeks flushed with adorable color. "Well, technically she's not my Charge anymore."

Mira clapped her hands and rested her chin on her fingertips. "Oh, this is wonderful news!"

And it was, but a sickening feeling churned in April's stomach at the thought of losing Daniel. "Wait a minute. What happened to my Charge?"

"Don't worry. I'll be taking care of him myself for now," Mira said.

"Why?"

She smiled and winked at her. "Because every newlywed needs a honeymoon."

Damian squeezed April tightly and kissed her on the cheek. "Thank you, Mira."

"You're very welcome. Now, if you don't need anything else, I've got a wedding to plan." With excitement in her eyes, she bowed her head and disappeared.

"So I've got you all to myself, with no interruptions?" She walked her fingers up his side and ran them through his hair.

"Mmm...whatever are you going to do with me?" He nuzzled her neck and nipped her earlobe.

"Oh, I've got some ideas."

"Oh, really?"

"Uh-huh."

"You know, now you can have your dream wedding. The dress, the flowers, everything you've ever wanted. You'd better go see Mira in the morning so she doesn't take over the planning."

She shook her head. "I don't need all that."

"Oh?"

"A wedding is one day out of thousands we'll spend together. I'll be happy with whatever Mira plans. I don't need a fancy dress or an elaborate ceremony. As long as you're there to meet me at the altar, that's all that matters."

"I'll be there for you. Every day, for the rest of my existence."

"Promise?"

"I promise."

EPILOGUE

April wore a simple white slip dress and carried a single lavender tulip. The grassy meadow and sparkling lagoon provided a pristine backdrop for the ceremony. And though it seemed like every Angel in the Realm showed up for the celebration, it was a quaint and intimate gathering.

Arm in arm with her grandfather, she waltzed down the aisle to meet her husband. A crooked smile reached all the way to Damian's eyes as he took her hand and pressed his lips to her fingers.

"You look stunning, April." He'd traded his usual jeans and t-shirt for a crisp white suit and tie, and his normally tousled hair was combed back from his face.

She trailed her fingers down his cheek. "You look like a dream come true."

He sucked in a shaky breath, and his eyes shimmered.

"Are you crying?" A lump formed in her throat.

"No, I just got some dust in my eyes." He pulled her into a hug and kissed her forehead.

"Ahem." Paul stepped in front of them. "You aren't supposed to kiss her until *after* I pronounce you husband and wife."

"Right. Sorry." He slid his hands down her arms and laced his fingers through hers.

They said their vows, and in an eloquent speech, Paul pronounced them husband and wife and presented them to the audience. Hugs and congratulations poured after them.

Ella waved and danced toward them. April stepped away from Damian to give her friend a hug.

"I'm glad you finally cracked your nut," Ella whispered.

"Me too."

She grinned. "And I guess the inside is as sweet as you'd hoped?"

"And then some. He's amazing. Thank you, Ella. For everything."

Damian wrapped his arms around her from behind and pressed his lips to her cheek. "What are you ladies talking about?"

"You, of course," Ella said. "Congratulations to both of you."

Mira hugged them both and took April's hands in hers. "Was the ceremony everything you wanted, dear?"

"It was perfect, Mira. Thank you."

All she wanted—all she needed—was to be with Damian. The celebration was nice, but the prize whose hand was joined with hers was the most incredible of all.

April married the man of her dreams, and she'd get to spend the rest of forever in his arms. The most extravagant wedding in the world couldn't compare to the way she felt for her Guardian Angel.

ABOUT THE AUTHOR

Carrie Pulkinen is a paranormal romance author who has always been fascinated with things that go bump in the night. Of course, when you grow up next door to a cemetery, the dead (and the undead) are hard to ignore. Pair that with her passion for writing and her love of a good happily-ever-after, and becoming a paranormal romance author seems like the only logical career choice.

Before she decided to turn her love of the written word into a career, Carrie spent the first part of her professional life as a high school journalism and yearbook teacher. She loves good chocolate and bad puns, and in her free time, she likes to read, drink wine, and travel with her family.

Connect with Carrie online:
www.CarriePulkinen.com